The Collected Tales of Nathaniel Darcy

A novel delight

by

ED NEWBERY-KING

Magic Words

Also by Ed Newbery-King

Do You Believe in Magic?

A contemporary fairy story, full of magic, transformation and growth, all lovingly nurtured within an overall theme of spirituality.

For young adults and available through Amazon.

This novel is a work of fiction. Any resemblance to people either alive or dead is purely coincidental. Names, places and all characters are born out of the author's overactive imagination (with more than a little help from angels and spirit guides). The author holds all rights to this work. It is illegal to reproduce this novel in part or in its entirety without written consent from the author himself.

First edition.

All textual matter
© Ed Newbery-King 2016
Published by Magic Words © 2016
All Rights Reserved.

Chapter illustrations, front and back cover are all by
Ed Newbery-King
Magic Graphic Design and Digital Illustration. ©

For the dear departed: my brother, Geoff, Mum and Dad, both sets of Grandparents, assorted Uncles and Aunts.

For Steven Strange, Sue Ruffel, Gwen Marr, Bill and Daisy Borrett and Audrey Miles (a wonderful woman) and my dear friend and source of much inspiration, the late great, Isobel Hughes. Most heartbreaking of all for me - my beautiful dog and sole (soul) companion, Cisco who went to doggy heaven in June 2015 and whom I miss every single day.

For the wonderful living – my sister, Carole and my brother, Ray, my nieces, Shelley, Susan and Louise, my nephews, Ben, Adam, David, Richard, and Martin. My Brother in Law, Mike, my Sister in Law, Sally, and my former Sister in Law, Margaret and all my other family members – you know who you are! For kindred spirit and medium rare, Lorna Hedges. For all of my psychically aware kindred spirits - Gill, Lynn, Sharon, Clare, Ann, Debbie, Charlotte, Laura, Jo, Kelly, Kayleigh, Serena and Lisa.

For Deana Milne (G'Day sheila!) For Donna Mayo, Donna Stamatin, Lisa Greener, Cindy Derousseau and Enid Young. Last but not least, for my former Thursday writing group friends, Ivy Blyth and John Compton – thank you both so much for your constant encouragement and help in keeping a literary spark alight in me, one that in turn, hopefully, will burst into a bright new spreading light, bleaching out all of the shadows in our darkened world, leading to more children reading books and exercising their imaginations in the process – phew!

Well, that's enough of me blathering on (who said, 'hear, hear'?)

Now what are you waiting for? Get reading!

Alan — we are the result of what we have been through — we have been through enough to realise that love is the key to everything

For Geoff

and love will bring a richness to life that will lead to our eternal salvation!

Thanks for supporting my work :)

Paul King 2020.

Preramble

Well, hello fellow bookworms and welcome to Nerdsville - 'cause, and I'm sorry if I offend you, having a copy of this book in your hands instantly makes you an honorary nerd in MY book - get it? My book? Oh never mind.

I imagine you're thinking, who the heck is this cheeky so and so and who on earth does he think he's talking to? Well, I'll tell you if you'll just be patient for a moment! Blimey - patience isn't just an antiquated card game you know!

My name is Mark. Mark William Andrew Hopkins, to be absolutely precise. Yes, I know, it's quite a mouthful isn't it! Doesn't help that when it's written out as initials it says, MWAH, which sounds scarily like one of those dumb air kisses, so many surgically enhanced Hollywood 'actresses' do on TV. Yeah right, Hollywood air kiss - where I live? I think not! Kiss of death more like, well, at *my* school at least, particularly after one of the trogs from the swamp hole I call school, noticed, MWAH, splashed across the cover of a well known trashy celebrity magazine, that he claims to have seen in a supermarket. Personally I reckon he bought it for himself to allow free reign to his, 'glittery' side! Of course, naturally, the, MWAH/me association then zipped around the school like an Olympic outbreak of nits. Ugh, school life - hopefully I'll be eligible for parole soon!

My friends aren't quite so 'out there' when it comes to nicknames, to them I'm Hoppy. Hoppy Hopkins - a name they jointly came up with. Oh don't worry, I can imagine what you're thinking, how lame is that! Sounds like someone from the 1940's, right? Silly twits - they mean well, I guess, and even went to great pains to point out to me how they'd come up with it, that it 'cleverly' stems from the 'hop' part of my surname, not that I needed an explanation - well duh! But I'm guessing you've figured that out for yourselves right? Even without a science degree! Incidentally, my sense of humour has been known to sink to sarcastic depths on the odd occasion - just saying! Hey, I never said I was perfect!!!

Anyway, where was I? Let me see - oh yes, I was introducing myself, wasn't I. Well, now that you know my name, you're probably wondering how old I am? Hmm? Well stop being so flipping nosy! Ha ha, got you - I'm just kidding again. Hopefully, you'll soon get used to my cruddy sense of humour or you'll be flinging this book in the nearest waste bin (unless, of course, it's a library book - I'll not be a party to any law breaking thank you!)

So, you want to know my age? OK. I'm sixteen and a bit and trust me, I'm really not trying to be precious here, but that, 'bit', makes all the difference to a young man desperately trying to break free from the dreaded pains (or chains as I prefer) of puberty. Now, you might be intrigued to learn (or not) that I live in Gloucester, or Glawsterr as some of the older folk around here pronounce it. Not familiar with Glawsterr? Really? That's shocking! A salubrious, (okay, go and look the word up, I can wait... tum-te-tum), place like this? Well I suppose I'd better describe it to you then. Yikes, where do I begin? For starters, and in geographical terms, Gloucester is a fairly average sized conurbation (ooh get me) in the south west of England (yee ha!) That's the country, to you and me. My Mum, Sandra, reckons Gloucester was ruined by developers in the 1960's, which, knowing that mum is blind to art or architecture, good or bad, is pretty darned amazing, let alone the fact that she can still remember anything of the 60's! Mercifully the stupid hippy planners back then didn't get their hands on our city's main treasure, and the reason we are classed as a city at all, our magnificent cathedral - ha-ha, something our nearest rival, posh old Cheltenham, lacks! So stick that in your pipe and smoke it you regency twits! Sorry about that, got carried away on a vitriolic cloud. Ah yes, a cathedral, something we have, that Cheltenham doesn't (tee hee).

Gloucester Cathedral is my absolute favourite building in the entire universe (outside of Uranus, teehee!) And hello! I realise being a fan of a big lump of historic architecture makes me sound duller than ditch water but I'm not, I promise you - read on intrepid readers (you won't regret it!)

Oh, it's no good - once again you've managed to wheedle the truth out of me so here's the thing - just why I like our cathedral so much. It's because of its position. Yes, really! It stands pretty much central in the city, seemingly rising out of the ground to look down upon its citizens (like Cheltenham does to Gloucester) almost looking like a fantastic giant's palace, and when one stands inside, looking upwards, one can't help (get me, talking fancy) but be in awe of how it was created, it makes one feel dizzy mind you, and it hurts one's neck but boy, is it worth it. I've asked myself many times, standing in an odd position with a crick in my neck - how on earth people in the 11th century managed to build such a complicated structure. Was it something to do with aliens methinks. Amazingly, I've read that architects of today still have no idea how it was achieved! Chew quiche on that Cheltenham! By the way, don't be fooled in thinking that this book is anti-Cheltenham, it isn't, but you will come to understand why comparisons are made as it progresses. Stick with it. Anyway, back to me. Hey, stop booing, yes you, the Cheltenham interloper, right at the back!

I live with my parents, and my 'utterly unalike' (I'll explain the reason for the quotation marks later) twin sister, Minty - yes, you heard me right. Minty's actual name is Minnie - (yeah, Dad loved the Beano as a kid) and a name that she, quite rightly, hates with a vengeance - the minx! I guess I got off lightly, I could have ended up being called, Plug or Walter! Last but not least, is my older brother, Paul, who, seeing as he is in the Navy, I hardly ever get to see because he's always at sea, see?

We live on one of Gloucester's older council estates, just about 3 miles out of the city and on a good day you can see clear across to the crematorium! Top that Laurence Llewelyn-Bowen.

Most of the houses on the estate are still rented but Mum and my Dad, Frank, decided to buy our house from the council quite a few years ago thinking that it might elevate us socially. Wrong! Picture this if you dare - Dad's usual attire comprises a string vest, jeans and slippers (even when he's out shopping) - you do the maths! We live in a fairly quiet area though, not one of those scary places littered with syringes you hear about in the news. OK, we DO have an old wreck in the front garden, NO, not Dad - a Ford Anglia on bricks 'cause the wheels got nicked a couple of years ago. I tell you, they'll pinch anything around here, I'd never dare bend down outside our house - I might get me bum pinched, 'Boom Boom' (yeah, thanks Mr Brush, for that one!)

Now I admit, I'm not the most gregarious (loquacious yes, gregarious, uh, no) person around, plus I am a teensy bit on the picky side, and because of this I only tend to have a small group of friends but none-the-less, as friends go, I could do a heck of a lot worse. My little posse (I know, makes me titter, too) keeps me grounded and keeps me laughing - what more could one possibly ask for? They get me through the long, dreaded school days with their crazy ideas and terribly lame jokes.

Here's the thing - one thing I can guarantee unreservedly is that whenever trouble looms ahead, I can be sure they will always be there, a couple of yards behind me!

We seem to spend most of our breaks between classes trying to find new places to hide out each time the classroom psycho's have discovered our latest lair. Must be a spy in our midst! We've been labelled geeks (and much worse) by the so-called, 'cool' kids at school (the ones who have iPhones, not android) but hey, who gives a rat's doo dah - let 'em think what they want. I'm not particularly cool, I'm well aware of it and that I possibly never will be cool and frankly, who cares? Hey, I was wearing cardigans before they were fashionable - yeah, get me, a retro trendsetter!

All I want is to make a good life for myself upon my departure from this dreadful institution (school), to not sink back into the primeval sludge with the other scummy troglodytes. Me? I'm going to be someone, so watch this space (man)!

Chapter Two

Most weekends finds me straining at the leash to get away from Glawsterr, sorry, Gloucester (memo to me - stop pronouncing it Glawsterr or I'll start to become like one of THEM and therefore, v annoying indeed), so I like to take the bus and head over to Cheltenham (I know, I'm soooo shallow!) to stay at my Great Uncle's house. I'll just refer to him as Uncle though, if you don't mind. He's an author, yeah honestly - me from a slightly Pikey family with an actual author for an uncle! He is Mum's mother's, i.e., my Grandmother's brother - just to put you in the picture.

His name? Oi, still being a tad Nosy aren't you? Well, okay then, it's Nathaniel. Nathaniel Darcy. Yes, I realise that he sounds like a Chick-Lit hero but you'd be utterly wrong - because he is nothing of the kind. You must have heard of him. What, you haven't? Blimey, I really think you need to get out more.

Oh well, whatever. Nathaniel is *the* smartest adult I know and if I say so myself, one feels it's beneficial, (that's me desperately trying to be poash, (as Mum would say, just for effect, and naturally - for her, mispronouncing the word) for me to stay in a different environment, where I'm not purely just one of three children but a totally separate entity, and in a place where I can enjoy listening at leisure to my Uncle's fantastic tales, some so tall that you can't see the end coming even when it's right on top of you. Fortunately for me, I get to have Nathaniel all to myself as Minty tends to be a bit prickly around anyone with an ounce of common sense, or years on the clock for that matter - personally I reckon she's a nut job but Nathaniel, well, he just says she is 'marching to her own tune', yeah, got that right, probably to the theme tune of the Clangers! I reckon she would rather die than go over to Cheltenham to shop and I have no intention what so ever of letting on that they have a T. K. Maxx store there!

This week, though, I felt like a change from the stinky bus and hopped (see - the nickname!) on to the slightly less stinky train instead, to 'Nam (as my inventive friend's have christened Cheltenham). I can't explain why, but train journeys always seem so much more exciting than bus travel.

I truly relish my weekends at Nathaniel's, particularly in the winter, sitting beside a genuine crackling log fire - (ours is a faux log fire - the moulded hollow 'logs' are made from fibreglass concealing a metal spinning fan-thingy over an orange light bulb!) Frighteningly realistic - NOT! Makes me cringe just thinking about it, but how I love settling down before the glow of real flames and getting comfortable in anticipation of one of Nathaniel's brilliantly weird, short stories. And yes, I do know (to all you 'greenies' out there) real fires *are* bad for the environment but only a real fire can help to create the right atmosphere to nudge his stories into life and I am sure that the odd coal fire once in a while would hardly do much damage, so please refrain from complaining, if only for the sake of fine literature, simply allow Nathaniel this one, small indulgence - thank you.

Actually, at this point, I must tell you how privileged you are with what I am about to share with you, for none of the following stories were ever intended for public consumption. However, as it's you and you have a nice smile (although, you might want to get that filling looked at right at the back), I have decided to give you a rare treat and if and when Uncle finds out, hopefully he won't be too miffed - although, to be honest, I can't imagine him ever getting snippy over anything - he's the coolest (and oldest) adult I know.

Yikes, I've done it again haven't I - been rabbiting on, that is (more hops!). So please, like me, get comfortable, in a place where you won't be disturbed, perhaps with some tea and biscuits nearby, for I am about to fill you in regarding my most recent visit to Cheltenham before I start to recite Uncle's latest story, a story of another train journey back in the mists of time when trains were still steam driven and you could buy 6 buns for a shilling - way before I was born, I hasten to add (and we'll talk again later).

....

Having made my way along the colourful terraced street leading from the railway station to the handsome square in which Nathaniel's house nestles in one corner, I stood outside in the bright winter sunshine and marvelled for a moment or two at the architecture of his Georgian terraced property thinking how grand it was in comparison to our bland 1960's semi. His lovely house is constructed from honey-coloured Cotswold stone, which makes it appear like a scrummy sponge cake in the sunshine. I must stress that when I compare it to our 1960's semi, I am not being snobby, well I hope not, anyway. It's more that I'm fast becoming an appreciator of wonderful structures - and now you may begin to realise why my friends are a select few and how I have a reputation as being a nerd and a half, or worse - a steaming great cream puff!

Nathaniel's house has all sorts of little embellishments both outside and in and it is such attention to detail that makes it stand out from most of the other houses in the square. I imagine he paid extra for the fancy touches like the gingerbread trim beneath the roof but boy, was it ever worth it!

Uncle Nathaniel lives alone, at least, that is, when his housekeeper, Mrs Bloomington isn't on site to fuss over him.

As if having built in radar, Nathaniel was peering down from his attic window and caught me, standing there like a twit with my nose in the air. He tapped on the glass, which made me look around to see where the sound was coming from. Eventually I glanced up to see his ruddy, bespectacled face smiling down at me through the patterned stained glass. He opened the circular window and called down. "Come on up dear boy, I am cleaning the attic out don't you know. The front door's unlocked."

This is something I find amazing, if not a little careless, frankly, for if you left a door unlocked where I live, somebody would probably run off with the door let alone anything else.

I made my way indoors and took my shoes off as I normally do. Uncle Nathaniel has thick wool carpeting throughout in what I consider to be an impractical shade of cream, and I certainly didn't want, or dare, to leave a dirty footprint anywhere. Heaven forbid, I'd never hear the last of it, so I hastily put on a pair of his outlandishly decorated Turkish guest slippers (from one of his many exotic jaunts) and then I proceeded to make my way upstairs. I had to dodge around another of his holiday nick nacks, a low hanging Turkish lantern - very colourful when lit up but very painful when not, if you are like me and forget its there and smack face-first into it!

"Ah, there you are young Mark," he called, peering down, owl-like from the attic aperture. "You wouldn't believe what I've unearthed – some of my old jotters from when I was in my first semester at Oxford! More to the point though, is that they contain a wealth of the first short stories I ever wrote!"

"Really?"

"Absolutely! They were all written during that rather turbulent time of my life when I was away from my parents for the first time and when I was not quite sure what I wanted to be. I thought I had lost my dear old books forever. I must say, I shall enjoy reading them again, for these are stories from a time in my life when I had the potential to be absolutely anything I wanted to be."

"Wow - how cool! So you have even more stories to tell me now?"

"Indeed I do!"

"Then they'll probably take me up until my twenties!" I laughed and Uncle smiled in appreciation.

"Well, I'm sure it'll guarantee many a return visit from you then my dear boy. A captive audience is better than no audience at all."

"Oh I'm hardy captive, Uncle! I love hearing your stories. To be honest with you, and without wishing to sound like a giant suck-up, hearing your stories has made me extra keen to do well in my GCSE's so that I can, hopefully, go on to Uni myself and study English Literature." At that, Nathaniel beamed a warm smile that indicated to me how much he appreciated my own appreciation.

"That would make me immensely proud my boy, immensely proud... Right then young Mark, this tidying up can wait for another day – are you ready for your next thrilling adventure?"

"I certainly am, I've been waiting all week for this."

"Jolly good. Mrs Bloomington has made us a lovely lemon drizzle cake to keep us going and today I have chosen a story with a theme related to your mode of transport this week."

I smiled benignly at this, knowing that Nathaniel couldn't possibly know that I had opted to use the train instead of the bus. We made our way downstairs to his sunlit study and he swiftly nipped into the kitchen to make us both mugs (bone china of course) of Earl Grey tea, and cut each of us a thick slab of cake. He then waited until I was comfortable in one of his plush chenille covered chairs facing the double French doors that led out to his garden, before he proceeded to read the story.

I am never sure how, but there's something almost magical about the way Nathaniel delivers a story that always seems to send me to the actual place. A gift, that's for sure...

Nathaniel waited until I was settled and happily tucking into my cake before saying, "I have taken the liberty of bringing this story a bit more up to date for it was set originally in the late Victorian period but as that time is oh so long ago, I thought it might have little relevance to you. It's still very much a historical piece in its setting but I think you'll find the revamped version a bit more relevant to you than the original Victorian version might have done. I do hope you enjoy your brief journey through the mists of time and remember to tuck your return ticket away somewhere safe. I call this story:

Train of Thought

The windswept station was alive with shadows. The sky, a heavy gun metal grey, had burst open causing torrential icy rain to dance on the deserted platforms and clatter like buckshot against the corrugated tin roof. Sheltering amongst the shadows and looking at his watch was Neil Watson, a man on a mission. Neil's watch confirmed what he had been dreading - that his train was late. He absolutely hated being late for work, especially having to apologise for something beyond his control to his smug faced boss.

"Damn it, are they ever on time?" He cursed. Just then a call came over the loudspeaker.

"Great Western Railways is sorry to announce the delay of the next train to Swindon which was due to arrive in Swindon at 08.50. This train has now been re-scheduled to arrive in Swindon at 9.40. Once again we apologise for any inconvenience. Hot and cold refreshments are available from the Turbo Café to eat in or take away."

"Damn!" He repeated.

Sick of the cold updraught from the rain that was now edging ever closer to where he was sheltering and noticing how cold his feet were in his impractical office type shoes, he decided to retreat to the waiting room as he had done many times before. It was not one of Neil's favourite places admittedly, for it always felt cold and unwelcoming and with an odd fusty smell that had a habit of clinging to the inside of one's nostrils for hours later. *All it would take*, he thought, *is a change of paint colour and a good heater to make it bearable,* but he quickly realised the flaw in his idea - if it was too comfortable it would attract wayward youths and other undesirables. He pushed the door open and oddly, felt suddenly light-headed for a second, as though he had stepped through a fizzy cloud of energy causing him to feel rather unsteady, but once he was completely inside the room he felt much better. He was amazed to see that it looked vastly different from the last time he had been there, only a few days previously. Now, the waiting room looked totally unrecognisable - just like something straight out of the 1940's.

"Wow! This is incredible," he said aloud.

"What's that then, young Sir?" Said a voice behind him. He immediately spun around and was confronted by an elderly apple-cheeked porter.

"I'm sorry?" He said.

"No need to be sorry my ol' butt," said the porter. "I just said, What's that then - what's so incredible?"

"Well you are for starters. Where did *you* pop up from?"

"Been 'ere awhile - been cleaning up behind this 'ere notice board. Them vacuees, their a messy bunch and no mistake," he muttered.

"Vacuees? What do you mean, vacuees?"

"What do I mean? Don't be joshing with me young Sir, you know full well what I mean – less of course, you're from another planet!" Said the porter wiggling two fingers above his head like feelers and smiling at his own joke.

"No," replied Neil. "I'm not from another planet! As I recall there haven't been any evacuees since the last war which, correct me if I'm wrong, ended thirty five years ago!"

"So you can predict the future then, can you? Mind you, with them clothes I reckon you *could* be from the future," he replied, chortling at his own joke. "By Crikey Sir, don't you be wishing your life away, we're only just into '42 - you sure you haven't had a bump on the head or summat?"

At that, Neil began to feel rather uncomfortable and didn't relish the thought of spending the next 30 minutes in a room with a complete nut-case.

To avoid eye contact with the porter, he glanced out of the window. The rain appeared to be easing off so he decided he'd casually make his way towards the café for a classic dodgy rail burger and a cup of tea. The porter looked up and watched him leave, but didn't say a word.

Neil was glad to be back outside in the fresh air but still the platforms were empty with not a soul to be seen, and looking around, he noticed more things about the station that looked different from usual. There were posters of a nostalgic nature on the walls, but then again, he thought, retro *is* back in fashion. He stood transfixed by a one penny chocolate vending machine. Touching the cream painted lever, the odd fizzy feeling washed over him again, making him shiver.

This is crazy, he thought. *Am I dreaming? Something doesn't feel right*. He shivered as a disturbing thought came into his head. *Oh blimey, I hope I'm not losing my mind like Mum did*.

In actual fact his mother hadn't lost her mind at all, she had suffered from severe depression after his older brother had been killed in an accident years before Neil was born. His mother had always felt guilty for failing to catch hold of the child seconds before he was knocked down.

Neil stood on the platform, feeling utterly confused. He was outside the place where the café should have been, only it wasn't there, in its place was a building called, 'The Tea Shoppe.' As he looked through the steamed-up windows it was clearly apparent that this was where his fellow travellers had retreated to during the downpour. He scanned their faces and was immediately struck by a similarity between them all - it was their clothes!

Not one of them was wearing anything bright, only dull, austere, one could almost say, 1940's fashions - all apart from one.

They must be making a film, he thought. That's probably it!

One person stood out amongst them, a woman. She reminded him of his mother somehow, just how she looked in his old family album. Even more so, because she was wearing a cheerful red poppy patterned dress, which stood out like a flame amid the general greyness of the scene. She had striking red lipstick to match. He distinctly recalled seeing his mother in a similar dress in one of the old photographs tucked away in a drawer somewhere. The scene looked like a special effect, one full coloured individual amongst a sea of grey. *Incredible*, he thought. As he made his way into the overflowing and stuffy shop, he shivered involuntarily. His mother would have described it as though somebody had walked over her grave.

Neil had quite a task in simply navigating his way through to the counter. As he did so, he found that couldn't stop himself from visually seeking out his mother's double.

"Yes," said the lady, sharply, from behind the counter, making him jump in the process. She was a tall, thin woman with equally thin grey hair pulled up into an unflattering pinned style. She had a down turned mouth that gave her the look of being miserable and it had been savagely attacked with bright red lipstick that was clearly outside the lip line in an attempt to liven and thicken the thin lips up. Neil couldn't help but notice that the lipstick had attached itself to her front teeth also.

"Uh...Pardon?" He said.

"Yes, next please!" She said over emphasising the words and momentarily flashing the red tinged teeth.

"Oh sorry - I'd like a quarter pounder please... with cheese!"

"You what?" Said the lady, rudely.

"You know, a burger with cheese?" He emphasised, starting to get irritated by the woman's rudeness.

'If you want a burger, go see the yanks at Fairford. We, young man, are governed by rationing as well you know. Now, how about a nice potato cake?"

Reluctantly he gave in. "Oh okay then, yeah, and a cup of tea please, you DO have that?"

The woman, smacked down a thick cup upon the tray in front of her, with her heavily nicotine-stained fingers touching the rim. It was filled with an equally thick deep tan tea that looked stewed. Neil immediately wished he'd asked for coffee. Luckily for him he spotted a counter seat spare, so he made his way towards it and sat down. He bit into his unusual cake, expecting it to taste disgusting but to his surprise, it actually turned out to be rather delicious. Neil glanced casually around whilst drinking his tea from the side of the cup the woman's disgusting fingers hadn't touched. The lady in red, he noticed, was not alone. She had a child with her, a little boy - well maybe not that little. He looked to be about 8 or 9 ish. He was busy pouring salt from the cellar making it form into little piles on the table.

"Andrew!" Don't do that you naughty boy - people have to use this table after us, now pack it in," she cried. The boy went scarlet as he suddenly became aware of everyone staring at him. He sank down into the chair and sulked.

"Don't get too comfortable, the train will be here soon and we don't want to miss it."

The boy didn't look up, for he was too busy sulking.

"Look at me when I'm talking to you, young man - you *were* naughty, you know!" But she quickly softened her tone and added. "Oh come on, let's go and get you a comic to read and some sweets for on the train."

The boy suddenly became animated once again and was off and running towards the door straight away.

"Andrew! For goodness sake, just wait a minute, please, I have to pay the lady first."

"Children," she said to the lady behind the counter who rolled her eyes in agreement.

By this time Neil had finished his unusual meal and stood up to pay the bill.

"That'll be one and three please," said the lady. He looked up at her over the top of his glasses.

"Pardon?" He replied, his patience with the awkward woman beginning to grow very thin.

"One and three," she repeated but this time with a sharper tone.

"One and three what? Asked Neil."

"Look young man," she said, "I'm just about sick of your attitude so just give me the money and be on your way."

Crumbs, he thought. MY attitude! What's going on? I guess the only way out is to humour her and pay her in old coins. He fumbled through his change and handed her an old florin hoping for the best.

"Well thank you," she said sarcastically, "nine pence change."

When he got out onto the platform he spotted the woman in red a few yards ahead of him, once again having trouble with the boy.

"Get away from the edge you stupid boy," she shouted. The child moved back slightly.

"If I have to come over to you I'll smack your legs," she called.

"But mum," he said.

"Don't 'but mum' me," she replied.

"But mum, there's a pound note on the track."

"What? Where?" She said, getting up to investigate. As she started making her way towards him, the train began its approach.

Neil stood watching, incredulously as if in slow motion, the boy suddenly leapt down to the track to retrieve the note. He could hear the woman screaming. He could see the boy's crouching form oblivious to any danger.

In a split second he made the decision. With all haste, Neil also, leapt down on to the track and with a superhuman effort, he swiftly grabbed the boy, hauled him back up onto the platform and then felt an immense impact.

Blackness.

Neil came to amid a sea of anxious faces. His vision swam in and out but as the picture became clearer and he recalled what had just happened to him, he suddenly started panicking and struggled to stand up. Having done so he quickly realised that amazingly, he was uninjured. Neil's head felt hazy but as his vision began to clear, he noticed immediately that none of the people from seconds before were anywhere to be seen - even the woman in red and the little boy were nowhere to be seen, the only people around him now were all wearing much brighter, modern clothes. Suddenly a man came rushing out of the toilets and ran over to see what was going on.

"Oh my god what happened?" He said, upon seeing the people gathered around Neil.

"Honestly, can't I leave you alone for a minute," said his brother - Andrew.

....

"Ohhhh, so it was his brother then? He must have actually gone back in time to save his own little brother, or rather, his big brother - is that right?" I asked.

"Yes - big brother who was then small! Strange eh? And who knows why these things happen Mark, some things are just meant to. There have been reports of time slips for years and it is my personal opinion that spheres of time, dimensions if you will, co-exist and that at certain times or under certain conditions they can inter-connect like two soap bubbles merging in the air causing all sorts of mayhem. So, tell me dear boy, did you enjoy the story?"

"Yes it was fab, Uncle, but I'm left rather puzzled about one thing, and it's not actually IN the story..."

"Oh yes?"

"Yes - how on earth could you possibly know that I caught the train this week rather than the bus?"

"Ah that? If I were to tell you all my secrets, I'd never have any surprises to spring on you would I? Let's just say that I have a good pair of eyes and ears and a very probing mind!"

Hmmm, very mysterious, I thought. *A probing mind eh - very mysterious indeed!*

Chapter Three

Later, when we were back downstairs I asked Nathaniel if he had ever considered getting his short stories published, so that everyone might enjoy them.

"Oh, I don't think they are good enough for that young Mark," He replied. "Do you know how many people are trying to get books published, my boy?"

"No. How many?" I asked.

"Well too many, that's for sure. Now drink your tea before it gets cold."

Too late. It was already stone cold, but I drank it anyway and without making a fuss, although if I had been at home I probably would have refused to drink it. It's just that I never like to show anything negative about myself to Nathaniel, it would feel as though I was letting him down. I sat for a moment simply enjoying the huge slice of cake I had also been given.

"Nice, Mark?"

"The cake? I should say so, it's absolutely scrummy. Mrs Bloomington bakes exceedingly good cakes!" I laughed at my little joke but Nathaniel just accepted the comment at face value. There was no TV in *his* house.

"Another story or have you had your fill for one day?"

"Always time for one more, Uncle and then I'll help you in the attic if you like – I love exploring attics!"

"Do that a lot do you?" Asked Nathaniel.

"Well no, actually, not as much as I'd like. Dad always gets crabby and orders me to stay at the bottom of the steps whenever he has to go up into ours. He's convinced I am going to step on the plasterboard and fall through! I don't know why he gets in such a flap, you can hardly move in there anywhere with all the junk he has!"

"Oh dear, sorry to hear that. Well I don't mind you helping me in *my* attic Mark, all good life experience I say. As long as you *do* stay on the boards! Now about that other story... More cake?"

I nodded vigorously, perhaps too much so. Once we were settled comfortably, Nathaniel opened his old Oxford jotter and selected another story.

"Now you won't be frightened will you?" Nathaniel had a mischievous twinkle in his eye as he always did when pulling my leg. I smiled back saying, "I think I'll survive!"

"OK, here I go then." Nathaniel smiled. "This one I imaginatively entitled:

A Ghost Story

It was mid winter, 1963 and bitterly cold. There was a shrill easterly wind whistling along Market Street in the village

Streepleton, that cut sharply through the telegraph wires, making them vibrate so much, that they created an eerie, unearthly sound like the wail of a mournful spirit. Such an ungodly sound somehow managed to make the already bitter temperatures seem even colder. In the distance, an ever-advancing wall of yellowy cauliflower clouds bubbled up menacingly like an oncoming avalanche about to swallow up an alpine village, but which, in actuality, were heralding the onset of an advancing snowstorm. Mary Westholm frowned as she looked up at it. Just seeing the cruel colour of the sky made her shiver and she immediately reached up to fasten the top button of her blue wool coat before hastily fishing into her handbag for her gloves. Mary then rushed, head down past a row of mismatched shops that had been gaudily decorated for Christmas, towards the bus stop to catch the bus home.

For once, the thought of sitting in the warmth of the bus replaced the feeling of revulsion she normally felt when confronted by the cloud of choking cigarette smoke billowing out as the door opened. She spied the usual crowd in the queue and couldn't help wondering why, even though they saw one another every night, no friendships were ever kindled and why nobody seemed to want to talk any more. But she also realised that by not attempting to make conversation herself, she was no better than them. *Must be a generational thing*, she mused.

Thankfully it didn't take long for a bus to arrive and the spaced out queue contracted so much that suddenly everybody in it was under cover. She immediately settled herself down and pulled her coat tightly around her, as the bus's heating didn't appear to be working. Ironic really, as in mid summer you could literally guarantee that the radiators would be throwing out heat on full power, making the bus incredibly uncomfortable (and even smellier). She attempted to look out of the window only to find it was coated with condensation on top of ingrained filth and because of this she began to feel rather claustrophobic.

The monotonous journey passed uneventfully and within less than twenty minutes she was home and attempting to hang her coat up in the hallway whilst Cisco and Toby, the family dogs, leaped and yelped around her, eager for attention.

"Got home just in time, love," called her mother from the kitchen. "It's just started snowing."

"Brrr, I'm glad I'm in. It's bad enough being half frozen from the unheated bus without getting turned into a snowman as well," she replied whilst patting the attention-seeking animals.

....

Later, after dinner, while Mary was settling down to listen her favourite wireless programme, there was a knock on the door. Mary's mother answered it. It was Stuart, her boyfriend.

"Oh hello Stuart, love," said Mrs Westholm. "Madam's in her usual spot listening to, 'The Goons'. Come on, hand me your coat – cup of tea?"

"Oh that'd be lovely Mrs W. Three sugars please. I tell you, I need something hot and sweet after what I've just been through - I feel pretty shook up."

"You what? Cried Mary, who had been half listening. What do you mean - shook up?"

"Listen, I'll tell you when your programme's finished. Let me get this hot tea into me, I'm blooming freezing." He then pulled a chair as close to the coal fire as possible and sat staring dejectedly into the dancing flames. Stuart, who was a printer by trade, had been asked to stop on his way home, and deliver some boxes of stationary to the church in Grassington Lane. It had been dark as he'd pulled up outside the church and he suddenly wondered if anyone would be in attendance inside. Stuart, who would be the first person to admit that graveyards after dusk are a definite no-no, was all set to drive away, to return the next morning, until something odd had captured his attention.

At first he'd thought it was a foreign body actually in his eye but after blinking a few times and rubbing it, he realised that it wasn't. The moving image to the edge of his vision was something real, right there, in the graveyard. What prompted him to get out of the cab and push open the ancient creaky gate, he couldn't recall but as he was relating the story to Mary, later, he started to remember a feeling of compulsion and conflict that he realised, must have been affecting his judgement.

Stuart recalled standing at the foot a grave, shivering, and being transfixed by the face of an angel carved into the ancient marble tombstone, and he recalled clearly, how the angel's inanimate face had a deeply mesmerising effect upon him and how, as he stared deeply into it, it had begun to change, subtly at first but then quite markedly. He saw another face, superimposed upon the angel's face. It was as though he was watching a silent movie - the face looked human, not a static carving, but a moving, human face - yet eerily pale and transparent. He remembered being able to still see the marble pattern and the yellow lichen beneath the face and he also noticed, just above it was a deeply carved name - *Jane Burdon*.

Mary held her breath.

"Your tea's getting cold Mary," said her mother punctuating the silence.

"Mother!" She snapped, annoyed at the break in her concentration.

"Oh sorry!" Replied Mrs Westholm in a huff.

None of this fazed Stuart who was still mentally half way between where he had been and where he now was. He monotonously picked up from where he had been interrupted.

"It seemed that no matter how hard I tried, I just couldn't look away, and the face seemed to grow larger and larger until I could see right into its eyes with a feeling of sheer, overwhelming sadness. It was all I could do to stop myself from falling to my knees and sobbing. I know - me, a big jessy! But I couldn't comprehend what I was seeing, for the face looked so young, a girl virtually, but by far the most shocking was that I could see her being set upon by a huge brute of a man and then he did it! He murdered the girl right in front of my eyes - there - in the very graveyard she lies buried! I could actually feel his vice-like hands around my neck getting tighter and tighter..."

He paused for a moment.

"It was so realistic, Mary, that I was starting to see spots of light dancing before my eyes and a feeling of sheer, overwhelming defeat. Oh God, it's hard to put into words, but Mary, believe me - I was conscious of the life ebbing out of the young girl's body as her neck was squeezed tightly by his monstrous hands! The poor girl, so young and so innocent!"

Stuart suddenly put his head into his hands and stared blankly at the floor.

"Oh Stuart, come on, you're here, safe now." Said Mary, tenderly running her fingers through his hair. "Safe and warm."

"I know, but I'm left feeling so confused by it all," he replied, looking up at her with his eyes still full of tears. "What does it all mean? Why was it shown to me? And look!" He pulled open his collar and showed her the marks around his neck. "Do you see? How could a ghost do that?"

Around his neck were red finger-shaped welts.

"My God Stuart - those are real bruises!"

"Well, yes - why, did you think I was making it all up?"

"No! I didn't mean that, it's just that I thought spectral hands would have no strength, no physicality about them. Sorry Stuart. What do I know about spirits? Not much it seems but you know what?"

"What?"

"I know I love you."

"Aw, I know you do, Mary. But do you love me enough to go with me back to the graveyard, tomorrow? I can't fight it, Mary - I know that Jane Burdon needs help, so I have to go back there. I *have* to."

Deep inside, Mary wanted to say no, not in this lifetime but, like Stuart, she felt as though she needed to help the poor girl's spirit to find some peace, so she simply replied, "Of course I'll accompany you. You don't need to ask."

"Phew, that's a relief. I can't tell you how much better that makes me feel. I wouldn't have thought that wild horses could of dragged you there."

No, me either, thought Mary, getting up to go to the kitchen where her mother was doing some washing up.

"Sorry I snapped at you Mum," said Mary, offering to make her mother a cup of tea as a peace offering. "It's just that what Stuart was telling me was so absorbing." She then proceeded to tell her Mother all she had been told whilst Stuart remained slumped in front of the wireless, eating his tea.

"I know that story," said Mrs Westholm. "It's all coming back to me now - it's actually a bit of a local legend. Jane something or other - I heard it years ago, and I remember it because it supposedly happened at my old church. The Vicar, back then, told me the story one day after choir practice. It seems that this Jane person..."

"Jane Burdon."

"Oh, OK. Jane Burdon was placing daffodils on her mother's grave on Mother's Day when she was violently attacked. The vicar also told me that by a horrible coincidence, the murderer is buried in the same graveyard. What makes it even sadder though, is that it happened on the girl's 16th birthday."

"Poor thing, it's no wonder she can never rest," said Mary.

....

At 5.00 o'clock the next evening, Stuart gently helped Mary up the slippery, snow covered steps of the old churchyard. She stopped to open some of the cellophane bags of the bouquets, for she hated to see the flowers suffocating inside. Stuart walked on in silence a few yards ahead.

"Where is the grave then, Stuart?"

He said nothing in return.

"Stuart?"

Still silence.

Then slowly he turned to face her. She noticed right away that his posture looked different somehow, not quite right. Broader, more hunched.

"Stuart?" She repeated.

His head was bowed but as he slowly raised it, Mary realised to her horror that his mouth was frozen in a grimace and his eyes looked wild and staring and then he began to stagger towards her.

"Stuart, whatever are you playing at? Stop it, stop it now - this isn't funny!"

He heard nothing, for his soul lay captive inside his own possessed body. Then, with his arms outstretched like Frankenstein's monster, he stumbled towards Mary, clearly intent on assault.

"Stuart! Stop messing about," she cried, trembling with fear and unable to move. Then, suddenly she became conscious of a glimmering shape right at the edge of her vision.

"Help!" She yelled out in desperation, but Stuart continued staggering towards her.

"Stuart! It's me, Mary!"

But he was beyond hearing.

Mary began stepping cautiously backwards, in an attempt to get away from him, but her foot caught on an exposed tree root causing her to stumble and making her fall to the ground. When she looked up, she gasped, for she could now see another face within Stuart's - a face so ghastly and bestial in appearance that it immediately made her legs go weak from shock. A wave of fear and the smell of putrefying flesh invaded her nostrils as two strong hands grabbed her savagely around the neck and began squeezing her throat tighter and tighter, causing spots of light to dance before her eyes. She could feel her feet literally leaving the ground as Stuart lifted her aloft like a prized specimen.

Now, as she struggled to stay conscious, she had all the confirmation of Stuart's story she needed but it all seemed too late, for she was on the verge of blacking out. Then, just at the point where she was about to lose consciousness, a piercing scream brought her back to her senses and the ever-tightening hands suddenly loosened their grip. Mary had desperately hoped to see someone coming to her aid for such was the pitch of the hysterical scream, but it seemed, nobody had heard her - the sounds were confined to the graveyard and to another time entirely. She looked at Stuart and saw that he was shaking uncontrollably as a glimmering shape was now entering his body. Mary watched, transfixed, for two faces could now be seen within his own, that of the beast but also the beautiful face of Jane Burdon – two spirits locked in battle within him.

"Fight him Jane - this is your chance to put things right," Mary instinctively found herself urging Jane's spirit on and in doing so, she started to see clearly, the girl's spirit growing in brightness and strength. The roles then quickly became reversed. As Jane's spirit was drawing strength directly from Mary, now it was Jane herself whose hands were around the beast's throat. As a consequence of this, the beastly murderer started to rapidly diminish in size and became paler in intensity, causing Stuart to suddenly slump to his knees. The monstrous apparition then continued shrinking until it became no more than a pulsating speck in front of them before it finally disappeared in a vivid burst of crimson light. Stuart too, now propped up on his elbows, was also witness to the incredible scene. Mary could see that the fight had taken a lot out of him for he was left him looking weak and pale.

Then, in front of the two of them, Jane's free-floating spirit hovered and was now bathed in a blinding white light. Slowly it turned to face them. Both were relieved and thrilled to see that Jane was now smiling happily and they could feel the warmth of her smile penetrating deeply into them, renewing their souls and giving them a unique insight into life after death. Amazingly, both Mary and Stuart now held the knowledge that Jane's spirit had been purified and although her lips had never moved they both clearly heard her thank them both and then, as she continued to hover before them, she said goodbye. Finally, her human form became like that of a whirlwind and shot upwards, into the heavens, throwing out a prismatic burst of colours before disappearing into the all embracing clouds.

Mary and Stuart remained staring upwards until suddenly, a noise behind them caused them both to spin around. They could hear and feel a deep rumbling sound coming from one of the graves. Both of them quickly moved back as far from the grave as they could get, for it had now begun to cave in on itself. Suddenly the entire grave imploded, leaving a gaping, steaming hole in the snowy ground.

For a second or two all seemed quiet but then the calm icy air was once again invaded by an ungodly howling. It must have been emanating from the killer's spirit for an apparition of a monstrous looking man had now manifested before them. Within seconds the apparition's features were pulled apart as Mary and Stuart stared in disbelief, into what can only be described as a spinning nebula of ectoplasm which spiralled crazily above the remains of the grave, causing a flurry of snow and leaves to rise upward magically as if dancing to some inaudible tune.

Stuart looked at Mary with fear etched upon his face and he instinctively pulled her tightly towards him. Mary buried her face into his jacket. Suddenly, with a loud *thoooom*, that made the earth around them, tremble from the shock wave, the entity was sucked into the grave cavity and with it, all traces of evil dissipated.

Neither of them attempted to move until Mary dared to glance across at Stuart. Though he could barely stop his teeth from chattering, he managed to say, "I don't think I need to ask whose grave *that* was."

"Or that," replied Mary, pointing. For in front of them was a white marble grave which, strangely, for December, was surrounded by fresh Daffodils, poking their pretty yellow heads through the snow. Jane Burdon had done what she had set out to do 150 years previously.

....

"Didn't scare you too much did it? Asked Nathaniel."

"Nah, of course not! Well OK, maybe it was a little scary. I might just think about it a tad tonight but it was another terrific story and creepily atmospheric."

Nathaniel smiled.

Just then I noticed a vase of daffodils on the dresser that I could have sworn hadn't been there earlier.

"Bit late for those isn't it, Uncle?"

"Oh my goodness, I hadn't noticed them. Must have been a bit of Mrs Bloomington's magic."

"Really?" I wasn't wholly convinced, for Uncle had simply side-stepped my question but I made a mental note that from now on I would wait and see what other amazing things happened to spring forth out of Uncle's stories and into the real world.

"Well that's quite enough for now - I don't want your mother accusing me of giving you nightmares! Let's go up and sort the attic out a bit, until Mrs Bloomington calls us for dinner."

With that we made our way back up into the attic to delve amongst the treasures that hadn't seen the light of day for many a year.

....

I cannot begin to describe the excitement I feel whenever I am faced with mysterious treasure (although many would refer to what I class 'treasure' as junk). Did I mention earlier, I am not a typical teenager? I'm sure I did. Well, anyway - I'm not! My absolute favourite programme ever is *The Antiques Roadshow* and because of that I know my Troika from Clarice Cliff and a heck of a lot more. Nathaniel thinks I have the making of a fine dealer of antiques.

"Here's something you may be interested in young Mark – Rupert the Bear annuals."

Unbeknown to him, he was displaying the Holy Grail of old books to me as I already have the start of a collection of my mother's (and mine) old Rupert annuals. These were different though, for they were far earlier editions, the much thicker annuals with wonderful matt covers and in pristine condition too. I felt as if I might explode from excitement as I shakily reached across to grab hold of the battered old leather suitcase that had been lovingly sheltering them for oh so many years and in doing so, had protected them.

"Do you like Rupert, Mark? Or are they too young for you?"

"Heck no! Like Rupert?" I cried. "LOVE Rupert, more like, always have, ask mum – I already have a small collection."

"Then you shall have these, but promise me you'll take the greatest of care with them! There's even a few original yellow Mary Tourtel ones!"

Mary Tourtel! I was on cloud ten, never mind, nine! I am sure Uncle knew that I would treasure them. To say I was the happiest 16 year old in an attic in Cheltenham would be an understatement. I simply couldn't stop myself from smiling (imagine someone with a coat hanger wedged sideways in their mouth – that was me!)

"Keep them in the case my boy, won't go far wrong if you keep them protected."

"You bet I will, Uncle, and thank you so much. I absolutely adore Rupert. Alfred Bestall's illustrations are ace!"

"Well as long as you don't start wearing yellow checked trousers and a red sweater!" Just then we were interrupted by the sound of, 'Yoohoo', coming up the stairs. It was Mrs Bloomington calling us down for our dinner and what a dinner it was!

"'Ope you don't mind, Mr D, but I decided, as master Mark was staying, to make something modern for you to enjoy, err, hopefully. It's something I like to call, 'Stargazey Pie with a twist'! The twist is that instead of using fish with the heads poking out of the pastry lid and which I'm sure master Mark wouldn't be attracted to, I have used German Frankfurters!"

"Sounds like a science experiment, Mrs B," I joked.

"Yes, a domestic science experiment!" Smiled Uncle Nathaniel at his own joke.

"You *are* a silly sausage," she said trying to hide a wry smile.

"Weiner we going to taste it," I remarked using the popular American slang word for hot-dog.

"Well right now master Mark," answered Mrs B, pulling a funny face and clearly not getting the joke.

"Good one, Mark," Nathaniel replied when she was out of earshot. I should have known that he would get my joke, he might be incredibly old but he is incredibly young at heart.

After we had eaten our deliciously unusual pie (with chips, peppers and sweet corn) Mrs B announced what we were to be having for dessert – Apple Crumble with a twist. When I asked what the twist was she did a quick rendition of the 1960's dance making us both chuckle.

"Someone's been at the cooking sherry again," he laughed whilst Mrs B was waddling away, back to the kitchen.

The crumble made me feel humble (feel free to ignore the rhyme!) I was in the presence of a domestic goddess and I savoured every moment. Uncle pushed his chair back a little and patted his stomach appreciatively. "Worth every penny I pay her," he joked. I was sure that Mrs B was worth more than pence and I was equally sure that Uncle Nathaniel was far more generous to people than he cared to admit to.

"I've got an extra surprise for you this week, young Mark. I've got us two tickets to the Everyman Theatre to see, *Blithe Spirit* - a play written by the late, great, Noel Coward. What do you think about that?"

"Really? You shouldn't have. You've already given me the Rupert annuals."

"Ah, but there is a purpose for me taking you to see THIS particular play. Tomorrow I shall be reading you a rather ghostly little tale entitled, *The Forbidden Room*, and you will, I imagine, see certain similarities with the play. Not only that, however, for *Blithe Spirit* is quite simply a wonderfully written piece of theatre and I want you to share in my enjoyment of it!"

"Then I am thrilled to be invited, Uncle," I replied.

Chapter Four

Turns out that Nathaniel had managed to get us seats in the upper circle where we enjoyed the best view, which was so cool! As it turned out, the play was both funny and spooky but never less than entertaining and as far as I was concerned it could have gone on all night as I really didn't want it to end. The sets looked so incredibly realistic that I started to think I might like to go into set design as a career. Mrs B had made us some home made sweets, Coconut Ice and Double Chocolate fudge to take with us. It's lovely being treated as someone special and I mentally noted that I must show my appreciation a lot more to Mrs B as she is, in my humble opinion, a rare gem.

Later that night, before going to sleep I pondered about the next story, trying to pre-empt Uncle and figure out what the general theme would be – then I went off into dreamland...

In my dream I found myself standing in the middle of a huge stage, all alone. There were two rows of small footlights and at each side, and way up high were huge spotlights (I think they are called, 'Super Troupers') shining directly down upon me, making the blinding, white glow the only thing I could see. Suddenly I noticed a figure forming within the light and it quickly started to take shape as it was getting nearer to me until I could clearly make out that it was Nathaniel. He wasn't dressed in his usual clothing though, he was wearing a multi-coloured jacket with long tails at the back, and he had on a red shirt, black trousers tucked into knee length black patent leather boots and a shiny black silk top hat.

An odd, wavering voice announced his arrival. "Ladels and Gellyspoons," it said, "would you please give a big hand for magician supremo, 'Mister Natty D'. This made me smile. I thought of Uncle Nathaniel as a rapper and it was, to say the least, a surreal and slightly disturbing, moment. Nathaniel smiled, bowed to the audience and then, with a wide sweeping gesture of his arms, he took off his hat. Instead of hair, a bunch of feathery blooms popped up from his head. He then proceeded to pull out of the hat, what appeared to be a white rabbit.

First came the ears, still came the ears, and still further came the ears. Then finally, a head appeared. This rabbit's ears must have been 5 feet long. Nathaniel asked me to take hold of one of the ears whilst he had the other. I could now see quite clearly that the 'rabbit' was a total fake and I started to pull as he instructed me to. We pulled and pulled until I started to tense up, for I could sense something was going to happen and sure enough, like a Christmas Cracker, there was a huge bang and a flash and as the smoke and acrid smell cleared, Nathaniel now had a rabbit's head where his own had been, whilst I, to my alarm, had been turned into a human-sized carrot. It was when the rabbit turned its pink eyes in my direction and I spotted its two vicious-looking, pointed, yellow teeth, that I woke up in a sweat.

What was the meaning of such a dream? Well, I think it was due to me feeling a bit special and also finding myself being popular (for once) if only as a snack for a bunny. Dreams can be very weird don't you think? Anyway, the very next day I was straight back up to the attic (slowly), for Mrs Bloomington had made sure I was stuffed from ear to ear with a full English breakfast, toast, cereal and a Cinnabun just in case I might still be hungry. It was a thoroughly miserable day outside which made me wonder what today's story might be about. One thing I felt sure of, was that the story would have an odd twist in it somewhere, for clearly, my mild mannered uncle had a dark and deeply mysterious side!

"Ah there you are! Mrs B can be very insistent, can't she! If you don't know how to say no to her you'll be in danger of exploding! At least you'll have plenty of energy now," said Nathaniel, smiling.

"Energy? Try lethargy! I feel ready for a nap more than anything else! Quick, give me something stimulating to do before I conk out!"

Nathaniel passed me a metal box. It had a lovely enamelled picture of a beautiful (if somewhat saucy) woman with wild blonde hair, on the front of it, she was holding a jewelled star.

"Her name is Pandora. Go on, open it..."

I tried to open the box but there didn't appear to be a catch or seam anywhere. No matter how hard I studied it, from every conceivable angle, the box appeared to be seamless (I was going to say 'seemed seamless,' but that would have seemed tres predictable!) I could hear something rattling inside but no matter what I tried, I simply could not get the blasted thing to open. Nathaniel stood watching, fascinated and faintly amused by my hopeless attempts to get it open.

"Well keep it near you because I feel certain that you *will* eventually figure it out and trust me, it'll be worth it - oh, and it's sort of connected to today's story... Shall I read this one here, in the attic? We can pull a couple of wicker chairs over."

Suddenly there was a huge flash of lightning followed seconds later by an enormous thunderclap.

"OK, sounds great, kind of atmospheric too. What's the story about then, Uncle?"

"Well, it's a story about relatives and how they are not all that they seem," he answered cryptically.

This made me wonder if he was referring to himself and it made me feel a bit nervous for the first time. Could Uncle have a skeleton in his closet? I thought.

"Well I'm all ears, bring it on..." And with that Nathaniel opened his bookmarked jotter and started reading. "This story," he said, "I call:"

The Forbidden Room

Imagine being all alone in a cavernous, isolated mansion with a wild, wintry storm raging outside making the window shutters slam against the wall and on top of that, imagine not having a working generator for light and heat...

Just imagine...

The rest of his family had gone out to a New Year's Eve Ball but Charles Winterbottom, being of a more studious nature, had elected to stay home to try to catch up on the thesis he had been dreading writing all Christmas break. The new term was looming ever near and he cursed himself once again, for leaving his assignment to the very last minute to tackle. Outside it was well below freezing with high shrieking winds that could easily have been earthbound souls screaming out for attention, and he was so glad that he had opted to stay at home in the warm.

For once, where he was in the huge house seemed almost cosy, making him feel more than content, immersed in his choice of classical music and happy with his own company.

He got up and made himself a hot drink and some toast which he slathered with butter and apricot jam and then he sat down in front of the cheery three bar electric heater, kicking off his boots and wiggling his toes in front of the glowing elements. With a sigh, for there were many more things he would prefer to be doing, he turned his wandering attention back to his thesis. Geography - not one of his favourite subjects but one that he knew only too well, he needed, if he was going on to become the archaeologist he wanted to be.

Soon the creation of the Great Rift Valley started fading as the sweeping strains of Pachelbel's Canon in D Major made his work focus less than clear. He stretched out his stockinged feet and flexed his toes a little, before the fire.

"Ah this is the life," he said, purposely biting into another piece of toast.

The lights flickered.

Oh no, he thought with a shudder. *Please no. Not the damned generator playing up again - please, anything but that!*

He carried on writing, to try and let the soothing music blot out his worries but suddenly the CD player stopped, leaving the house in a cloaked silence until Charles heard a familiar, unwelcome sound. It was a distinctly odd kind of mechanical grating sound, a sort of cla ch... clach...unk. No sooner had he made the mental connection as to what the noise was, than, in an instant, all of the lights and the fire were extinguished; the generator had finally died. "How many times have I told Mum we need a new one," he muttered. "They've only been gone an hour for goodness sake, and now this! So much for living in the middle of nowhere!"

And so, with much grumbling and stumbling about blindly, knocking of shins and knees by bumping, first into the table and then into the chairs, Charles located some candles in the cupboard beneath the sink where fortunately, he recalled seeing them, and then after sending his wooden pencil box crashing to the floor in a clattering explosion, he discovered some matches, he'd also remembered seeing, in one of the lower desk drawers.

"If only my ability to retain geographical data was as sharp as my ability to recall where candles and matches were kept!" He cursed.

After more bumping and cursing he made his way outside to the former tack room that now housed the generator. The shrill wind whipped about his thin frame and he half turned to go back inside for a coat but then thought better of it.

The tack room smelled of burnt oil but was still fairly warm, and yet despite its warmth, it felt decidedly unwelcoming to him, as though he was an intruder and had disturbed something. All he hoped was that he wouldn't need to stay there too long.

For more than half and hour he tried in vain to get the old generator going, but as he wasn't terribly mechanically minded and the generator was positively ancient, he soon conceded defeat and headed back to the house. Once inside, he noticed instantly how the atmosphere of the house had changed in the short space of time that he had been gone. He could immediately feel the hair rising on the back of his neck - for the house didn't seem to feel like home anymore, it felt almost as if it was alive, brooding and watching him - and vengeful with it. The whole scenario unnerved him. He had never liked the dark as a child and if he was to be totally honest with himself, he still, had never really come to terms with it.

He felt a fluttering in his stomach. Uh-oh, he thought. What a time to need the loo.

He had a choice, there was a toilet at the back of the tack room and which was hardly ever used and therefore, full of spiders and god knows what else, or there was the family bathroom, upstairs - in the dark! As he wasn't keen on spiders or rats for that matter, he opted to use the one upstairs. For security he locked and bolted the back door and after a few seconds of mental debate he gingerly began to make his way up the grand sweeping staircase.

The ancient, creaky house had a permanent smell of beeswax and always reminded Charles of a museum. Each step he climbed, made the mahogany stairs creak and caused the candle flame to flicker erratically, making the portraits on the walls appear to sway. This made the faces of his non-smiling, dour faced ancestors, appear to look distorted and devilish, instead of comforting and familiar as they would ordinarily look.

When he reached the top of the staircase, he quickly rushed into the bathroom so fast that he almost caused the flame to go out. He then just as quickly bolted the door.

The bathroom was fairly small for such a large house but at least it was cosily decorated and would be easy to illuminate with the candle, as well as being easier to keep warm. It was also a good place to plan his next move. Amazingly, the candle managed to light up most of the room, revealing the wallpaper that featured a lovely repeated rose pattern, which had always made him feel safe and secure. This time, however, the garland pattern caught his eye, for it looked different somehow.

Charles peered closer, his eyes still adjusting to the dim candle light and as he did so he noticed that where there were normally bunches of cabbage-like roses - in their place he could see eyes, millions of eyes where the roses should have been! He couldn't believe it. Every eye felt as if it was burning right into him, all of them were glistening and blinking realistically. Charles looked away, blinking himself, several times and rubbing his eyes, unable to comprehend what he had just seen. Then, quickly, in a moment of bravado, he glanced back at the wall and was greatly relieved to see the rose garland design back on the paper as normal.

Pull yourself together, Charles, stop being a baby, he thought. *That imagination of yours is going to land you in the nut house.*

Once more, the toilet was back to feeling safe and warm as he sat down to assess the situation. He didn't know why, but he found himself thinking about his sister Clare. She had always had the best of everything, clothes, birthday and Christmas presents even the most attention. It was probably, he reasoned, because she was the only daughter. Once, at a point when he and his brother Craig were annoyed at the continual show of favouritism towards her, from their parents, they'd played a rather mean trick on her.

They had sneaked into her bedroom one night and built a large dark figure out of boxes, brooms and a few toys. Later when Clare had calmly walked into her bedroom, before she'd even had the chance to switch on the light, she found herself confronted by a huge, hulking monster, half lit by the hall light. Poor thing. How she screamed the house down.

In retrospect, he could see that it was his parents who were at fault, not Clare. The old guilt feelings came flooding back as he thought of the time that elapsed before they became friends again. He had to laugh though, she had gotten her revenge by digging up worms and putting them under Craig's and his, bedding, he shivered as he thought of the slimy shock they got.

Bet she's dancing away now, he thought, *and no doubt Craig is up with the DJ hassling him to play his choice of records - why on earth didn't I go with them?*

Just then, Charles suddenly became aware of a further drop in the temperature. It was as though a window had suddenly been thrust open causing a terrific blast of icy air to blow across him. He noticed his reflection in the gloss-painted door and to his horror, he saw what appeared to be a tall shimmering figure behind him - a figure with burning, coal-red eyes. He spun around but there was nothing to be seen. Then, in a state of panic, he rushed back out, onto the landing. *Who needs a laxative with a mind like mine*, he thought, half crazily. For a moment, he stood outside shaking, not knowing which direction to go in. Then like being hit sideways, an awful thought occurred to him.

"Uuhuuuugh," he shivered. It was just around the corner - *the forbidden room.* In his family there was one bedroom that had always been known as such. When he was a child neither he, nor his siblings, were ever allowed inside it. Whenever he asked what was in the room and why it was always kept locked, he was always told the same thing, "Your Great, Great, Aunt Isobella died there." Needless to say Charles and his brother used to tease their sister mercilessly, telling her that Isobella's body was still in there - mouldering away in her bed!

Now, to him, the old joke didn't seem so funny. He recalled the day, just after he had turned sixteen, on a chilly autumn evening, when he had once again asked his mother to tell him the truth about the room.

His mother had started to get annoyed and began to say what she had always said, when suddenly she stopped, mid sentence and then to his surprise and astonishment she admitted to him that she had not, due to their tender ages, told them the whole truth, but that now, was the right time. Then she proceeded to tell him the full story...

....

"Your Great, Great, Grandmother, my Great Grandmother, May, told me this when I was eighteen –"

"It happened back in 1873, that was the year everything changed. The house had been a happy place, full of joy and the sounds of children laughing. My older sister, Isobella was expecting her first baby and staying here while James, her new husband, was away fighting the Boer's in South Africa. Unfortunately, Isobella was not in the best of health and most days she would languish in her room and we would hardly ever see her. Occasionally she would wearily come to the door and shout at us children to be quiet. Mother reasoned that it was because, not only was she expecting her first baby, but that she was also terribly worried that her husband would never come back home. Soon there was an even greater need to worry about her for she suddenly went down with a dreadful fever and had to be nursed both day and night. After three days, Isobella dismissed the servants with a demand to be left alone and then in the early hours of the very next morning a terrible scream echoed through the corridors. There was a great sense of panic in the house but everyone knew where the scream had come from.

Being a terribly inquisitive child, I wriggled through the tight group of family members and servants gathered around the bedroom door and I shall never forget the sight that met my eyes. Isobella my beautiful sister, was lying at an odd angle across the bed, her hair no longer auburn but as white as snow, as was her face which was fixed, as if frozen in terror, mid scream and with clouded, bulging eyes, frozenly looking down towards her waist. My eyes followed her gaze. There between her legs amidst blood and fluid, giving its last few breaths was a hideously deformed baby. It didn't look human. It had no eyes in its bulbous and misshapen head and horribly deformed arms and legs that sprouted from it, for there was no body as such. Where there should have been hands and feet there were what I can only describe as pulsating lumps of flesh - totally without pigment and transparent, revealing thin blue veins beneath it. The pitiful creature's breathing was laboured - and its tongue lolled out as it fought to suck in life giving air.

The staff, upon seeing the horror, either fainted or ran off to be sick - to my shame, I admit that I must have fainted and when I came to, I was back in my bed. The doctor tried to convince me that I had dreamt it but I knew it was no dream. Later, the doctor told mother that he thought the worry of Isobella's husband being away, fighting, coupled with her being pregnant and highly strung in temperament, was possibly conducive to the baby's deformity. The shock of seeing the deformed baby must have immediately driven her insane and caused a massive, fatal heart attack. Both mother and child, were buried in the grounds and from that moment on the room was permanently locked up and the key removed."

Charles stood shivering outside the toilet knowing that the dreadful room was so near. Suddenly he was rooted to the spot, for he could hear the sound of material swishing and the distinct jingle of a chatelaine, accompanied by a low whispering. His feet felt as though they were cemented to the floor. *Come on legs - move*, he mentally pleaded. They moved - in the one direction he had no desire to take.

By this time, the candle, which had burnt down to a pitiful stub, was struggling to illuminate the dusty displays of miserable looking stuffed animals along the route and yet still managed to make their shadows dance on the ceiling. He turned the corner almost afraid to look. The shock, even though he secretly half expected it, almost took his breath away. For the first time ever, the door to the forbidden room was wide open.

"Oh my God," he said aloud. A shivering wave then coursed through him, racking him in spasms. With great determination, he tried to turn around but it was as though he had become a puppet with somebody else pulling his strings - towards the open doorway.

He closed his eyes. He didn't want to look inside the dark room for fear of what he might see, and yet, at the same time he felt compelled to. As his eyes adjusted, he could just about make out the outline of a four poster bed. Everything, sheets, pillows, drapes, were covered in thick grey dust. The smell alone nearly choked him.

Then his worst fear - the stub of candle blinked out. Suddenly, his back felt terribly exposed in the yawning blackness and he peered over his shoulder along the gloomy landing. To his terror he could once more hear the sound of swishing crinoline and the jingling of the chatelaine, and it was getting closer.

He had no choice - there was nowhere else to go.

He rushed into the darkness kicking up the choking dust. The room had the same layout as the other bedrooms in the house so he instinctively ducked into the side dressing room, by feeling his way along the wall. He was painfully aware of the swishing sound coming to a stop as he hid, trembling in the dressing room. Shivering uncontrollably, he peered through the gap in the door expectantly. He had no idea what he would see and hoped upon hope that it was just his overly imaginative mind simply playing tricks upon him. Then he noticed a yellow glow at the edge of the bedroom doorway and his heart felt as though it was fighting to break free from his chest. The glow increased until it was moving into the bedroom.

He knew it was Isobella.

Peering through the gap, he could see the shimmering incandescent glow surrounding her. Although he wanted to look away, he felt compelled to stare at her face and he shuddered. It was skeletal. But no - it was changing, into the beautiful face of his Great, Great, Grandmother and in her arms was a perfectly healthy looking baby. The glow increased until it became intensely white before fading away entirely and for the briefest of seconds Charles felt elated until he tried to open the door to make a run for it, for to his horror where his hands should have been, were lumps of flesh covered in pulsating growths, blue veined and transparent.

....

"Oh my word, THAT one was HORRIBLE!"

"Do you think so? Answered Nathaniel. "Horribly bad or horribly good?"

"Good. Horribly good - but bad, with a miserable ending for poor Charles," answered Mark with a frown.

"Hmmm, I must admit, they do seem to be getting darker as I go along - must be because I was beginning to find my stride at university. Perhaps I should leave them in the attic?"

"Not a chance, I can take it! It's not just the story though, it's the way you read them - you probably don't realise it but you have an uncanny gift of making the listener feel as though they are actually there - in the story. That's what truly makes them so chilling."

"Really? Then I'll take that as a complement," he replied. "Nothing like a good immersive experience my boy, is there. Enough for now though, actually, I have just had something of an epiphany..."

Nathaniel caught me looking puzzled for a moment.

"In other words, young Mark, I've just had a brainwave! How about *you* writing a story to read to *me*? If nothing else it'll show me how much promise I suspect you have."

"Oh, I don't know - I could end up looking a right twit. Suppose you think my work is rubbish? You probably won't want to upset me by telling me the truth..."

"Untrue! I would never lie to you, Mark, don't you worry your little noggin about that! You have nothing to lose but much to gain."

"Well okay then," I said. "I guess I'll give it a go. I have been kicking around an idea for a few days actually, but I can't promise that my punctuation will be the best..."

"At this point I'm more interested in what you have to say rather than how you express it grammatically," replied Nathaniel, shuffling some loose notes into a tidy bundle.

So there it was, my mission for the day or rather, the evening and it left me feeling both nervous and excited at the prospect of having my work considered by a professional author.

Chapter Five

It was now evening. We had just eaten our dinner (Roast Guinea Fowl, if you're interested, with wild mushrooms and all the trimmings followed by Lemon Meringue Pie and whipped fresh cream). Nathaniel called it Mrs B's heart attack special.

After reading a copy of *The National Geographic*, whilst waiting for my dinner to go down, I gently knocked on Nathaniel's bedroom door. "Uncle, are you disturbable?"

"Hold on one moment dear boy," he called back. I could hear a strange sliding sound and a click just before he came to the door.

"Just finishing something off," he added cryptically. "One day I'll tell you all about it. Right then, what do you have to entertain me with?"

"Oh nothing much, only the première of my very first short story! I'll try to make my narration interesting but it's bad enough allowing you to hear my pathetic attempt of a story compared to yours, let alone having to try to read it with nervously forced enthusiasm."

"Oh nonsense Mark, you'll do fine - it's not as though I'm a stranger is it? Come on in, take a seat."

I sat on Nathaniel's Lloyd Loom chair by his window and he sat on the edge of his bed. I tried my best to scan his room to try to ascertain where the sliding sound had come from but as far as I could tell, it was just an ordinary, though beautifully furnished, bedroom. I was aware that Nathaniel might be wondering why my eyes were darting everywhere and why I was being so inquisitive so I immediately stopped it and proceeded to tell my story. "Ready?" I asked him. He nodded and so I began. "Right then, away we go and I have called this one:"

Careful what you wish for

Alex was so excited. At last, after so long, he had actually found the nerve to ask the girl he most admired, out on a date and she had accepted! Tonight was going to be their first night out - a meal followed by a movie. For him, it was as though Christmas had come early but at the same time he felt that his patience and efforts had justifiably been rewarded because he had been working up the courage to ask Summer Rayne (no kidding) out on a date for months. Alex's flat mate, Ivan, could not believe his friend's good fortune, he knew that the mysterious Summer was a prize wanted by all the guys in the village of Hatton Coate (also, no kidding). Secretly he wondered what Alex had, that he did not, but then he felt ridiculous for thinking such a thing, for Alex was as gregarious as Ivan was reclusive.

"It's too amazing," said Alex. "Someone as plain as me doesn't deserve such a fine beauty on his arm."

"You don't think very highly of yourself do you," answered Ivan. "Why do you think she is too good for you?"

Alex walked towards the window that overlooked the village square and by sheer coincidence he saw Summer gazing in the window of a new age crystal store.

"She has class, poise, a good education - and I've heard rumours that she comes from a fine family and me? I'm an orphan - virtually a street person."

"Oh for goodness sake, why are you always so melodramatic about yourself? Who are you – Charles Dickens reincarnated? You are her equal, get that in your head and never lose sight of it."

Alex considered his friend's opinion for a few minutes and realised that he was absolutely correct and yet, deeply ingrained, the nagging doubts refused to go away; the damaging feeling of inadequacy. Just then he suddenly felt his face flush and his stomach started to gurgle. A feeling of panic surged through him - *God, I hope I'm not coming down with something*, he thought. As if that were not enough, his throat then started tickling which brought on a coughing fit. As he rushed to the tap to fill a glass with water, his nose suddenly felt completely blocked up and yet still managed to drip without cease.

"Oh fabtasdik, I godda code dow."

"Oh, don't be daft, you can't get a cold *that* quickly. Your stressing about your date! Look, why don't you have a nap so that you are bright eyed and bushy tailed for tonight," said Alex.

"Ub, baybe your right, baybe it's by allergies blaying ub. I'll set by alarb clock for five. Hopefully I'll be feeling a bit bedder then. Just in case by clock doesn't go off can you give be a call blease at five?"

"Of course I will, stop worrying."

Alex made his way to his bedroom and crawled under his duvet. He was soon in deep slumber. Almost immediately he started feverishly dreaming. He saw Summer coming towards him down a winding golden path that shone so brightly that he was forced to squint his eyes, but the closer she got to him, he suddenly realised that what he had thought had been a path she was on, was actually part of her - she was half glittering serpent and when she was merely inches from his face he saw to his terror that she had a thin green forked tongue flicking from side to side detecting his presence. Summer's snake eyes were small and half domed and reminded Alex of cabochons of haematite. He tried to scream but nothing would come out. He then tried to run, but found he was rooted to the spot. All he could do was to close his eyes as Summer's yellow fangs pierced the skin of his neck, pumping poison into his bloodstream and making his tongue instantly start to swell grossly large inside his mouth. As he struggled to breathe he became conscious of a an odd sound - a rooster crowing, and it got louder and louder.

"Alex!"

It was Ivan calling him to make sure he had heard his cockerel alarm going off.

"Oh dab, I feel awful, trust be to ged a code..."

"How about some hot lemon?" Asked Ivan.

"I deed a biracle nod a hod lebud," whined Alex.

"You could try something from *my* country, tastes utterly vile but boy does it work!"

"I duddo, I don't want to get any sigger..."

"Then cancel your date, If she is keen she'll understand."

"Do way, Ib nod bissing this one. How ofden do I go out? Dever, thad's how ofden. Dope. I'll dry it, id for a peddy, id for a poud, dat's whad I say."

"OK, give me half an hour and I'll knock you a batch up."

As Ivan walked away he turned back to add. "And be sure to take off any metal jewellery!"

Alex pulled a stunned face at this request but Ivan just smiled. "Just in case," he added, as he made his way into the kitchen. Alex smiled back weakly and pulled his fleece robe tightly around his shoulders. Within minutes he had nodded off again and was quickly back in dreamland.

"Here, take this…" It was Summer again, this time he was tethered, staked to the ground and lying spread eagled in a desert somewhere. She was bending over him holding a green leaf, dripping water droplets into his mouth. "It'll make you worthy of me!"

"Ugh, what the…" He awoke to find a teaspoon shoved between his lips.

"It's OK, the vile taste will quickly wear off." It was Ivan, he was feeding Alex some of his potion and it had awakened him.

"Blibey. I can feed myself you know!"

"Sorry, I just thought you be better off unconscious when you take this as it tastes so utterly vile.

"Why, whad's id it?"

"I can tell you some of the ingredients, for instance, onion, garlic, chillies, horseradish, pimento, lemon juice, Manuka honey and three tablespoons of whiskey. Added to this are a few drops of Belonka Boing, a lesser-known Transylvanian liqueur, impossible to get hold of these days."

"Crikey, by boor stobach," moaned Alex. "I do feel butch bedder already though."

"Good, it's an ancient recipe and let me tell you, how privileged you are to have had some. It's worth the vile taste to feel great again."

Alex wasted no time and rushed towards the bathroom to gargle with mouthwash.

"You're welcome," shouted Ivan good naturedly.

By the time he was due to leave the flat, Alex felt fine. It was as though he had never had the cold. Because of this he fell into the trap of thinking that it had not been a proper cold at all and that it was just coincidental that the concoction of Ivan's had appeared to work so well.

There she is, he thought, as he saw Summer waiting for him across the square. She was standing beneath a spotlight that illuminated her blonde hair, giving it an almost unearthly glow.

"You look radiant," he said as he stepped towards her.

"Why thank you. What a lovely thing to say - you look pretty spiffy yourself!"

Hmm, he thought. *Pretty spiffy? Why not hunky or dead sexy? Pretty spiffy makes me sound like a geek - a geek from the 1940's at that!* "Thanks," he replied, half smiling and offering her the crook of his arm.

"So, where are we off to then?" She asked, linking her arm through his.

"Well, I thought we'd have something nice to eat and then, if you are good (*oh boy, why did I say that*, he thought, *I can't believe how nerdy that sounded*) I thought we might meander over to the cinema to watch a movie - of your choice, naturally."

"Sounds great," she replied as they walked the cobbled street. *A little too short and sharp*, he thought, almost as though she meant to say, 'sounds excruciatingly dull!'

"Well, here we are..." Alex gestured with a sweep of his arm revealing to Summer his choice of restaurant. "It comes highly recommended. My flat mate, Ivan, comes from Transylvania and assures me the Chez Dracul is the absolute perfect place to visit when you have the urge to sink your teeth into something yummy," (*god, I'm so lame*, he thought).

"Ha, ha, ha, you are so funny, can't wait to get stuck in."

Blimey, thought Alex, *I do believe she meant that! Perhaps my smooth tongue is working its magic for once. Yeah baby, Mr Charm is back in the city, even if it is actually it's a village!*

By this time all thoughts of colds and their cures were long forgotten.

"Would you care for a drink whilst waiting for your table," asked the waiter. Alex looked at his date - Summer seemed miles away in thought and in the strange blue light of the booth they were in, though he hated to admit it - she looked almost evil.

"Summer? What would you like to drink?" He asked her.

"Ooh," she replied, suddenly brightening up. "I'd like a Bloody Mary please and what about you, Alex?" The waiter smiled and his face turned from Summer to Alex.

"Might I recommended *Dark Victory* Sir? It's our house ale and devilishly delicious."

Alex nodded and soon they were both looking at one another as they sipped their drinks, Alex couldn't help noticing that Summer's eyes didn't blink once.

As his drink got lower in the glass, the more Summer seemed to get a little bit fuzzy in his vision. It was hard for him to define what exactly felt wrong but something odd was happening and it wasn't the feeling of being tipsy. Suddenly his nose felt heavy and his throat felt tickly. Then it was as if someone inside his head had turned a tap on, for as before, his nose started to run uncontrollably. He fumbled in his pockets for a tissue but unusually for him, he had left home without one.

"Blibey," he muttered apologetically. "Seeb to ab a code all of a suddud, exuse be but I bust visit the bens roob a binute."

"Oh okay, see you in a minute," answered Summer, sweetly.

Alex rushed into the toilets, hardly able to see because his eyes were streaming so badly. Inside he retreated into a cubicle and with the aid of toilet paper he tried his best to clean himself up. Just when he thought he had it all sorted and felt calm enough to emerge, he had the sudden urge to start coughing and because it had caught him unaware, it made him involuntarily wet himself. He shrieked, "Noooo, God no!" For now, in the last place on earth he wanted to draw attention to - in the groin area of his stone coloured trousers, there was an unfortunate wet patch. "Oh God, dake be dow," he cried. Then he had a moment of crisis-fuelled inspiration. The hand dryer! Knowing he was still alone in the men's room, he stealthily nipped out of the cubicle and turned the dryer on. It was nowhere near his groin area so out of sheer desperation he took his trousers off and held them up against it.

Naturally, half way through the procedure and with the toilets now having a somewhat unpleasant warm pee aroma, somebody just *had* to walk in.

"I had an accident," he said sheepishly. "Wader sprayed out of the tap all over by drousers," he lied.

"Really? The man replied, looking not at all convinced. "Would you like me to get somebody in to help you?"

"Dow! Dow, thank you, I'b dearly done, really!" And he was. He felt a sense of relief flood through him until, as he was exiting the toilet, he had another coughing fit. This time to his utter dismay he felt an even worse sensation - his bowels had relaxed at the wrong time and to his absolute disgust and shame he had no doubt that he had just pooped himself.

"Well I give ub, clearly I'm beant to be thingle for the west of my life!" Without a thought for Summer, who had been watching

Alex intently, from the moment he had moved crab-like out of the restaurant, hoping to God that nobody noticed him, until he suddenly raced outside and disappeared into the night.

When he arrived back home he was amazed to find that Ivan wasn't in. Ivan, the man who never went out at night! Ivan the recluse! He was glad though, at least he had no need to explain the awful facts to him. Realising he had left Summer adrift at the restaurant he quickly had a shower, put on new clothes and hared back to restaurant. As he peered through the window he saw to his amazement a huge commotion around the table where he had left Summer sitting.

He rushed inside dreading what might confront him but nothing could have been worse than the reality of what met his gaze. Ivan was unconscious on the floor as Summer, or what had been Summer was crouched over him, her fingers tipped with what looked like transparent suckers attached all over Ivan's bare chest. Pumping upwards through the suckers, he could see Ivan's blood coursing out of his body, into hers. Alex did what came instinctively to him and pulled Summer away from Ivan. Summer turned to face him and with a deathly glare, she screeched and hissed at him, and he knew it was something that would never leave his memory. Then, with a flash of grey and brimstone yellow, she vanished, still screaming like a banshee into the night, leaving a sickening smell of sulphur in her wake.

As Ivan came to, he saw Alex leaning over him and whispered weakly, "Eew, what is that awful smell? Have you let one go?" But in reality he knew full well what had happened. He explained to his rather puzzled friend that he had raced over to the restaurant to remind him not to drink alcohol but he had been too late. Alex rolled his eyes. Ivan went on to explain that after he had decided to keep Summer company until Alex returned from goodness knows where, she had suddenly begun acting strangely and quickly became transfixed, staring at an evil eye pendant that Ivan was wearing around his neck. In a split second she had laughed like a babbling idiot and suddenly lunged at Ivan, ripping his shirt open and instantly putting him under some kind of hypnotic staring spell.

Now as he looked at his bleeding, blotchy friend, Alex realised how lucky he had been - it could so easily have been him. Ivan looked up at him with an almost apologetic look and whispered the word, 'succubus'.

Alex vowed two things as they made their way home after spending most of the night in the emergency room - never to eat in a Transylvanian restaurant ever again, and never, ever to let Ivan make him a potion to cure anything - fangs very much!

Chapter Six

As I closed my writing book I glanced out of Nathaniel's bedroom window and I noticed that the scene outside now looked distinctly different to how it had been when I started the story. It was now dark and in the square, every eight feet or so were little pools of yellow light from the Victorian-style street lamps dotted around the central park area. I looked over to Nathaniel and was surprised to see that he had his eyes closed.

"It wasn't that bad was it?" I asked.

"Hmm?" Came the reply. "Oh - I wasn't asleep! I was miles away - in a place with a succubus on the loose! My word! Tell me this young Mark, how on earth does a boy of your age come up with such a theme? Succubus indeed! I would never in a million years have expected you to know anything about such a thing! I guess I must be a bit behind the times. I was shocked, no, not shocked, delighted, by your mastery of storytelling - and at such a tender age too."

I didn't know what to say for a moment, of course I was thrilled inside, that he actually liked my story and not, as I feared, ready to pull it to pieces, literary-wise. Not so keen about the, 'tender age', bit though - *I am 16* for goodness sake - practically a man!

"Really? Wow! I can't believe you actually enjoyed it. I never get any praise like that at home!"

"Do you share your stories with your family?" He asked.

"Oh no. They might not like them."

"Well there you are, you're your own worse enemy. If you want to get on in life you must be prepared to share your talent with the world or you'll end up living in obscurity like me."

"You're hardly living in obscurity, Uncle. You have a lot of loyal followers and ardent fans."

"Hmm, thank goodness none of them have discovered where I live yet," he replied, with a wink.

As I glanced out of the window again, I noticed a very tall man entering the park, walking an almost impossibly small dog, a Yorkshire Terrier from the look of it. However, from my viewpoint it looked like a bit of fluff on a stick!

The man must have easily been six foot five if not more and I could plainly make out his long, sallow features as he walked beneath a street lamp (although, come to think of it, the yellow tinge was possibly due to the lighting). He had a thin, miserable looking, droopy moustache that curled at each end as though he had waxed it and shaped it around something like a pencil. On his unnaturally pointy chin he sported a tiny v shaped beard and all in all his whole look reminded me of a Victorian villain. I must say, it seemed to me, rather an odd time to be taking a dog for a walk and I felt compelled to watch them both. Uncle Nathaniel came up behind me to see what I was looking at.

"What's so fascinating? Oh him! Yes, that's Dr Acula from the surgery on the corner. He's from Transylvania you know - yes, I've known Vlad for years. He's got a skin condition that prevents him enjoying the sunshine and he tends to make up for lost time in the evenings – always up to something in the wee small hours."

No way, I thought. *Nathaniel's having me on! His name was Dr Acula - Dracula! He's from Transylvania, like Ivan in my story! Not only that, but his Christian name (Christian, hah, that's a laugh) is Vlad, as in Vlad the Impaler, the real person that the character, Count Dracula by Bram Stoker, was based upon!*

"You're kidding, right? About his name and that he's from Transylvania?"

"No, not at all dear boy, all true."

"Oh great, that makes me feel secure - not! I'll have to keep my eye on him and keep my windows securely fastened."

"Oh he's completely harmless, it's his dog you should worry about! Do you know what he called that minuscule mutt?" His question made me jump.

"No. No idea."

"It's Fang! Can you imagine, a wee little thing like that called Fang. Clearly has a sense of humour - Dr Acula that is, not the dog!"

So there it was again, yet another connection with a story and this time it was connected to MY story. This house was certainly harbouring many secrets and I intended to find out just what! As it was getting late I decided it was time for bed but not before Nathaniel had brought me some cocoa and a plate of Mrs B's home baked choc-chip cookies. You can guarantee that at No 49 Farfrum Square (which was actually closer to a circle), you'll never go hungry.

Later, as I lay in bed pondering the days events, I thought back to Dr Acula and it set me thinking about the other people in the square. As I haven't got a clue who Uncle's neighbours' are, I guess it must have played on my mind because that night I had yet another weird dream!

In the dream, I was standing, looking out of my bedroom widow which also overlooks the square and to my surprise there seemed to be a big street party taking place. I could see that all around the perimeter of the park were odd-looking lights on tripods. Inside the park itself were all of the square's residents including Nathaniel and they were all waving placards with messages such as, 'Save Our Square', 'Say No to the aliums' - the last one I guessed was a spelling error and I felt determined to march over and point it out as Cheltenham is no place for spelling slackers, Gloucester perhaps, but Cheltenham, pretentious regency capital of the south west - never!

I put on my dressing gown, stepped into my pink bunny slippers (well it WAS a dream!) and marched purposefully into the night.

Something didn't feel right though.

To my utter dismay (and terror) I noticed that the 'tripod' mounted lights were actually moving in on the crowd. The residents were being rounded up as though they were cattle.

"Be off with you," shouted one chap in a mackintosh and tweed cap and waving a copy of *The Echo* newspaper at them. With a blinding flash from what I had mistaken for lights, he was turned into what can only be described as a large steaming kebab.

"Eeew, Charlie is charred," said a little girl holding her nose.

"Don't look dahling, take mummy's hand." And with that, the child's mother extended a robotic hand.

"You're not my mummy," cried the child. Suddenly there was a second smaller kebab next to charred Charlie - it was the girl! And in her place stood an evil automaton. As I cowered in the shrubbery, too afraid to do anything other than shake, I watched until one by one the whole square were replaced by dodgy looking replicas and kebabs.

"Ma, ma, Markkkk, velcom." It was my worst fear, I had been rumbled by a crude copy of Uncle Nathan. "Do do do beep beep dosh dash be o-o-overly concerned lad ad," it said.

"Noooooo, I cried, you're a big tin fake," I said, kicking it in the tin shin. "I'm going to call the police!"

Suddenly the lights went out, plunging the square in total darkness. I took the opportunity to run. Disturbingly, the house I ran into was not Uncle Nathan's, it was Dr Acula's! Fortunately he was no threat as he was propped up by his front door - a kebab in a cape and looked about as threatening as a blancmange.

"Mark!"

Strange? It was as though someone was trying to get my attention.

"Mark?" The square was starting to go all wobbly around the edges and I watched fascinated as Dr Acula's kebab body trembled.

"Mark? Are you awake yet?" It was Mrs Bloomington, dear Mrs Bloomington with a nice cup of tea for me - suddenly it was morning and life was normal again! I immediately leapt out of bed and glanced out of the window at the square. It was now bathed in dappled sunlight and do you know, just for a second I could have sworn I saw a greasy, fly covered kebab propped up in the entrance to the park.

Ten minutes later as I made my way, bleary-eyed to the breakfast table, Nathaniel asked me if I had a good night's sleep.

Probably tipped off by my constant yawning. I told him about my odd nightmare.

"Oh that's nothing, this house seems to feed on imaginative people - the more imaginative you are, the worse the dream seems to be."

"So there's nothing particularly odd about your neighbours then," I asked.

"Well, I wouldn't be so sure about that! Apart from Dr Acula and the old lady next door who seems convinced that she's a cotton reel - the number of times she's turned up on my doorstep bound up in thread! Many of them only seem to come out after dusk, very strange, but then again, I suppose I shouldn't really be peeking through the curtains late at night..."

"Maybe you should get a telly?" I suggested.

"Oh no, not on your nelly, I'll have no telly!" Nathaniel smiled at his dodgy rhyme.

At that point, Mrs B whizzed into the kitchen, yes, whizzed, I have never seen her move so fast before - truly.

"In a rush aren't we dear?" Enquired Nathan.

"Ooh Mr D, I've got such a list of things to do today, more than a woman of my 'youth' should attempt - fresh flowers to be bought, a stew to be prepared with a surprise pudding, cleaning, polishing and shopping for tomorrow..." I could feel an attempt to procure my assistance by the devious housekeeper or was I just being horribly suspicious? Either way, before I had time to regret it, I had opened my mouth to volunteer to help her.

"Well Mrs B, what would you like to relegate to me? Name it and it shall be done!"

"Oh Master Mark, I couldn't impinge upon you on your weekend break, truly I couldn't."

"Shall I clean the windows? I insisted.

"No, I couldn't ask you to."

"Please? I don't mind doing a bit of cleaning."

"Alright, it's a deal then, the windows it is."

Mrs Bloomington smiled a lovely sunny smile and I sat mentally counting just how many windows were to be cleaned - 18, that's all, only 18!

Chapter Seven

My maths must be pretty rotten because no matter what I tried, I couldn't make the number of windows outside the house equal the number of windows I found inside - clearly something didn't add up! The ground floor checked out properly, it was only when I got to the first and top floors that my maths failed me. From the outside there were a further two windows, one on each of them. Then a thought came to me; there was one room I recall that Nathaniel said I must never go into, right at the back of the attic. Oh yes! And I recall hearing an odd click from behind his door yesterday. I was intrigued and I only had one day left to figure it out as later that very evening I had to be heading back to Gloucester courtesy of my dad's hair raising driving.

Dad - I haven't really mentioned him have I? I guess you're dying to know more about my family eh? Particularly as I must seem so keen to get away from them. Well, I'm sure you know the feeling of being like a cuckoo in a blackbird's nest - as though you had been born into the wrong family, wrong life? Well that's how I have always felt, it was as though someone upstairs had made a humongous boo-boo and the stork, or whatever, had dropped me off at the wrong house.

Why do I think that? Take dad - please! Just take him and leave somewhere, like outer Mongolia perhaps!

My Dad is the kind of man, good taste decided to pass by, oh I know, you're going to call me a snob but truly, you should see what he wears - I swear he dresses in the dark. Shell suits never died out with my dear papa, neither did having the tongues exposed on his silver trainer boots (and he wears such clobber all the time - even to parents and teachers meetings and he's well into his 50's). He's the only person I know who will wear a hoodie (tucked in) with a tie - oh, and sometimes, slippers!

Mum met him when he worked on our family's farm - she was 18 and he was 19 or something like that. I think Nanna wanted something better for Mum, but Dad's rustic charm, (I know! Can you imagine?) Must have won her over - go figure!

When I asked Nathaniel how he and Mum could possibly be related he said. "Mark, I must point out that my younger sister, your Grandmother, Katherine, is equally, if not more gifted, than I, after all - like Minty and yourself, we too come from good stock. It was just that Katherine chose a different pathway in her life, as academia never really appealed to her. In any case, back in those days it was much rarer for women to go to university and our father, a true man of his time, put more effort into seeing me off to study. It made me feel terribly guilty but what could I do?

"Later," he continued, "when we inherited a farm from a late Aunt on your Grandfather's side, it was down to Katherine to run it. Your Grandfather, Sam was away doing National Service so run it she did, and with great success, I might add. Neither she nor Sam, needed a college degree to show how well they could run a farm - everything they achieved was the result of sheer hard work and common sense along with an instinctive knowledge and innate love of the land."

"I had no idea!" I said. "I don't often get to see Nanna Katherine these days, she's so frail now that I am always afraid that I might say something to upset her - maybe it's time our family made more of an effort to go and see her."

"She'd love that, Mark, and make sure that Minty goes along too, it might broaden her horizons somewhat."

"Hmm, maybe," I replied. *If I have to*, I thought.

....

You know that I like and appreciate antiques, right? (Hopefully you've been paying attention). Well Dad loves car boot fairs and is a collector of everything. To him everything has a value. Consequently our house is almost chock-a-block with what he calls treasure (and I call trash!) We have half a dozen cars and motorcycles lying dismembered in the front and back garden and blocking the side entrance too. It's truly embarrassing. Luckily Mum isn't quite as bad, although a fair bit of Dad's ways have morphed into her. You can't stand up straight in the bathroom due to all the knickers and tights hanging from our home-made line. I tell you, I have to put up with having one tight leg each side of me if I want to look in the mirror, and I end up looking like a spaniel.

Dad, get this, even came home one day with a selection of second hand underwear for me from a car boor sale that he'd poked around and found in a box! Now do you see where I'm coming from? The neighbours love him though, he'll do anything for anyone and I think that his chest hair poking through his string vest really excites the women, you can just tell by the way they move in closer to be near to him when he is telling one of his infamous dirty stories. Mum smiles proudly, knowing that he is faithful to her and that she has got something they all appear to desire. Makes me laugh. What Nathaniel thinks of it all I cannot imagine. Please, please don't misunderstand me though, I DO love my family, they inspire me, only without them realising it.

Anyway, back to my conundrum - the more I checked Nathaniel's windows, the more I became convinced there was an extra window in Nathaniel's room and an extra window in the attic. All I had to do now was to find out, via my mastery of suspense and cunning, how to access them. I realise that I could just ask Uncle, but in my heart of hearts I am sure he would come up with some excuse or other. Then I had a master plan ping into my head - I'd write another story based on what I think is behind the two windows and watch hawk-like for Nathaniel's reaction! If nothing else it will be a way for me to probe him about my poor maths! Alas, time was now running terribly low for this weekend so I shall make it my number one priority for next Friday night. Oh yes!

By the time I had cleaned all the windows I felt shattered (no pun intended). With perfect timing, Nathaniel peered around the lounge door and asked if I was ready to hear another story and indeed I was, more than ready, let me tell you. I needed a break from the norm and a well-deserved rest. No sooner had he opened his jotter than Mrs B came in with tea, cakes and biscuits. I watched her as she carefully placed the tray onto a pouffé and waddled over towards me with a deadpan look upon her face. I wondered what I had done wrong, but she grabbed both of my ears and gave me a big kiss for helping her. I felt my face reddening but I was really pleased to know that she was happy - doesn't take much to make someone's day (only 18 windows!) Nathaniel smiled and waited until the tea was poured before commencing with the story which he christened:

The House

"It's gone! This can't be right, buildings don't just disappear overnight - do they?" Thought April.

She dismounted from the bus and stood shivering in the cold, unable to grasp what she was seeing. Across the road she noticed a rather seedy looking cafe, whose lit neon sign, a dirty pink, was attempting to look inviting but instead it simply buzzed and flickered as though it was short circuiting which simply made it look intimidating. However, amid all the old office buildings flanking it, it was the only place open for her to head for. April stood, as if frozen in time and watched the blurred lines of heavy traffic in front of her. It was late afternoon and the rush hour was in full swing making the road difficult to cross.

It's ridiculous, she thought. *A house can't just simply disappear!* Her mind was in utter turmoil as she attempted to navigate her way through the choking traffic.

By some miracle she managed to make her way, in her dream-like state, across the road to the other side. At one point she inadvertently took in a lungful of fumy air and was hit by a wave of nausea that rippled through her, making her legs feel as though they would give way at any moment. As if that wasn't more than enough to contend with, after struggling across the busy road, she discovered to her dismay that the door to the cafe appeared to be stuck fast. Pushing as hard as she possibly could, didn't help at all until suddenly, it flew open outwards, causing her to almost lose her footing and fall backwards against a parked car.

"April?"

Looking up through a spinning haze, her eyes focussed on the owner of the voice.

"Marcus? Oh Marcus, thank God it's you."

He extended a hand. "Here let me help you. You must have tripped. Hey, come on now, stop trembling - come inside in the warm and have a seat, you don't look at all well you know."

"I'm not surprised, Marcus. I thought I'd never see you again what with the house gone."

"The house? Gone? What on earth are you talking about?"

She looked puzzled for a second by his sharp comment.

"Look, come and see for yourself." She pulled him over to the window. "Oh! But It's there now, I, I…"

"You're probably just tired, April. It's one of those days! It hasn't exactly been good for me either. My day started out quite normally, I got into my car, was driving to work when I suddenly found myself standing outside my own house looking across at this cafe. I don't know how I got there or what had happened to my car. One thing I am definitely sure of though, is that my house is OK as you can well see."

He pointed to it.

"Come on," he said holding out a hand. "Lets go back to my house and have a stiff drink, I think we both need one."

Sitting in front of Marcus's lovely warm fire, April savoured the delicious glowing warmth of her cognac. She swirled it around in the crystal globe and allowed her mind to wander. Oddly, she could no longer remember crossing the road, only sitting down in front of the fire with Marcus, as he fussed over her, attentively. Stranger still, she discovered that she was wearing her favourite blue velvet dress even though she would normally only wear it for very special occasions.

April looked up and caught Marcus smiling at her and she suddenly realised how deeply she loved him.

She smiled back at him before lapsing back again, into her daydream. *It's funny*, she thought, *how people always said that we were perfect for each other.* April had always felt that if the need ever arose, she would lay down her life for Marcus, no question about it.

Now, for some reason, the thought made her shiver - even the cognac was beginning to lose its warmth. Then, as before, a rising wave of panic began to surge through her.

"Marcus, I don't feel at all right... Marcusssss... "

Suddenly she felt as if she was being flung backwards at an alarming speed All around her in a blur were fields of wheat.

"Oh my God," she screamed. "Marcus, your car - look at your car, it's on fire!"

"What are you saying, April?" He walked over to her and put his arm around her shoulder, tenderly. "You look like death warmed up."

"Oh Marcus, stop it!" she sobbed. Then she found herself back in his house again, in front of his fire. "I don't understand - what's happening to me? I just saw your car on fire in a field! Something feels terribly wrong ..."

"No, no my love - there's nothing wrong with you. I had a vision too. I saw you lying in the entrance to a field, I was about to wake you up when I was suddenly back here again. Even stranger was that I swear I saw my mother, just at the edge of my vision, beckoning to me."

"That doesn't make sense, your mother's been dead for years. Wait! Marcus, there's more coming back to me now. I was on the bus! Yes, it's all coming back to me now. It was this afternoon - I think – there was a man in a strange hat sitting a few rows ahead of me. I remember a sense of familiarity about him and now I'm certain that it was my Grandfather! I remember thinking that he didn't quite seem to belong into the overall picture, like a piece of jigsaw that doesn't quite fit. Oh my God. It's all clear now, I'm remembering - I know what happened to me – to us."

EPILOGUE

April had been on her way to meet Marcus to go and view a piece of prime property - the cafe, with a view to purchasing it and updating it to attract all of the local businessmen in the area. Marcus, worried that she would be late, raced off to pick her up from the bus stop only to have a tyre burst on him. This is how the evening newspaper reported it:

"Today, local Estate agent, Marcus Tate, caused the death of his fiancée, April Stevens, due to a bizarre set of circumstances. Mr Tate's blue spitfire swerved out of control on the main Cirencester Road when a blow-out to his tyre occurred forcing him to collide into Miss Stevens whom he had been on his way to pick up from the bus stop. The car then crashed into a nearby field and burst into flames killing Mr Tate. Witnesses said that an old man could be seen waving frantically from the bus window seconds before it happened. Miss Stevens died at the scene."

"We're dead, Marcus? DEAD? Then our lives are over!"
The sun was low and Marcus stood holding his hands out.

"No April. There is no such thing as death. Here, take my hand, I want to show you a wonderful place."

....

"Ooh, goosebumps time again," said Mark, rubbing his arm. "I love those weird, twisty tales."

"Spooky enough for you, was it?"

"Well it made the hairs on the back of my neck stand up for sure." I waited for a moment before committing myself out loud before saying. "Uncle? I've been thinking – next weekend I'd like to have a go again – you know, to read you a new story. I haven't written it yet but my personal mission is to make it as strange as I possibly can, maybe even stranger than yours!"

"A challenge eh? Ooh, I do so love a challenge," he replied, rubbing his hands together excitedly. "It's like the good old days that actually weren't that good in hindsight, only this time tis the pen that must be mightier and far more piercing than any sword!"

Chapter Eight

In what seemed like no time at all I was back to reality with my upcoming GCSE's and all the pressure associated with trying to do well in them. Curriculum-wise, I am naturally drawn to English literature and language (as you have probably gathered) but also to art and history. I'm not too bad at geography but just a pathetic dweeb when it comes to maths and science. Still, I aim to at least, get a pass in each of my subjects - if nothing else, one is most determined!

One annoying kid in my class is hell-bent on causing as much disruption as he can and consequently, it always affects the rest of us. If he messes up, we are all punished by having to do detention. That's the thing about school life, it's rarely fair - do you not agree? Why do teachers fail to comprehend that it is unfair to punish the whole class for the chaos caused by one jerk! I'll give you an example of what he's like. We have an old lady teacher (well she looks old to me - gotta be at least a 100) who takes us for religious studies. Most of us are keen to do well in this subject, not because we are a bunch of religious suck-ups oh no, it's because as a GCSE subject, religious studies tends to be an easy option and boy, with some of the other subjects, we need the odd easy option, trust me. But Robert Punnet (yeah, a right strawberry if I ever saw one) is too thick to realise that he is threatening our 'easy ride'.

Whenever Miss Pew (yes, I know) has her back to us, Punnet blows spit balls through a pea shooter to try and hit her on her tightly rolled bun. The poor dear suffers from really thin, snowy white hair and not a lot of it either, and it's always styled the same way, into an unforgiving bun so tight that we all wondered if she might be partly oriental. She tries to continue writing wobbly text on the blackboard as misfired spit balls land from all directions onto the board with a splat, dangerously close to her chalky fingers. Occasionally she'll feel one hit her head and spin around surprisingly fast for one so ancient.

"Who did that?" She'll bark out with her face reddening by the minute, eyes bulging and red like two radishes, corded neck veins standing proud, making her resemble a constipated tortoise. "Come on, one of you spat at me and I demand to know who!" Naturally nobody ever answers her but you know what it's like at school, you tend to go red in the face even when you are innocent.

"Very well then, I shall get the Headmaster and he will winkle the truth out of you!" As she turned to go, another spit ball hit her square on the ear and by this time we were all rolling about laughing because she had used the word, winkle. With that she turned tail and fled to the Headmasters office. Punnet smirked like, well, a moron smirking! His friends told him that he had really gone and done it now, and that he had gone too far. He replied by calling them a bunch of pouffs and promptly flipped everyone the bird! Suddenly the door burst open and Mr Glassell, our 'beloved' Headmaster stormed in with the cowering figure of Miss Pew peeking out and grinning triumphantly from behind him.

"Right. I demand to know who has been disrupting this class. Come on, only a snivelling coward would remain silent."

Silence hung over the classroom like a shroud. Time appeared to stand still as we watched the Headmaster's hawk-like eyes scanning our faces. Miss Pew did exactly the same. The pair of them reminded me of hideous gargoyle's. Suddenly Miss Pew tugged at Mr Glassell's sleeve. He lowered his head to offer his ear to her (she was barely five feet tall and he was a monstrous six foot five, at least!) With laser like accuracy, Mr Glassell's eyes locked in on Punnet who was now looking more like a puree. He had sunk so low into his chair that he was barely visible and had a, 'who me?' look upon his normally waspish face.

"Robert Punnet - did you, or did you not fire spit balls at Miss Pew whilst her back was turned?"

Silence.

"Very well, let me put it another way. If the rest of you know that Robert Punnet is the guilty one, please raise your hands."

Mr Glassell stood glaring at us, hands crossed, twiddling his thumbs. Naturally most kids were afraid of lunatic Punnet but one, shall we say, dopey, kid in our class raised his arm and this suddenly gave the others courage to do so. And so it was that Punnet was named and shamed in full view of everyone and guess what? Yes. We all got detention - ooh and the dopey kid? He got a black eye and a major wedgie too - and let me tell you, he was wearing really old-fashioned underpants! Me? I couldn't wait until Friday evening when I was going back to Nathaniel's and back to some culture. Now all I had to do was to fit my new story in between all of my dreaded homework.

....

Finally, hours later it was finished - my very own masterpiece, if I say so myself and I must say, what an odd tale it is too!

No sooner had I put my pen down than the telephone rang. I could hear Mum cursing deliberately loudly that she was not the only person in the house, then, hearing her lift the receiver, I peered over the banister to get a better idea of who she might be talking to and to turn my satellite-dish ear to get the best reception. I could see Mum wiping her floury hands in her apron which was a total waste of time as the hand piece was already covered in flour along with most of the floor.

"Oh yes?" She said. "I see, really? Goodness, how very poash (as Mum pronounced 'posh'). OK, Nathaniel, I'll tell him - thanks, love, for letting me know." With that she put the receiver down and yelled up the stairs. "Mark?" As she saw me, she lowered her volume.

"Nosy! That was your Nathaniel, it's about tomorrow."

"Oh no, I don't have to stay here do I?"

"Oh charming, can't wait to scurry of to Cheltenham can you," she complained. "Well don't go jumping to conclusions - he phoned to say that he was having an unexpected guest this weekend, a distant relative of ours that I, for one, have never met. She's Nathaniel's cousin, Madam Clarice something or other - spelt, C, l, a, r, i, c, e, but pronounced, Clareece - apparently! She's a world famous medium, so he gushingly tells me, and he is looking forward to introducing you to her - never mind your dear, sweet mummy!"

"Oh right! So, we have a world famous medium as a relation then, eh? Cool!"

"Doesn't take much to impress you does it, my little baby. Come here, let me cover you in hugs and flour!"

"Mum, leave off!" I protested.

Quicker than a politician leaving a sincerity seminar, I felt so relieved. It had been a stressful week at school and quite honestly, I desperately needed a change of scenery and being at Nathaniel's was as good as being on holiday.

"What's for tea Mum?' I asked.

"Chicken and mushroom pie, mash and peas followed by plum tart and custard - is that good enough for Sir?"

"Sounds lush!" (Well, you can take the boy out of Gloucester but... I'm sure you know the rest!)

Chapter Nine

By ten, the next morning, I was at Nathaniel's door, eagerly waiting to be let in. Dad had quickly driven off which was just as well as his hair was looking utterly ridiculous as per usual, it badly needed washing and was sticking up all over the place. He hadn't shaved in days, either. I reckon he must have thought that he had been given a gift from the gods when stubble became fashionable! When I asked him if he was planning to go outside looking like that he called me a cheeky blighter and said that the ladies liked the rugged look! Rugged? Ragged more like. He looked like a beggar!

Nothing appeared to be happening so I rang the doorbell again just to be sure. Nathaniel has a weird, antiquated looking bell, the kind you sort of pumped in and out to get it working. Why he didn't get a wireless chime I'll never know, although, I suppose it wouldn't really suit his style. Suddenly I could hear movement coming from within and then I heard the door chain coming off. Mrs Bloomington stood before me with tears streaming down her cheeks.

"Blimey Mrs B, whatever is wrong?" I asked her.

"Onion tartlets, that's what's wrong! Her Ladyship, Madame blooming Clarice, if you please, insisting on certain foods to enhance her, 'speereet powers'! She's a Madame alright, a right little Madame, (but you didn't hear that from me!") She added as an aside.

I had to laugh. This was one weekend I wouldn't want to miss for anything!

Mrs B announced that Nathaniel was in the summer house in the back garden with Madame Clarice so I looked around for the guest slippers. Surprise number one, they had been taken! I quickly ran upstairs to drop my bag off into my room. Surprise, number two. My room was no longer my room. Clearly Madame Clarice had taken a liking to it, for the place was festooned with crystals and candles, angels and Buddha figurines. I was a bit put out but decided to reserve judgement until I met her. For the time being I left my gear on the hall chair.

"Oh Mark," called Mrs B. "I forgot to tell you that your room has been commandeered by Her Royal Highness. Nathaniel wants you to use the gold room next door to it."

Hmm. I was not impressed. Takes more than mere gold to impress me. Still feeling miffed, I put my bag into the gold room and closed the door because, for some odd reason, I felt that Madame Clarice might be a bit on the inquisitive side. Having done that I raced downstairs in my socks (and the rest of my clothes!) to go and meet the mysterious Madame C!

At first glance, as I entered the sunny garden, I couldn't see any evidence that anyone was out there, that was until I heard what sounded like the mating call of a hyena. I have never heard such an alarming sound before and it was coming from the octagonal summer house at the bottom of the garden. I was inches away from the door when another burst of the unearthly sound pierced my ears. As I stepped inside, I could see the source of the noise. Nathaniel was making a strange looking woman go into fits of laughter as he read from his journal. Upon seeing me he abruptly stopped reading.

"Mark! Dear boy. I was just reading something to my charming house guest, too risqué for your young ears though. Please, let me introduce you to my cousin, Clarice from Provence, France no less."

Well! I have never seen so much make-up on a person who isn't a clown by profession.

"Sharmed," she appeared to say. She held out a be-gloved hand, covered in rings and then she waited. I was a bit unsure of what was expected of me, should I bow, curtsy or what? I looked at Nathaniel for direction and he inclined his head as if to say 'go on' and made what appeared to me as a slight puckering of his lips. I took this to mean, 'kiss the hand'. This I did. Madame Clarice made a strange trilling noise and smiled at me warmly.

"Eez sharmon, sharmon boy," She patted the seat next to her. "Please seat." Well that's what it sounded like to me at least, so I obediently sat next to her.

I noticed a large basket of strawberries from Nathaniel's garden and asked him If I could try one.

"Of course you can dear boy, had a bumper crop this year so fill your boots!"

"Bumperre crop," said Clarice stifling a giggle. "You are such a silly head, Nannypoo!" At that she gave Nathaniel a soft nudge on his shoulder. I looked at him quizzically. He returned my puzzled look.

"I can only presume, dear boy, that bumper crop sounds like something else in French! As for Nannypoo, alas I must admit it, that is a nickname Clarice christened me with when we were both les enfants - quite honestly, I had almost forgotten it!"

"You will always be my little Nannypoo, Nathaniel," she said with her eyes crinkling up as she smiled. She then turned to me and I thought, uh-oh, here we go.

"Ere Mak, I 'ave sommsink por vu."

I was intrigued. She reached down beside her and picked up a handbag that resembled a pink, furled, theatrical curtain. It had a bamboo handle and pink tassels at either end. Was I imagining it or did her arm go into it, almost up to her elbow? The bag seemed deeper on the inside than on the outside. She fumbled and fumbled until...

"Ah, ere eet ees - et voila!" She motioned for me to hold out my hand which I did and whilst concealing what she was holding, she placed whatever it was into my hand and then folded my fingers around it. I was afraid to look. It felt odd. Like a bit of old tree bark perhaps.

"Go on Mak, take a look, eet won't 'urt you," she urged. I looked at Nathaniel, and saw him smiling, knowingly. I had the feeling that I was being set up in some way and it felt a bit uncomfortable and unfair. Gingerly I opened my hand.

"Ugh, what is it?" I shrieked, dropping it.

"No worry. Eet ees a geeft. A great geeft to you from Madame Clarice. Peek eet up. Eet's a monkee paw and can breeng you mash luck!"

"Ugh! Not very lucky for the monkey though, was it!" I replied.

"Now, now, Mark, don't be ungrateful," said Nathaniel. "Madame Clarice would not have given it to you if she didn't think you needed it. Come now, be polite and give her a kiss as thanks."

I was in a tight spot. Even though I didn't really want a severed monkey hand, I felt I had no choice but to pick it up and thank Madame Clarice for it. "Thanks very much," I said clutching the very thing I wanted to fling as far away from me as I possibly could. Through gritted teeth I then said, "It's very unusual." I then leaned forward to kiss the cheek she offered. It was like kissing a powdered doughnut and I could hear a contented purr as I kissed her.

"Eet's not preety but eet's powerful - you wet, you weel learn to love eet."

I nodded and backed away thinking, *Hmm, I don't think so*'. How can anything chopped off some poor creature have anything positive about it?

"So Mark – have you been creative this past week? I've been telling Clarice all about your story telling skills," said Nathaniel.

I felt a bit shy at the prospect of a perfect stranger, oh alright, a perfect faint relation, hearing my latest attempt, even more so because she was French and might not understand what I was trying to say.

"Well I *have* written another story, Uncle, as I promised you I would, but it's a bit unusual and I'm not sure Madame Clarice might understand what I mean."

At this she shifted in her seat and appeared to make a huffing sound. Clearly I had upset her.

"Mak, my Engleesh is perfac. I know 'ow to read and understand ze language goodly. Please recipe your leetle story, I weel know what you tell."

So that was that, with Madame Clarice unwittingly making a point of demonstrating how poor her command of English was, admittedly, it was still a whole lot better than my French. I then sat back in my chair and began to absent mindedly twiddle with the monkey paw, until I realised what I was doing. I waited until Madame Clarice's eyes were not on me and than I deftly shoved the vile thing into my shirt pocket.

"OK, Madame Clarice, Uncle Nathaniel - for your delectation (I could already see her looking puzzled) I present my latest short story and I call it:

Yin and Yang

This is a sad tale of sickness and shame, which revolves around two men, identical twins in looks but oh so different in personality. They lived in a large terraced house that they'd inherited after their parents had died. Fairly quickly, they realised that living together was going to drive them apart, as they were both so different, so the house was effectively split in two, height-wise.

The one half, like its occupant, Joshua Brown, looked fairly normal. Joshua, who was a textile designer by trade, conducted his work from the upper rooms. His twin, Leviticus (their parents had been pious Christians) lived a very different life in the other half of the house, choosing to occupy the lower rooms with his bedroom in the basement.

Poor Leviticus was cursed with a debilitating condition - he was agoraphobic, (this is when a person can't stand to be amongst others) and as a consequence, it made him extremely reclusive. By the time five years had passed, he had become so reclusive, and it had affected his mind to such a degree, that he literally wanted to fade into the background, so-to-speak. Eventually, Joshua realised dismally, that Leviticus, who refused point blank to see a doctor, a specialist, or indeed anyone from the medical profession, was never going to get better.

One day Leviticus pleaded with Joshua to design some wallpaper for him. Which Joshua did. It didn't stop there though, for once it had been done, he demanded some matching material. He wanted the material so that he could get a suit made which would allow him to be able to sit and blend in front of a wall all day and all night, to simply be inconspicuous. Joshua refused at first because he thought that if he did as asked, Leviticus would, almost certainly, never get better. His twin had become so absolutely set in his ways that he refused to eat anything unless Joshua did as asked. Eventually Joshua felt he had no choice and conceded defeat but on one condition – that he would have nothing more to do with his brother until he admitted he needed medical help.

The house from the outside looked perfectly normal, it only had one front door, Leviticus never left the house so there was no need for another. If anyone was of a curious nature, they might have wondered why there were less windows inside than outside.

In spite of not being on talking terms with his twin, Joshua still cared deeply for him and made sure he had a hamper of provisions delivered each week. He would unlock a revolving book-case and slide the hamper through. As long as there was an empty hamper returned each time, he began to feel more relaxed about his brother's welfare.

One day, to his horror, Joshua noticed that the hamper hadn't been touched in a week. In a panic he called out to Leviticus to check that he was OK, but he got no response and felt a cold chill running down his spine. *It's no good, I must venture through to his side to see if he is OK,* he thought. He was terribly worried at having to do this, for goodness knows what he might find. Joshua knew he had little choice and so, trying to think positive thoughts, he made his way through. Immediately he was struck by how tidy it was. He had imagined Leviticus living like a hobo, but no! His half of the house was decorated immaculately. Each room had matching wallpaper and curtains as he expected them to, but more than just that. Somehow his twin had furnished each room with sumptuous antiques and Joshua immediately realised two things – his brother was both a thief and a fabulous interior designer. He continued looking around and was soon in one of Leviticus's two reception rooms. It was whilst he was calling out his brother's name, that he heard the door to his half of the house suddenly slam shut. Instantly he spun around only to hear a distinct sound - the door being locked. He immediately sprinted across the room to try to get out but he was too late. He had been caged inside like his brother had chosen to be.

"See how YOU like it, dear Joshua," laughed Leviticus from the other side. "I'm going to enjoy pretending to be you."

"But I thought you wanted to live in isolation," cried Joshua.

"Oh really? Perhaps it was easier for you with me out of mind? But you had no idea of my life at night, dear brother, which was thrilling and adventurous and cured my agoraphobia don't you know! You simply MUST try it sometime dear twin of mine. Oh, and don't worry, you'll get exactly the same food I had to endure every week of every month of every year!"

And so it was. The people who knew, or rather, who thought they knew Joshua Brown, couldn't believe how gifted he had suddenly become, for he played his role to perfection. As for the real Joshua, he searched high and low to find the way out that Leviticus must have used but as yet, has never discovered the secret window behind the mirror.

What he did discover though, was that if he sat long enough in the same position, wearing clothes that blended in with the wallpaper, he could actually meditate and dream that he was anywhere he wanted and well, that couldn't be so bad – could it?

....

"My word Mark, they are becoming deeper and deeper. I loved it for its unusual subject matter – I think you are going to be a great writer one day, do you not agree Clarice?"

"Well, eet was an odd leetle tale. A man oo wants to wear the wall paper ees crazy no? Should ee not be locked in the loony been?"

I tried to explain, that although Leviticus had problems, Joshua still loved him and wanted to look after him. Of course Leviticus saw it rather differently after living alone for so long.

"The thing is though, Madame Clarice, all the time Joshua thought his brother was never going to get better, Leviticus was sneaking out at night and having a great time whilst his brother was inside, worrying about him."

"Well Mak, I don't like thees Leviticus, ees dupleecitus," said Clarice while fumbling in her bag once again. "Eh, I make a rhyme no? Now, where eez eet. Oh, where can eet be?"

"Have you lost something dear," said Nathaniel.

"Yes. I wanted to show Mak a peecture of me when I was 'is age, I think eet would shock eem. Ah, ere eet eez." With that Clarice fished out a small photograph that was housed in an enamelled art nouveau frame.

"Look at eet Mak and tell me what you see!"

The minute I touched the picture frame, let alone saw the picture, I felt my fingers tingle. There was something magical at work here. As I looked at the photo I couldn't believe my eyes for it was of a girl, a beautiful blond girl around my age and just behind her was, well - me!

Chapter Ten

Before I had a chance to respond, Nathaniel asked if we were ready to hear his latest offering. Madame Clarice winked at me and tapped her nose as if to acknowledge a secret between us and I instinctively knew that we would be discussing the photo later. At this point Mrs B appeared with tea and cakes, her timing was impeccable, as always, and I managed to catch a slight dip of her eyebrows as she approached Madame Clarice.

"Thanks Mrs B, you're a star," I said, because, in my opinion, she didn't get half enough praise due her. Mrs B gave me a lovely sunny smile and quickly returned back to the main house.

"Right then," said Nathaniel. "Here we go - I call this one:

The Cottage

"Are you hot, Deana? I tell you, I'm beginning to wish I'd left my coat in the car," said Phil, grimacing.

"I know! It's absolutely roasting out here but I'm not even sure of where we parked the car, I hope you are."

"Well I think I know - at least I hope I think I know. Wasn't it back through those trees over there?"

Deana wasn't so sure but followed Phil faithfully as they set off in the direction where he thought they had parked. They were both in America enjoying a holiday they had won in a local Halloween competition back in England, which is why they were now in Salem, Massachusetts, and lost.

"It's hard to believe that this is where there used to be a lot of witches," said Phil.

"Don't be daft, said Deana You don't believe in witches do you? Back then, in the days of the witch trials, if you had something as innocuous as a mole in the wrong place or a snaggly tooth you could find yourself in danger of being branded as a witch. It's disgusting how we used to treat people," she replied, glaring at him.

"Hey, I'm not the villain of the piece. Can't say that I've ever really thought about it in any great detail before, but I guess you're right. When you think of what those poor people went through - must be a heck of a lot of restless spirits hanging around!

"I hope not," said Deana looking upwards, "It's starting to get dark and I don't relish the thought of spending the night outside in a strange country full of equally strange spirits. Come on, let's see if we can find a high vantage point to be in with a better chance of spotting the car."

As it happened they were in the flattest part of Salem so Deana's suggestion, though good, didn't turn out to be much use to them. Once they had finished looking for a hill, the sun had disappeared and they were both starting to get irritable.

"There could be bears or wildcats out here," said Phil. "Or murderers!"

"Oh great, if we don't get possessed, we get shot or eaten."

They continued to stumble about in the darkness for what felt like hours with Deana clinging onto Phil's' sweater.

"Hey, that's cashmere - if you stretch it you're in trouble!"

"I know it's cashmere, I bought it!" She snapped.

They were both on the point of exhaustion when Deana noticed a dark shape in the distance - it was a small building.

"Phil, look, " she cried.

He looked to where she was pointing.

"Hey, is that a house?" He said. Maybe we can shelter there."

She pulled a face. "Shelter? It could be a hide out for murderers, winos or druggies, or Charles Manson type killers, you know what this country's like!"

"Deana! You have to spoil everything don't you. You pessimist. Mind you, all joking aside, you do have a point, this isn't exactly Gloucester. Why don't we just sneak up first and see if the place is empty," he said, in a whisper.

And so, stealthily, they made their way to the building. Up close, it looked pretty much like a typically English cottage. It had very thick, whitewashed walls but liberally covered in disgusting graffiti and the door was just about hanging off it's hinges, having long ago been kicked open by the looks of it. Reluctantly, they both stepped inside. Deana immediately fumbled about in her handbag and fished out a lighter.

"Thank god for women's handbags," said Phil, relieved to see a welcome flicker of light. They quickly located some sticks and weeds to put in the fireplace and soon had a warm, if smoky, fire going and even in its state of disrepair the cottage suddenly emitted a magical hint of cosiness. Amazingly, Phil managed to find a couple of ancient tallow candles in a cupboard beneath a pile of old newspapers. Once the spitting candles were lit, they lit up the room with a dull yellow light. The moody light and the flickering shadows the candles created, made them both look different.

"It's a good job we brought some sandwiches with us, I'm starving," said Deana.

"Yeah, and we've got those cans of coke too," said Phil.

"Can of coke," she replied. "You've had yours already."

"OK, OK, what ever happened to sharing?"

"Sharing, what would you know about that? Hey," she said, as she looked around, "you know, this place is kind of cosy really, quite homely in a funny kind of way - don't you think?"

"Sort of", he answered flatly. "Fire smells a bit unusual though and I don't relish sleeping on this floor, you're liable to get a rattlesnake up your trouser leg."

"Or a scorpion in your pants," Deana shuddered as she said it, yet giggled none-the-less.

"Ugh don't," added Phil, crossing his legs.

After they had shared Deana's drink, settled down and eaten something, Deana said, "Phil, can you pass me those newspapers please, It'll be fascinating reading them."

"Yeah as long as nobody's peed on them. Can you throw me the lighter a minute, please."

He opened the cupboard to get to the papers and as he pulled them out something fell out from beneath them and landed on the floor - it was a folded piece of paper. He bent down to pick it up. It looked ancient and in turning it over he saw that it was fastened with a wax seal.

"Ooh what's that?" Asked Deana, her huge eyes missing nothing, despite the gloom.

"It looks like a home made envelope but it's got a seal on it. I'm going to open it!" Said Phil excitedly.

"No, let me, let me," whined Deana, like a child at Christmas. He smiled and dutifully handed it to her. Deana smiled back and then carefully turned the ancient envelope around, her fingers probing every contour and then she opened it, carefully. She was fearing it would disintegrate at the slightest touch. Inside was another piece of folded paper that looked as if it was taken from an old book or something and as she carefully unfolded it she was delighted to discover a cross, a simple metal cross.

"Look at this! A cross! It looks so old. I wonder who it belonged to?" She cried.

Phil was equally curious as he slipped the lighter back into his pocket and then sat reading the newspapers. Deana sat down quietly next to him, seemingly mesmerised by the twirling cross on its leather thong, suspended from her hand.

"Isn't it lovely. Simple, yet strong. Just holding it makes me go all goose pimply, she said, as much to herself as to Phil.

Nothing much more was said that night, they were both so tired that they cuddled up together in front of the meagre open fire with Deana holding on to the cross that she had now fastened around her neck.

Inside the cottage everything felt calm.

Deana found getting to sleep to be quite difficult at first, mostly due to the strange animal noises from immediately outside but also from the dancing red shapes in the fireplace. The flames created an almost hypnotic effect and she felt herself being mesmerised by them. Suddenly, from somewhere nearby came a strange clicking noise.

Probably a Death Watch Beetle, she thought, which then started her wondering if a Death Watch Beetle was a real insect or purely an omen of death as a white owl is meant to be. Following a few fretful turns, she finally managed to settle down to sleep after a final glance at Phil's sleeping form.

She was soon in a state of deep sleep and dreaming...

....

At that point in the story, Nathaniel paused. He had heard his front doorbell ring and no doubt was expecting Mrs. B to come rushing in at any moment. He said he was expecting a delivery and I felt he wanted to make sure he could spirit whatever it was being delivered, away upstairs with as little fuss as possible from us.

"Sorry about this jarring break in the proceedings both of you," he announced. "I'll just be a moment and when I return, I shall resume with the story - please amuse yourselves for a moment won't you? Have some more strawberries!" With that he got up and dashed off into the house.

I peered out of the summer house doorway to try to see Mrs. B. Because of the linear layout of Nathaniel's house, from where I was sitting I could see clear through to the front door. Mrs. B was just closing it and there at the foot of the stairs I could see a rather large and oddly shaped package. It was as if Nathaniel knew I was spying on him because he stood in front of it as he closed the back door so I couldn't see any more. He had forgotten all about the intercom extension in the summer house though and Clarice and I could hear everything.

"Ooh Mr.D. You don't want to be doing that, it's really 'eavy- get young Master Mark to 'elp you," she cried. Nathaniel declined her suggestion, saying, "No, no I don't want anyone short of you my dear, knowing about this delivery. Some things are best left out of sight!" Then, we could hear a lot of huffing and puffing, clearly he was lugging the whatever it was up the stairs and gently cursing - it *was* Nathaniel, after all! No doubt he was wishing that he was a young man again and how much easier it would be not to have so many secrets.

What can I say? Madame Clarice and I were looking at each other, equally embarrassed. I couldn't think of a thing to say in response to what we had just overheard so I chose to be deadly silent, and swinging my legs like a little kid. I looked at Madame Clarice, she was pushing out imaginary creases out of her skirt whilst all of the time humming a strange little tune in her inhumanly high voice that to me sounded like utter torture to my ear drums. She had the weirdest and highest voice I have ever had the misfortune to hear. Suddenly she looked me in the eye and asked, "Would you like a bonbon, Mak? They are the very best - made for over wan 'undred and feefty years by a confesshioner een Paree - 'ere, try one!"

I peered into the crumpled bag she was holding out to me. Inside were a mass of what looked like boiled sweets, patchy with powdered sugar on them and all clumped together.

"Go on," urged Clarice. "They are, ow you say, delashious!"

Delashious! Good grief, this is going to be a long couple of weeks, I thought. Then carefully, trying to avoid a snowfall of powdered sugar, I pulled the side of the bag down and selected a purple coloured sweet expecting it to taste of blackcurrant. Wrong! As far as I was concerned, notice how I said *was* concerned, the only nation to make sweets properly were the British, so to say I was not expecting much from Clarice's crumpled bag is a gross understatement. It took a fair bit of prying to get one single sweet free from the clump but having done so I bravely popped it into my mouth and started to suck it. I must be honest, I really wasn't expecting too much. At first it just tasted sweet but then all of a sudden the flavour came flooding out of it - It was lemon! Purple but lemon - such trickery! But it was also a symphony of deliciousness, so tangy, so deliciously sour that I could feel little jets of saliva shooting out from the sides of my mouth.

"Madame Clarice," I said. "These sweets are amazing!" Clarice smiled. "I am so gled you lak them Mak, 'elp yerself tu anotherre..."

Despite the sweet connection, I was now beginning to feel decidedly uncomfortable, sure, it was OK having to chat about goodness knows what for a few minutes, but now my second sweet was almost sucked away to oblivion. I glanced across at Clarice hoping she wouldn't catch me doing so - wrong! My eyes met hers and out of sheer embarrassment I smiled. "Looks like we've been stood up," I said.

"Uh? Stud oop? We are both seeting down silly boy, why would we want to be stud oop? Do you want anotherre bonbon, is that eet, is that why you want to stand oop?"

I turned away from her and rolled my eyes. I then took a deep breath and stood up to reach across to select another sweet.

"Ah, see? So I was right, that ees why you wanted to stand oop non?"

I was going to try to explain but thought better of it.

"I think I'll just go and find out where Uncle Nathaniel has got to, I get the feeling that he has forgotten all about the story."

Clarice appeared to understand this much better than I expected and nodded, saying, "OK Mak, while you are dooeen thet, I will jus' goo and refresh my face - mek myself gorshush again non?"

I smiled, raising both eyebrows and nodded.

"Be back in a jiffy," I replied leaving Madame Clarice looking puzzled again. As I was stepping through the French doors and into the lounge I bumped into Mrs B. "Where are your slippers? I 'ope your feet are clean young man," she said.

"I haven't got any and yes they are clean," I replied. "I haven't been on anything other than the path and that is spotless, see?" I gestured with a sweep of my arms to the path to prove my point.

"OK, young man, I'll trust you. Now what have you done with her Ladyship then - you've never gone and left her alone with all those strawberries?"

I think my guilty look answered for me and suddenly from Mrs B there came a flurry of activity as she strode off to save the bloomin' fruit, as she put it!

Soon Nathaniel reappeared and we both headed back to the summer house. Quickly he resumed his narration of the rest of his witchy little tale, possibly to avoid any awkward questions from either Clarice or me.

....

"Good day to thee Miss Mary, how fare thee on this fine morning."

"I am most well and most pleased today, thank ye kindly for asking, Master Pendleton. I have just been given a most effective remedy to ease many unfortunate maladies of the head," replied Mary Carrington, the local physician.

"Is that a fact, Miss Mary? And where did thou get this... concoction of yours pray tell," he added.

"Oh, why twas sent to me by traveller from a beloved cousin of mine in the far north. Tis a simple herbal remedy made with

God's own creations and should be of great benefit to the whole village."

"How can ye be sure tis just a herbal remedy and not a dangerous or wicked potion of some sort?" He asked accusingly.

Mary was shocked by his sudden change of tone.

"Master Pendleton, what, pray tell, is the matter with you. You know perfectly well that I am known hereabouts for my vast knowledge of herbs and medicines and may I kindly request that you respect as much. I know a herbal remedy when I see one, I use only God's creations in my work"

"Careful what you say Miss Mary, it may be God's creations that you use but with a bit of alchemy it can very easily become something evil if you..."

"Don't say it," she interrupted, anticipating the end of the sentence.

"... are a witch," he spat out the words.

"I beg your pardon sir," she cried out in alarm. "Please, be mindful of what you say," she looked around, grabbed his coat lapels and pulled his head towards her mouth, where she whispered, "Do you want me put to death? What on earth's got into you," she pleaded.

"Twould all fit together nicely. You living all alone, you making your mysterious potions, and, let's not forget - you have yourself a familiar!"

"A familiar? My cat? Surely you cannot believe what you're saying."

"I believe in what I see," he insisted. "My eyes do not lie."

"James, I live alone because my beloved husband died shortly after we came to live here. I make soothing lotions and remedies to help the sick and ailing and my cat is just that - a cat. Now please, I beg of you, stop this madness and stop making such wicked accusations or you'll have my death on your conscience."

Pendleton simply replied with, "Nice bit 'o land you got here, Miss Mary, too much for one person I'd say," before he bid her farewell, whistling gaily as he went.

So that's it, she thought, *blackmail*. She shivered as she closed the door knowing full well that the matter was far from over.

Meanwhile, as Deana's dream was unfolding, Phil, unknown to her, was also part of it.

"The woman is a witch I tell thee, she be making the devil's own brew to take away our very souls, I've seen it with my own eyes," said Pendleton to the village preacher.

"Tis a very serious accusation thou makest, Master James, Miss Mary is a god fearing woman and a devout Christian."

"She poses as a good Christian woman to fool us all as Esau fooled his father. Should we trust someone who interferes with God's creations to form new ungodly substances?" He pleaded in a most persuasive tone.

The preacher sighed. "I will question Miss Mary myself before I cast any judgement upon her."

....

The cold winds of autumn whipped across the preachers face stinging his eyes as he rode slowly and reluctantly across the windswept open plain towards Miss Mary's isolated little cottage. He could see Blue grey smoke spiralling sideways from her chimney as he drew closer.

"Good morning to thee, Miss Mary," he said tipping his hat as she answered the door. "Tis a cold one especially to a man of my years."

"Nonsense Father, thou art young yet, please come inside and warm yourself by the fire." The preacher did as asked and rested himself by the hearth.

"Wouldst thou care for some hot ginger cordial, and maybe some fruit cake?"

"Sounds most appealing, thou art truly a fine hostess," he smiled.

Whilst she was preparing his meal, the preacher looked around the room to see if Master Pendleton's fears could be proven in any way. He was just putting a china lid back upon a pot when Mary came back into the room just in time to witness it. She looked crestfallen.

"Oh Miss Mary, whatever am I to do. Please, I beg you, forgive me. I really must apologise and I think I need to be totally honest with you." He then told her exactly about his conversation with James Pendleton.

"He is a wicked young man and would see me burned as a witch. All I want is to be a physician and to help people," she said. "Did he tell you that he thought I had too much land for one person, I bet he did not."

"No, indeed he did not, said the preacher. "And that's interesting – so what do you think he is up to?"

"He accuses me of being a witch but Father, tis my land he is after. I pray you must stop him before this gets out of control."

"I'll do all that I can my child. Now, rest easy, I for one, am certain that thou art not a witch and I must talk to the village elders before Master Pendleton gets to them or the elders may be easily swayed by his fanciful notions. I must tarry along now. "Thank thee kindly, Miss Mary, for the drink and the cake, both delicious. Now worry you not, put your trust in the good Lord," he will protect you, he shouted as he galloped away.

Mary stood at the window watching him getting smaller in the distance and all the while she felt her hope diminishing along with him. All she could do was to hold her crucifix tightly to her chest and pray.

Poor Mary, little did she realise that her fate was already sealed, for at that precise moment, James Pendleton was entering the home of Thomas Ludwig, most senior of the village elders. Not more than a half an hour later, Ludwig had made up his mind enough to call a meeting with the rest of the elders. A gathering was hastily arranged in his drawing room. As the frenzied people debated Mary's guilt or innocence, an intense darkness permeated amongst the elders. That same evening a unanimous vote of guilty echoed throughout the house for as far as they were concerned Mary Carrington was, indeed, a witch.

Around nine o'clock, two people were chosen, together with the priest to go and arrest her. Naturally when she found out, Mary was utterly devastated and tried in vain to proclaim her innocence, appealing especially to the priest.

"You'll have a chance for your say at the trial my dear, all is not lost, the lord is thy shepherd - remember," said the Priest, taking her right hand and patting it reassuringly.

"At least I have my cross," she said aloud. "Tis my only comfort."

Mary was then pushed into a dark room at the end of a cowshed that had only one small window, covered by a rusted iron grille. The room smelled dreadful, it was tiny and overrun with rats and all manner of insects that crawled over everything. She didn't dare sit down for the first hour but eventually had to give in or drop from exhaustion. In the dim light she sat crying and tried to avoid looking at the insects crawling upon her.

Phil suddenly awoke, he looked around the room, realised he wasn't in a cowshed, turned over and went back to sleep and immediately re-entered the dream. Deana was also in dreamland unknowingly sharing the same dream.

Mary awoke with the sunlight streaming through the bars of the window directly into her eyes. She immediately shook off all of the insects that were crawling on her and shuddered. She had bites everywhere upon her body.

By midday it didn't appear as though she was going to be fed so upon hearing footsteps nearby, she cried out for help. Who should walk in but none other than James Pendleton.

"You! Look what your lies have caused. I am no more a witch than you. You know full well that my words are the truth. I am no witch and I never have been. Do you not feel remorse for the suffering you are causing me?"

"I will never feel remorse - ever." He paused. "Dost thou not remember the little boy, years ago, that you had punished for stealing from your garden."

Mary looked blank.

"When you still lived in Bessom, at the Mill, he paused again. A little boy with a thatch of red hair?"

"You? She cried, as the old memories suddenly starting forming in her head. But you have black hair."

"No, not me," he spat. "My brother. And for the great misdeed, the savage crime of stealing three turnips from your garden, he was whipped mercilessly and sent to the colonies where he died from his infected wounds. The shock of it all caused my mother to drop down dead in front of us all. You - you deserve nothing less. I've been waiting a long time to get even with you and believe you me, revenge never tasted sweeter," he hissed.

"Oh bless my soul, your brother! Twas not I that wanted him punished that day. Twas just an unfortunate coincidence that on that very day, Master Ludwig was visiting me, he insisted that the boy be punished saying that the devil had to be beaten out of him, you must believe me, for I truly had no part in it and no idea it would lead to the boy's death. My heart goes out to him. I'm so sorry for what happened," she said, nervously playing with the cross.

"You can forget being sorry and you can forget that." With that he reached in and yanked the cross out of her hands. Now even that had been torn from her.

"Noooooooooo," she screamed and lunged at him to retrieve it. But he was too strong and pushed her aside making a hasty retreat.

"Thief," Mary cried. "Thief, give me back my cross..."

Cross, the world spun around in Deana's subconscious mind. Her hand automatically tightened around the object. She felt strange, detached, floating. She knew that she was dreaming and yet found it impossible to get awake. It was as if she was spinning faster and faster which began to make her feel quite nauseous until with a jolt, she awoke - still in the past.

"What? This can't be right, this just cannot be right, this is not happening. It's night time, I'm asleep - but it's daytime and I'm awake?"

Somehow she had transcended the dream state and slipped into Mary's past life.

Her hand felt wet. She was flat on her back and turned to see what was causing the wet feeling and saw that her left hand was trailing in a lake.

After getting up and after pinching herself to see if it was all real, she looked down at her legs and was shocked to discover that she could see straight through them to the grass behind her and it suddenly struck her that she was in all senses of the word - a spirit. However before she had any chance to analyse things further she had to quickly duck behind a hedge as two women came ambling towards her and, as she was dressed so differently, she thought that it might cause a commotion.

After the women had passed by, Deana suddenly thought, that in theory, anyway, she probably wouldn't have been visible to them anyway. She decided to test the theory. With all the energy she could muster, bearing in mind that she still felt half asleep, she raced up to the two women and jumped out screaming in front of them. They simply carried on walking, completely oblivious to her spectral shenanigans.

This must still be some sort of dream - it's the only logical explanation - well I hope it's the only logical explanation, I don't relish the thought of being dead - not yet anyway, she thought.

She followed the two women, as it did indeed seem the logical thing to do. They were approaching a town square and once there, they both stepped inside a large whitewashed wooden building. Deana gingerly pressed herself against the wall - and promptly fell through. It was the Courthouse. She could see Mary down at the front with her hands shackled behind her and the Chief Elder, opposite, who was addressing her.

"And as a consequence of this, we the jury, find you, Mary Carrington, guilty of practising witchcraft. You are a devious and evil woman and because of your wicked ways you shall be burnt at the stake this very night. No more chances will you have to ply your evil trade. Does thou have anything thou might wish to repent?"

Mary slowly and wearily raised her eyes to the judge. "I have nothing to repent my Lord because, as I've told you time after time, I am a good Christian woman, ask Master Pendleton, he stole my cross - the very symbol of my faith."

A worried look crossed Pendleton's face as he sat watching from the gallery, Deana saw it.

"The woman is up to more trickery, wouldst though believe the word of a witch against mine," he urged. "Believe me friends, I have never seen her, 'Cross', and I sincerely doubt it ever existed - what in the Lords name would a witch need with a cross?"

This proved to be the final straw for Mary who collapsed sobbing onto her knees. "He lies, he lies," was all she could manage to yell before she was dragged away.

A silence fell throughout the room. Pendleton kept his eyes to the ground but still managed to exude an air of confidence for such was the degree of his duplicity. In his twisted mind he was singing for he'd be glad to see the witch burn. One thing puzzled him, however, and that was where the cross had gone after he had taken it. One minute it was in his hand and then... *Still*, he thought, *at least it is all going as planned.*

Meanwhile Phil, who had also been privy to all that had been happening in Deana's dream, had become part of the same past events along with her. He 'awoke' to find himself lying next to the same lake as Deana had done. In the distance he could see Pendleton storming through the town and knew in his heart that he must follow him. When in the centre of the town, which was no more than a couple of dozen buildings, Pendleton met up with his 'friends' - *all vagrants by the look of them*, thought Phil. Like Deana had, before him, Phil suddenly became aware of his transparent state and quickly realised it must be some sort of bizarre waking dream and started to question just what kind of weeds they had thrown onto the fire. He moved in closer to see if he could be seen and to hear what they were planning.

"The harlot shall get what she deserves," said one, completely oblivious to Phil's presence. "We jus' forge a note where she admits it all and leaves us 'er land and we all come up trumps."

"You've done us proud Jamie my boy, with 'er gone nobody will remember the past," said another red haired character who resembled Pendleton so much that Phil felt sure that they must be related. "We've always stuck together eh," he said nudging Pendleton, "just like brothers should."

Brothers! So he's not dead at all, they are all in on it. One, quite rightly, gets punished years ago and now their all enjoying his revenge. My God what times these are! He thought about it for a while and came to the sad conclusion that things hadn't really changed that much in the twenty-first century.

Meanwhile, on the other side of town, a pyre was hastily being built by villagers, a little too keenly for Deana's liking. Part of Mary's punishment was to be suspended in a wicker cage next to the pyre as it was being built.

Deana tried in vain to comfort her but it was of no use, for as she wasn't actually a physical being in Mary's time, she had no way of getting through to her.

"Deana!" Shouted Phil excitedly upon spotting her across the square. He ran over to her. She spun around and her face broke into a smile. "Phil? Uh, what's happening here? What are you doing in my dream?"

"Excuse me, you're in my dream... at least I think so."

"Whatever - does it matter whose dream it is? She replied. Isn't this weird? So, how long have you been here? Do you know anything I don't know?"

"That's impossible to answer! I've been dreaming of you, here, so I figure I know the same as you, said Phil looking around the town. "Did you mean about us, or Mary?"

"Both," she answered.

The next half hour was spent trying to piece together all of the fragments of the historical puzzle that they found themselves to be a part of.

"And," added Phil, "have you noticed that as well as seeing 'here', you can also see, albeit faintly, the room back in the cottage!"

Deana looked puzzled for a minute and stared vaguely and let her eyes relax a little, then she said excitedly. "Hey, you're right, Oh wow, I can even see us asleep."

"Well," said Phil. "I guess if the cottage is haunted it's naturally, or unnaturally as the case may be, going to affect both of us, mind you I still wonder what exactly we threw onto that fire."

"What do you mean."

"Some sort of drug shrub?"

"No way! Do you think so? Anyhow, if you're right about the cottage being haunted I guess it would affect both of us. I've been trying to get through to Mary but she can neither see nor hear me."

"Well I feel sure that we're meant to be here for the - execution," he whispered the last word. "I've never had such strong instincts before about anything," he said.

"Same here," agreed Deana, looking first at the pyre and then at the Mary's crumpled form in the wicker cage. By this time quite a crowd had gathered around them and through them.

"Damn, I can't say that I'll ever get used to this," said Phil looking at his invisibility.

"Me either," answered Deana wistfully. "Has to be the most extreme form of dieting!"

Just then a man strode forth holding a flaming torch aloft proudly, as if he was taking part in some kind of noble ceremony.

"Oh God, they're going to light it, I can't believe it," said Deana, her eyes pleading with Phil to do something. "I can't look!"

"What can we do? We're not solid."

Suddenly the whole scene erupted into a frenzy of blood lust and Mary was viciously dragged from the cage kicking and screaming.

"I am not a witch," she cried, as she was roughly tied to the stake. "I am innocent!"

At this point the eldest of the village elders strode out of his chambers to address the crowd. "Thank you, good people, thank you for turning out to see this wicked creature removed from our society. On this, the 16th day of March, in the year of our Lord, sixteen hundred and fifty five, you, Mary Carrington, under God's law, are hereby sentenced to death by burning for the crime of Witchcraft. May the Lord God have mercy on your soul."

He then turned to the torch man. "Light it."

As the flames took hold, Deana suddenly realised what she must do.

"Mary? MARY! Take this," she screamed. And with that she threw the cross as physically hard as she could towards her. Phil understood and willed it to work.

"They both watched the cross as it twirled through the air towards Mary, and it seemed as if time had been paused for a moment as the cross sailed away from them. Mary looked up. She turned her gaze directly upon Deana and then lowered her head forward to try catch the cross. Miraculously, the cross twirled around in the air and then looped itself around her neck.

Someone in the crowd witnessed it and fainted. An Elder also witnessing the sudden appearance of a cross dangling around Mary's neck, called out in alarm.

"Water! Dowse this fire, for we have surely been given a sign from the Lord."

The crowd roared with a heightened mix of awe and displeasure. Children selling sweetmeats booed. Pendleton, who was standing at the very front of the crowd gasped. He couldn't believe his bad luck. "Damn her," he said loud enough for many to hear. "Come brothers, all is not yet lost."

Mary, had now been hastily cut down and was, fortunately, mostly free of injury apart from a couple of bruises from stones that had been thrown at her, and some smoke inhalation.

The Elder motioned his brethren to follow him. Inside his chambers he announced that he was going to be retiring, for his judgement appeared to be no longer sound. Word went out that Ephraim Bailey would accede him. By this time most of the crowd had dispersed. Mary was left alone, pondering upon whom the spectral woman was who had managed to throw the cross to her.

"Forgive us Mary, please. We have all been fuelled by one man's word against you. Perhaps this has happened to teach us all a lesson," said a spokesman for the Elders, apologetically.

"Perhaps, answered Mary quietly, perhaps." And with that she found herself alone in the square. She carefully made her way towards Deana.

"Who are you," she whispered, making sure that no one could see her talking to herself.

Deana looked at Mary, amazed that she could now see her. "My name's Deana. Deana Cross," she replied stepping out of the shadows.

"Of course, whispered Mary. "Deana of the Cross - it all fits. Ah, but who is this with you?"

"Phillip Milne, I'm Deana's fiancée."

"Good names, for good people. How can I ever repay thee?"

"Listen," said Phil to both Deana and Mary. "We can talk about all of this later - I overheard Pendleton say to his brothers that this wasn't over yet and I'd be willing to bet that they're up to no good and I'll also bet they are heading towards your cottage right now. Mary, you need to get someone to drive you home as quickly as possible. It shouldn't be too difficult as they are all tripping over themselves with guilt. Deana and I will meet you at the cottage."

Phil turned towards Deana. "Now we need to think hard, try and focus on the cottage."

Suddenly they were there, as was Pendleton and his entourage.

"Think she's got away with it does she? Well, lets give her a nice warm welcome home... Now pass me the tinderbox," he said to his brother.

"They're going to burn the cottage down. We can't let them do that - we're asleep inside," said Phil frantically.

"Yeah but we're asleep in the future," answered Deana.

"Well, the cottage didn't look like it had been burned down at any time to me, Deana. Don't you see, by saving Mary, we've already changed the past. We can't let them burn this place, it isn't meant to happen."

"Well what do you suggest we do?"

"Pass me the lighter, I'm going to try to scare them."

"With a lighter? It isn't very intimidating is it?" She replied.

"Well wouldn't you be alarmed if you saw a flame appear out of nowhere."

"I see your point, I only hope you can make them actually see the flame."

"Don't worry, I've been thinking about that, it seems that if we really concentrate, together, we can do it. I noticed that it only seems to work when we are in an emotive state so get it in your head that they are going to burn us alive. Picture us both in flames... I'm going to light the lighter now, okay, and when I do, start chanting 'murderers,' like I do - ready? Right, now!"

"Murderers, murderers," they repeatedly chanted as Phil held out the flame under each of their noses. James Pendleton suddenly saw the flame and leapt back in shock.

"Demons! She must truly be a witch! She'll be upon us in no time. Out of my way, I'll not tarry here a moment longer," said Pendleton pushing his brothers aside who, being of little intelligence but blessed with speed, quickly picked up on his actions and overtook him. "Wait for me," he cried out after them.

"Hopefully that's the last we'll see of them," said Deana.

"Well they've been dead over four hundred years - how weird is that!" Answered Phil.

"Ugh, it is," she shuddered, "isn't it. All of this is. So, what should we do now? How do you reckon we can get back to our time?"

"Well you could try clicking your heels together three times and saying 'there's no place like home,' but, as this is not Oz I don't think that we'll be too successful! I think the answer's probably lying here in this cottage."

Slowly they walked up to the cottage and opened the door. It didn't look so very different from how it looked in their time. The minute they stepped into the room they were back in their own bodies fast asleep.

The next day when Deana awoke and saw that Phil was still sleeping, she didn't wake him up immediately, instead she walked over to the cupboard where he had discovered the envelope. It was lying on the floor where it had fallen. She carefully bent down to pick it up and noticed that it was once again sealed with sealing wax. Turning the envelope over she was amazed to see that it was actually addressed to her. As she carefully opened the envelope, she shivered. Inside it, once again, was an object wrapped in ancient paper, which upon closer examination were actually pages torn from a bible and she could still make out the text which was from Mark 12:30-40:

'And you shall love the Lord your God with all your heart and with all your soul and with all your mind and with all your strength.' The second page said this: 'You shall love your neighbour as yourself.' There is no other commandment greater than these.' And the scribe said to him, 'You are right, Teacher. You have truly said that he is one, and there is no other besides him. And to love him with all the heart and with all the understanding and with all the strength, and to love one's neighbour as oneself, is much more than all whole burnt offerings and sacrifices.' And when Jesus saw that he answered wisely, he said to him. 'You are not far from the kingdom of God.' And after that no one dared to ask him any more questions...'

Deana smiled, she was glad to learn that Mary's faith was strong. Finally as the last wrappings came free she found herself holding... The cross? Instinctively she put her hands to her neck where it should have been but then remembered that she had thrown it to Mary.

There was also a letter...

"Deana and Phil, how can I thank thee both, I am now old and death grows ever near but I have never forgotten ye both. Deana, thou flew through time itself to aid me when I called out from the threat of an early death and the consequences of your bold actions are still being felt. Do not fear, for all has been good since that day and my cures which always were so pure in their nature are purely the results of my valuable knowledge of plants and medicine. One day on a higher plane thou and thy betrothed shall be justly rewarded but, for now at least, please accept this cross which bears your name and which I'm sure you are familiar. The cottage can be home to ye both if you want it. Til the day we meet again..."

Mary Carrington
of Salem, Massachusetts.
29th day of September, 1699.

"Full circle. It's all come full circle," muttered Deana to herself. Then she notice that the letter was folded at the bottom and proceeded to unfold it and it said –

"I have no further need of this cross, I want you to wear it proudly, you who saved me from a certain death. This may surprise you, but I have always been in contact with the spirit realm. Some have called me a witch, some have called me a saint, but they are only names. My faith in the Lord above has always been unbreakable. You might call me a hedge witch but I prefer to be known as a healer."

Deana just stood with her mouth hanging open. Then, shaking Phil awake she said, "Phil, you are not going to believe this!"

....

Madame Clarice suddenly sat bolt upright and peering at Nathaniel over the top of her elaborate half moon glasses said, "Magnifico, you 'ad me on the edge of my shair - 'ow you come up weeth eet, Nathaniel?"

"Well that's the million dollar question my dear, all I can say is that as soon as my pen hits the paper, the story starts writing itself - one could almost say that it's a kind of magic!"

"Well bravo! Did you enjoy eet, young Mak?" Said Clarice, patting me on the leg.

"Enjoy it? I loved it! It felt so real, as though I had been transported into the past and I almost want to know what happens to Deana and Phil afterwards."

"Really? I never really considered what happened to them after," answered Nathaniel. "That's really the point of short stories. Perhaps I should re-visit them in another story some time. Who knows, maybe the cross is more than it appears to be... And what about Mary? Somehow she had the rare ability to be able to reach out and touch the mind of another, even from so long ago. Wouldn't you love to be able to do that?"

"Ooh you tease," said Clarice, not giving me a chance to reply. "You'll be writing a crazy story about me next, non? I'll 'ave to watch my step over the next few wicks eh?"

Wicks? Errrr, weeks even? It suddenly hit me in the face like a wet kipper - wicks? Clearly Madame Clarice was going to be a semi permanent fixture for a while and I would have to put up with it. I can't explain why I felt that way, I guess it's because I consider Uncle Nathaniel mine and mine alone - Minty isn't interested and quite frankly I don't want to share him! At that point my insane mental rant was interrupted by a familiar trilling sound as Madame Clarice showed her appreciation of another of Nathaniel's humorous quips.

"Sauce!" She said, pushing him away with her hand. Poor Nathaniel nearly went flying off the end of the couch.

For a brief, and I mean - brief, moment there was a lull in the conversation until Madame Clarice turned her attention once more, to me!

Chapter Eleven

"Mak, 'ere. Come 'ere and seet next to me." Clarice patted the cushion on the chaise lounge. "I want to tell you all about thee monkey paw - quite a story - make you eyes poop out!"

Oh dear, I wasn't sure I wanted to hear such a story let alone have my eyes poop out! I was quite conscious of the paw prickling my chest whilst still hidden in my breast pocket. It gave me the creeps just thinking about it.

"Where eez eet," she asked me.

I fished it out and held the sorry looking thing aloft.

"I'm sorry Madame Clarice but I feel really sad for the monkey - surely there are only going to be negative things associated with such a brutal act?"

"Leeson to the story Mark, eet weel change your, ow we say - tune, no?"

With that she again, patted the seat of my chair, which she had pulled tightly next to hers and then, once I had sat next to her and making sure that she had Nathaniel's full attention, she proceeded to relate her story. To make it easier to follow, I have transcribed it into the Queen's English (you can thank me later!)

The Tale of the Monkey Paw

Back in the early part of the 19th century, in what was once known as The British Honduras (now, Belize), there lived an English family of Jesuit missionaries. The head of the family felt that it was their mission in life to bring the Lord to the native tribes upon our planet and to set them on to what they considered to be the right course in life. They knew that in order to gain the trust of the indigenous people they were to meet, they had to be seen to be meeting them halfway so-to-speak, rather than revealing how shocked they were by their somewhat alarming, (to our culture of the time) traditional practices.

Week after week the family were invited to attend many of their hosts' strange ritualistic ceremonies and at times the missionaries found it hard not to show their outrage at what they were witnessing. They did, however, feel protected by the Lord, for each morning they asked for his protection and understanding for the entire day ahead.

Over the coming months the tribe grew more accustomed to the strange white people attending their ceremonies but still they appeared to be resistant to any suggestions of change. They seemed to have ceremonies for just about everything – birth, death, manhood, female flowering, hunting, communing with the spirits and even, heaven forbid - earth magic. Yes, all of these things were considered by the missionaries to be heathen practices to be stopped.

As the months rolled on, the missionaries became more and more disillusioned by their lack of progress. There were five missionaries in all, Samuel Johnson, he was the father at 43 years old, Madeira Johnson, the mother was 39. Charles Johnson was their eldest son at 19 and then followed, Colette, 16 and finally, was young Albert at 14. The children were all remarkably bright and were having more success than their parents at changing the views of their young counterparts.

One day, Charles was helping a group of pre-manhood ceremonial young men to construct a bamboo hut. Everything was going well and it seemed to be taking shape with the precision of a military operation. As the last pole, the main support for the centre of the building, was being pushed into position, Charles slipped on some wet earth. As he fell forward he instinctively put his right hand out to save himself but he caught the rough edge of a bamboo half pole. In an instant his hand was severed at the wrist and for a moment, as he watched it happening, time for him appeared to stand still. When he realised that it was not a dream but in fact real, and he saw the blood pumping from the stump at the end of his arm, he fainted.

When he awoke, later that day he felt disoriented and confused. He couldn't understand why he had been sleeping in the day. Suddenly a half remembered image came into his mind – of a bloody stump! In a flash he sat up and held his arms aloft. Both hands were there! It must have been a nightmare.

Charles rubbed his eyes and checked his hands once again. "It's true," he cried, "my hands are undamaged." It was only when he got out of the low cot he had been sleeping on, that he spotted the blood trail on the floor, that led away from the bed, and it worried him greatly. He followed the bloody trail to a place where a small group of the natives were all huddled together.

They were looking down at something on the ground. Charles peered through a gap in the circle of people and was sickened when he saw the body of a monkey - with one paw missing. Suddenly everyone started looking upwards for a commotion had broken out in the treetop canopy. Hundreds of Howler monkeys were screeching at them and throwing anything and everything down upon them. The dead monkey was a large male and it had been their leader.

Charles began to feel odd, not at all himself. The villagers around him seemed alien somehow and the clothes he was wearing felt tight and unnatural. He could not help himself, a primal scream issued forth from his lips as he felt the need to escape, to join his brothers and sisters - in the trees. Screeching like the others above him, Charles ran towards the nearest tree vine and started to climb it. It felt easy and so natural to him, as though he had been born to it. Within minutes his clothes were in a heap on the jungle floor, along with his humanity.

By this time his family had gathered beneath the trees waiting for him to come down, but to no avail. Samuel Johnson could only watch through tear-filled eyes at what used to be his eldest son. He knew at that moment that his family could do God's work no longer, for they had broken one of Moses' ten commandments, deliberately. But, you might ask, what had actually happened after Charles had lost his hand?

As he was lying on the floor losing his lifeblood, his father tried in vain to stem the bleeding by keeping his son's handless arm raised high whilst tied with a vine. By this time all of the villagers had encircled them to see what was happening.

"Go away you savages," shouted Samuel, angrily. He cried out to the Lord in desperation, hoping and praying for a miracle. Rakkata, the Shaman of the village stepped forward and offered to save the boy's life but Samuel roughly pushed him away saying, "He is at God's mercy now."

"Father please, don't let me die," cried Charles, weakly.

There was a battle commencing in Samuel's head but the look on Charles's face was more than he could stand. Suddenly Samuel stepped back and motioned for the Shaman to take over. Rakkata took control and ordered the youths of the village to kill a monkey leader and cut off its right paw. This they quickly did and dumped the poor creature's body on the ground before him. Rakkata glared at them for showing so little respect and fully intended to punish them later, for the elders of his people held a deep respect for all things - dead or alive. The Shaman then performed a ritual in which the monkey paw was bandaged to Charles's stump.

As Charles lay thrashing about, surrounded by the chanting villagers, something incredible happened, he could see the spirit of the monkey entering his body and at the same time, the pain in his arm was no more.

Suddenly the Shaman motioned for everyone to stop singing. He bent forward and carefully unwound the bandage on Charles's arm. Samuel inched forward preparing to be disappointed but no! It was a miracle – not a sign of the dreadful injury. Charles had a perfectly unblemished, human hand again. The Shaman insisted that Charles should be allowed to rest, for a transmutation of the species had taken place and such a thing always rendered a person exhausted. Rakkata stood back expecting praise from Samuel but the missionary wouldn't so much as look at him. Samuel felt sick of heart at what he had allowed to be done to his son and heart sick at his lack of faith in God. Briefly, it had all seemed worthwhile to him whilst Charles was sleeping, seemingly, once again in perfect health. However, within minutes of his son's miraculous recovery, Samuel's elation quickly turned to despair, when Charles was suddenly swallowed up by the great jungle, leaving the distraught man forever heartsick and his family, never the same again.

....

"So what deed you mak of eet, Mak," asked Clarice.

"It was a bit gruesome! Sad and sort of strange but a strong indication that's it's not a good idea to mess with magic - or nature! Clarice?"

"Yes, Mak?"

"How did you get hold of the monkey paw? And how can you be sure the one in the story is one and the same?"

"My paw? Ooopsie, *your* paw. Why eet 'as been passed on to me from my papa, Robert. Eet has been en famile for shenerashion - you see, Alberre Shohnson was my Great, Great, Great, Grandpapa, so 'e wud be a fent relation of yours, too! We 'ave known always eet to be the 'and of 'Sharles Shohnson, a missionary and last year I 'ad the story come to me in a psychic meditation. Now eet is infused with mashic – but weell eet be lucky, for shou?"

Well, I was not convinced, but I smiled and acted as though I was truly impressed. Truthfully though, if an animal is killed in such a horrible way, or a human, for that matter, you can't tell me that there are going to be good vibes running through whatever is left of it. As far as I was concerned I was going to put the horrible chopped off paw in a drawer in my room until the day Madame Clarice was due to go home, then I would sneak it back into her bag. Creepy thing - the monkey paw, not Madame Clarice (although?)

As it had turned out to be such a lovely day, Nathaniel surprised us all by saying he was going to take us to visit Woodchester Mansion, a well know unfinished building just outside Stroud. From what I have read and seen on TV, it is now a protected bat sanctuary which, ordinarily, is more than enough to fill me full of excitement but there was more to come. Full of zeal, Nathaniel related a story of how, in the mid 1800's, the mansion was mysteriously abandoned by the workmen building it. They left their tools and ladders where they stood and where they have remained until this day. Clearly something pretty bad must have scared them away, otherwise they would never have left their tools behind, for they would have cost a small fortune in those days.

It is rumoured that a fight broke out between English builders and a French stone mason resulting in the stone mason's death but it is widely thought that the place is haunted by more than one spirit, and by spirits from more than one time period at that. Just as well then, that we are visiting it on a sunny day rather than a dismal night but, like all the best laid plans, little did I know then, that things were going to take a different course entirely!

Chapter Twelve

Oh boy! I had to open my big yapper didn't I. No sooner had I said to Nathaniel that at least we had good weather than it immediately, or practically immediately, clouded over with big black cauliflower shaped clouds. The air went kind of weird too, all wrap around warm and uncomfortable, like when you know the flying ants are going to swarm, making you shriek like a girly when they get in your hair (or is that just me?)

"Good job I brought a couple of these," said Nathaniel, as he turned the car into the long approach that lead to the mansion. "Always carry a brolly in England, Mark. Always!"

"Eet look ivil out there," squeaked Madame Clarice. OK, perhaps not 'squeaked' exactly but kind of like that, all babyish and frankly, a bit irritating.

"Eet weel ruin my do eef I get a wet 'ed," she whined.

I told her not to worry - there'll be nobody to see her - just the ghosts! As for me - I wasn't afraid of getting my hair wet, water's fine, flying ants - no flippin' way. I aimed to take a run into the mansion anyway, no chance of any raindrops landing on me! Dad's always saying that I am thin enough to dodge the raindrops (note to any child psychologists reading this - that's how to set a child onto a very wobbly pathway in life!)

The approach was longer than any of us had expected and I was thinking that the 'mansion' must really be quite small to have stayed out of view this far in but then, as we turned a corner, it suddenly appeared in its imposing magnificence, all darkly honey-coloured and huge! I looked up and saw that there were tattered sheets of plastic flapping from some of the unglazed windows, like shrouded spirits. The sky by this time was like slate grey cotton wool with little wisps of white.

"Stratocumulus," said Nathaniel as he helped Madame Clarice out of the car. "There'll be thunder soon, you mark my words, Mark."

"Yes I think there will, Will," I replied jokingly. Madame Clarice looked at me oddly. "Why you call Nathaniel, Weel? Ees not 'is nem? You a strenge boy, Mak!"

Clearly she had a problem with the British sense of humour, or perhaps it was just me she had a problem with. Didn't worry me unduly though, in fact, it made me want to tease her all the more. Hey, don't blame me, 'tis the mansion, something evil lurks in the shadows so it do!

"Yes, welcome, welcome," said a thin, buck-toothed tour guide as we stepped through the front door. "Normally," he said, "in inclement weather we would call off any tours but as you were non contactable, we have decided to make an exception. You are the only party here so you have the place all to yourselves, well, apart from a few spirits and the infamous black dog. You won't be scared will you?"

He said the word, 'scared' like Vincent Price might have said it, for effect, but he didn't fool me for a second, I KNEW I was going to be scared and it didn't help that the lighting inside the mansion was hardly sufficient for such huge rooms. I also knew about all of the supposed ghosts including the black dog that is meant to be a sign of impending death. Yeah, thanks Google!

Casting my eyes from floor to ceiling, I tried to gauge what kind of style this building would be classed as. Theatrically Gothic I'd say. You really need to witness it yourself though, as it is definitely a one of a kind, building! One of the first wacky things I noticed was an unfinished fireplace - halfway up a wall! There are also corridors that serve no purpose whatsoever. We wandered into one room and there was a kind of inverted pyramid in the floor directly in front of a fireplace. The equally scary guide informed us that where we were presently standing, had been designated by many psychics as a vortex - an opening where spirits can come and go (bit like the airport only breezier!) We were advised not to stand in it or we could be (a) possessed or (b) feel nauseous and dizzy or (c) disappear completely only to reappear in the spirit realm. Great! Personally, I'd settle for b!

"You won't run off alone now, will you sonny Jim," said the guide invading my personal space and spitting on me in the process. I was now aware that a globule of his crinkly middle-aged spit had landed on my bottom lip and the thought of it was totally grossing me out.

"No, no way." I replied before using my shirt sleeve to rub my lip furiously in case I should catch cooties or turn into a buck toothed middle-aged clone of the guide.

"Goooood," he gasped expelling ancient tea breath. "Children should be seen and not heard eh?" The last comment was aimed squarely at Nathaniel, who smiled unconvincingly, (to me that is). The guide, who seemed more than pleased with his 'presentation' then turned and swooped upon Madame Clarice, bending forward awkwardly to grasp and kiss her bejewelled hand.

"Enchanté, Madame," he cooed, extending his rubbery lips. Clarice giggled girlishly into her other gloved hand.

"Monsieur, charme," she replied breathlessly.

If I had been there with any of my friends I would have been miming the finger down throat action, but as I was friendless, I just made do with the pleasure of visualising it.

"If you want me at all, especially you, Madame – I will be in the foyer on sentry duty, wouldn't want anything to creep up and ravish you!"

Clarice coloured up and squealed with delight at the over familiarity shown to her by the guide. What is it with middle-aged people? As long as a sentence has a bit of innuendo thrown in, they are more than happy! Personally, I was glad to see the back of the guide as he plodded away on his spindly legs, back to his little dark corner like a spider, but why, oh why, was he was wearing a hunter's outfit and a pith helmet?"

"Eez sweet," said Clarice, straining her neck to watch him as he turned the corner. He clearly knew she was watching him and you could see he was trying to enhance his stooped (or should that be - stoopid!) walk, to look like, what he considered to be, sexy. He then promptly turned his ankle causing him to fall awkwardly into a Swiss Cheese plant before crumpling to his knees.

"I'm all right," he called. "I meant to do that." We watched as he dragged himself onto the chair, shuffling papers with one hand and rubbing his aching ankle with the other - but he knew we were watching him.

"So where do you want to go first?" Asked Nathan, turning away from the unintentional comedy.

"Well I'd like to veeseet the leetle girls room first, all thees 'anging about een drafty 'allways meks me want to go," answered Clarice.

"OK. Then afterwards, what say we go into the chapel area and sit awhile to see if we can tune in to anything? Think you can sit quietly for 15 minutes, Mark?"

"Oh *I* can!" I deliberately angled my eyes over to Madame Clarice to indicate that perhaps 15 minutes of silence might be an impossible task for old chatty Clarry. Nathaniel smiled back and then gestured with a sweep of his arm for Clarice to lead on as we made our way upstairs to where the toilets were.

The stairs were wide and draughty and the steps themselves, like the mansion, were scaled up so that it felt like you were venturing upwards into a giants house.

As we approached the first floor it occurred to me that it was an odd place to install modern toilets for they just happened (or did they!) to be next to the infamous and extremely scary bathroom that featured a kind of sarcophagus bathtub and a shower stall, both carved with many strange animals and symbols, where, it is rumoured, some poor girl was once murdered. Charming!

What is it with women and bathrooms? Men are in and out in minutes and women? They just take forever and a day, they have to check their hair, check their make-up and goodness only knows what else they check. Well, we waited patiently for 10 minutes! Ten whole minutes, for goodness sake!

I asked Nathaniel if I should knock on the door. He said no, let's give her a few more minutes and if she still hasn't made an appearance then he'd knock. At that moment the door opened and she came stumbling (literally) out and collapsed (kind of) straight into Nathan's arms.

"Why whatever is the matter, my dear," he cried. "You look so pale, have you seen something?"

Clarice looked him square in the eye and in a high wobbly voice squeaked, "no, not a sausage but I desperately..."

"Yes," he urged.

"... desperately..."

"Yes, go on," said I.

"Desperately need a cake, my sugar levels 'ave dropped! Now I sorely need the pastry!"

"Oh my word," muttered Nathaniel discretely into my ear. "It's going to be a long night!" I had to laugh though for as we made our way to the chapel, Madame Clarice was desperate all right, desperately rummaging through the bag of provisions we had brought along, ferreting for a pan-au-chocolate, and in the space of a couple of minutes she had devoured two and started on a sausage roll! As long as she didn't eat my share, I was happy - anything to calm her down a bit and keep her mouth occupied (and we hadn't even started any psychic stuff yet!)

Quietly, possibly due to a show of reverence or possibly because Madame Clarice still had a gob full of sausage roll, we silently filed into the chapel. The room was austere and bone-chillingly cold in fact, you could see your breath as you exhaled (apart from, yeah you guessed!)

"Are you feeling brave enough to each sit in a different corner?" Asked Nathaniel, looking first at me and then at Clarice who was now patting her greasy lips with a lace-trimmed handkerchief.

"OK, I'm mega keen to test my courage - so yup, I'll do it," said I.

"And you dear," said Nathaniel to Clarice. "Are you happy to sit alone in a corner for, say 15 minutes to see what you might pick up on?"

"Oui, you should know by now Nathaniel, I am not one to be scared easily, non?"

Nathaniel smiled warmly but I knew what he was thinking, I reckon Madame Clarice was not being completely honest and personally, I couldn't wait for her to get the creeps!

So began our first vigil, for that is what serious Ghost busters, sorry, *Paranormal Investigators*, call an expedition such as this). I was thrilled beyond belief and I know that my school mates will be sooooo flippin' jealous when I tell them all about it, assuming I last the night!

Suddenly, as I sat alone in the darkened corner, the reality of our situation dawned on me and it seemed as though the blackness was pushing forward, trying to press itself upon me like an inky stamp. I felt as if my eyes were on stalks because I was trying so hard to see something, anything, in the pitch-darkness. On the one hand I wanted to see something or at least, I wanted my eyes to adjust, so that if nothing else, I could see the room. But on the other hand I was wondering just how I would react, if I *were* to suddenly see a full on phantom. It didn't happen though, after five minutes (well, it felt like 5 minutes) there was still nothing more than impenetrable blackness.

"Oohee!"

"What was that?" Asked Nathaniel.

"Wasn't me," I replied.

"Clarice dear, was that you? He cried. No reply. "Clarice, dear? Are you OK?"

"*Qui est cela ? Qu'est-ce qui m'est arrivé ?*"

"Who said that, Nathaniel? It certainly wasn't Clarice!"

"Oh my! I believe, dear boy that Clarice is channelling. What she just said was: Who is this? What happened to me? Hang on, I'll ask her who she is. *Qui sont vous. Quel est votre nom?*"

"*Mon nom? Je suis Jaques Garrault. Pourquoi sont vous ici dans l'obscurité. Où sont je?*"

When I asked him what it meant in English, Nathaniel said: "My name is Jaques Garrault. Why are you here in the dark? Where am I?" Nathaniel then replied to the voice by saying: "We are studying this house, it is said to be haunted. That is where you are, in Woodchester Mansion. Are you always here? What is your occupation?" The answer came back:

"*Je ne suis aucun esprit, je suis un maçon en pierre - est-ce que ce n'est pas évident? Où sont les autres, ceux qui me détestent et me veulent mort?*" This, Nathaniel excitedly told me, meant: "I am no spirit, I am a stone mason - is it not obvious? Where are the others, the ones who hate me and want me dead?"

How thrilled was I! Actual two way conversation with an actual dead person!!! Nathaniel then asked the spirit what year it was - "*Dites-moi s'il vous plaît quelle année est cela?*" and it replied, "*Mais 1868 évidemment - sont vous la pagaille été à la tête?*" I asked what it said and Nathaniel laughed and replied, "Why, 1868 of course - are you muddle headed?"

Nathaniel then said. "I think we had better bring Madame Clarice back now, Mark, it can be dangerous to leave them in a trance state for too long. I will just thank Jaques for talking to us.

"*Le merci Jaques, nous devons aller maintenant mais j'espère que vous avez un soir plaisant, vous n'avez personne pour craindre, Dieu Bénissent.*"

That was closer to the truth than I realised!" Said Nathaniel. I asked him why.

"Well this is what I said to him. "Thank you, Jaques, we must go now but I hope you have a pleasant evening, you have nobody to fear. God Bless."

Do you see? I said he had 'no body' to fear!"

"Oh dear," I groaned at his poor joke. Talking of groans, at that precise moment Madame Clarice returned to us. "Ow my 'ead eet 'urt too much. Did I fall to sleep?"

Nathaniel filled her in on what had just happened. *"Dans une transe, vraiment ? Incroyable - a pitié je l'ai manqué pas?"* Said Clarice, apparently.

Uncle then explained to me what she had just said.

"In a trance, really? Incredible - pity I missed it no?"

We all laughed and were only too glad to be leaving the chapel for the kitchen area where the spirit of a serving woman has been said to haunt. The kitchen sounded cosy but of course it wasn't, in fact it was even grimmer than the chapel. What I would have done for a few minutes by the cheery glow of a coal fire.

"Oops sorry," I said as a woman rushed by me laden with trays. She carried on and completely ignored me.

"Who were you talking to Mark?" Asked Nathaniel as we explored the scullery.

"The maid of course, didn't you see her? She almost knocked me flying."

"Mark, Clarice, myself, the guide and you are the only ones here - you know that, right?"

"What? Then... She must have been a ghost? Oh my god, I've actually seen my first real live dead ghost and she looked as alive as us!"

"You saw a spirit?" Said Nathaniel. "That's something I have never seen, how marvellous for you!"

"Blimey, I've just seen an actual spirit! I wondered where she went?"

"On her merry little way, I shouldn't wonder. She probably does it over and over again. Well done you though!"

Madame Clarice was noticeable by her absence but we soon discovered her eating a packet of stinky cheese and onion crisps in an alcove that used to be a larder (according to a sign).

"Pay no attention to me, I am so 'ungry I could eat a 'orse. There nothing in here that makes me theenk eet ees 'aunted!"

"Apart from the ghostly maid I just saw!"

"Whut? You saw a phantom in 'ere Mak? Mercy me, I feel 'ungry just theenkeen about eet! Peraps you are a leetle beet psychic!"

And it was that throwaway remark that set me thinking. Maybe I am a bit, you know, psychic, maybe it's my destiny to be a great medium instead of just a lacklustre small. Sorry, spooky situations bring out my tragic mirth! Perhaps I might visit the local spiritualist church one of these days, when I am brave enough. Perhaps.

"Uncle Nathaniel? I'm just going out into the hallway a moment to see if I can pick up anything else with my new spiritual radar."

"OK, Mark but don't go wandering off or you could hurt yourself. There are a lot of uneven surfaces and holes to fall through let alone what could happen to you if you meet the dreaded black dog!"

"Oh really? Black dog indeed, I'm a bona fide ghost buster don't you know!"

As I stepped out into the hall, I noticed that it now appeared to have a different atmosphere about it, rather than how it had felt earlier. It had become bitterly cold and felt downright menacing. Once again my eyes strained to focus as I scanned around myself, for I felt as though someone or something was always there, standing doggedly next to me. Suddenly I distinctly felt a hand squeeze my shoulder and I was almost too fearful to turn around to see who or what it was.

"Mak? I need the toilet again, would you be as kind to escort a lady upstairs while I veeseet the leetle girl's room?"

"Yes, it was Clarice, able to speak for once because, amazingly, her mouth wasn't full. "You made me jump Madame Clarice, I thought you were a ghost or something!"

"No, just a very beautiful French lady, no?"

"Uh no, uh, yes!" *Boy*, I thought, *nearly walked into that one, good job I'm a quick thinker*. Clarice held out her hand so that she could hold on to me as we climbed the stone steps up to the first floor.

"You weel wet for me won't you Mak, I'll be just a moment or two."

Yes, I thought. I've heard that one before. I explained to her that if I wasn't directly outside the toilet when she came out, I'd be next door in the scary bathroom. Brave aren't I? No? Stupid then. I know I shouldn't have gone in there alone but it was so close and you know, boys will be boys and all that!

Turns out, there was a pathetic little light in the grand bathroom and even though it was utterly dismal, it still managed to throw disturbing shadows across the walls. As I was walking in, to my left was the big carved bathtub, totally over the top in its design and really very creepy. It looked like the sort of place you might kill something, you know, to let the blood drain away? I then made my way to the end of the room, still checking out the left side. This was where the odd shower room was and where, as I mentioned earlier, for those of you paying attention, some poor girl, it is rumoured, was murdered in a ritualistic killing. Of course, it could be nothing more than an urban myth. Either way, the shower heads look weird and have strange creature carvings upon them and me, being as brave as I am, elected to not step inside the shower enclosure for fear of finding myself trapped in there with something truly ghastly.

"Ooee, Mak! Are you still 'ere?"

It was Clarice, true to her word, for once, and just a moment or two later she stood in the doorway wafting clouds of dubious perfume in my direction making me cough.

"What a dreadful place, I wouldn't be caught dead in 'ere! Needs a woman's touch - perhaps a few, 'ow you say, doilies?"

Oh yes, that probably *would* keep the ghosts at bay. Some scary doilies!

"Come, let us go back to Nathaniel, 'e weel be wondering where we are and I could do weeth a beeskeet and a cup of tea!"

A beeskeet? She was hungry again? Thank god I am not ship wrecked on an island with her, I know women like to nibble on your ear but hey - I'm a genius, not a snack!

Chapter Thirteen

As we made our way back downstairs, my eye was drawn to an area directly ahead of us. I couldn't see very much at all due to the darkness but never the less, I am pretty sure that, just for a moment, I saw a bright green burst of light coming from within the scullery. I asked Madame Clarice if she had seen it but she said no, although, apparently, she sometimes sees lights when she is particularly hungry! Still excited by it, I rushed in to ask Nathaniel if he'd seen the green light but to my surprise he was nowhere to be seen - so much for his advice about not going wandering off! It was then that we heard an odd sort of sound, a bit like, well, kind of like a... dog growling! Suddenly Clarice's hand was firmly attached to mine and to be honest, in the pitch dark, I was glad of it. The growling, that seemed to be coming from all around us, began to rapidly increase in volume and then we could hear what sounded uncannily like claws on the flagstones as whatever it was, prowled around us.

The thing sounded angry and emitted a low guttural growl that seemed far too real and far too menacing for my liking. We were both scanning the area around us, constantly, when, all of a sudden, to our amazement, we could both see two eyes! They were like two fiery embers floating in the blackness. Clarice screamed, if you could call the thin strangulated sound issuing from her lips, a scream. I could feel her body trembling and for someone in regular contact with the dead, I now realised that she was, in fact, nothing more than a big ol' wussypants!

"Hot chocolate?" It was Nathaniel, he had been visiting the guide. He was holding a tray with three hot chocolates and biscuits. Everything was suddenly back to normal.

"Did you hear it?" I asked him. "The Growling? It was the black dog - well, actually it could have been any colour because we couldn't really see it but we certainly heard it and we both saw its red eyes - it was so cool! Wasn't it Clarice?"

"Eet was notheen, I 'ave seen mush worse than that Mak, eet was just a leetle puppy lost een time."

"And you were trembling because...?"

"Because I was cold, foolish boy, no othere reson. I am in touch weeth the speereets, why should I be scared?"

"Beats me," I replied, thinking that Madame Clarice was clearly a bit of a fraud but still keeping my mouth firmly closed to avoid upsetting Nathaniel.

"My word," said Nathaniel. "I haven't seen a sausage yet but I suppose that is for the best eh? Ghostly sausages are never going to be front page news, that much I am certain of, now come on, drink your hot chocolate up because I have just learnt of a great place I want us to visit next."

The hot chocolate was, I wanted to say warm and comforting but alas no, it was tepid and powdery, however, it DID taste very chocolaty and went down well with the chocolate chip cookies. I couldn't help but watch Clarice, yes I know it's rude to watch people slyly but you should have seen her get through half a dozen cookies, it was a race to get my hands on one before they all disappeared - truly!

Once we had all eaten, Nathaniel proposed that we march forward and begin our next vigil upstairs. This was to take place along a cold, echoey corridor where voices had been heard, voices of, amongst others, American airmen, apparently, who had been billeted at Woodchester Mansion during World War Two. Luckily I had brought along a voice recorder of Nathaniel's so that I could try to get some EVP's (Electronic Voice Phenomena) caught on tape.

All I needed to do was to set it recording and then ask a series of questions such as, What is your name, how many spirits are with you etc. I had to remember to allow enough room for their ghostly replies though.

It kind of makes my head swim thinking about it, for instance; how can ghosts speak when they have no voice box? No tongue, no lips? I tell you, this world we live in is full of mysteries and most of them are only mysteries because we are so governed by what our well conditioned scientists tell us, that there is no room for anything not based on what we already know - or do not know, as the case may be! Do you get what I mean? It's like aliens. Scientists insist that if advanced aliens living light years away from us, did exist, they still would not be able to visit us on Earth because to travel so far across such vast distances in a space vehicle would be impossible. They will not even entertain the notion that these super intelligent beings, far advanced than us, could probably move inter-dimensionally and not conventionally via antiquated rocket power as our scientists expect! Well, I say, never confine yourself to earthly thoughts! Let your mind expand and just watch, your intellect will blossom in the vastness of space as surely as a dropped piece of buttered toast will always fall butter-side down. Well that's my ten pence worth, see - didn't I already say that I was not your average sixteen year old!!!

As we made our way to the first floor hallway, we were all struck by the all invasive cold that permeated every space. It was so chilly that when you spoke, your words came out in clouds. The fact that the windows were unglazed didn't help, it allowed a damp mist to form and which shrouded the lower half of the corridor. As you might have gathered, those of you paying attention that is, along the corridor, it was not completely dark. There was a single yellow light that broke through the unglazed windows, that weakly, and I mean *weakly*, illuminated the hallway, and with the lack of glass in the windows, there was a constant sound of flapping from the torn plastic sheeting that offered us no protection from the elements, whatsoever.

"Eet weel be cold non?" Said Clarice. "Perhaps, theese once I will seet eet out. I theenk I weel keep the guide company for a leetle beet yes?"

Before Nathaniel had a chance to get Clarice to change her mind, she had waddled off to seek out the source of (a) some free flattery and (b) more biscuits. Hmmm, maybe I should swap those around! I was actually glad that Clarice had decided to give Nathaniel and I some time ghost busting time together. I felt that Nathaniel had more chance of seeing something himself without Clarice near by than with her - don't ask me why but that's how I felt.

"Well, just down to us two lads then eh? Are you OK? Won't be scared will you, boy?"

"No! Have I been scared yet by the many things I have seen? Well, have I? Have I?"

"OK, Mark, put your eyes back in, I was only asking! But I guess it DID sound a wee bit patronising now that I come to think of it."

"Just a tad! I'm not a baby, Uncle. I'm sixteen! I'm sorry if I was a bit snappy back then it's just that Madame Clarice is meant to be the expert here and frankly, I am not convinced that she is all that she claims to be." I had said more than I intended to but as I was with Nathaniel I was sure he would understand. Wrong!

"That's a hurtful thing to say, Mark. Clarice has shown you nothing but kindness since you arrived and you really should respect her and her vast experience of the paranormal. There is an awful lot I could tell you about the dreadful things Clarice and I have witnessed over the years but now is not the time and in any case, after that comment, I don't feel you deserve to know… I'll pretend I didn't hear those unkind words about her so let's just carry on with our experiment and make Clarice proud of our attempts to get in touch with her world. Eh?"

"But…"

"No buts Mark, just behave yourself, that's a good boy!"

I was suddenly relegated back to being just 'a good boy'! I hated being classed as a boy, I was a young man - not a 'good boy'! What am I - a dog? Ooh I felt spitting mad now, Madame Fraudice had driven a wedge between Nathaniel and I and that made me annoyed! I wasn't being mean was I? She does appear to be a big fake doesn't she? Oh well, no use being a *bebby*, I wanted to be treated as an adult so I decided to just get on with the job at hand and duly switched the record button to on. I waited a couple of seconds and then asked my first probing question.

"Is there anyone here?" I waited a few seconds again and asked. "What is your name," followed by, Are you alone here" and then the big one, "Are you the spirit of an American serviceman?" I let the recorder run a little longer and then played back what I had recorded.

"Couldn't you have waited until we had finished the vigil? Said Nathan, clearly still a bit miffed.

"No! I deliberately wanted to double check that we, sorry, that I, was getting something or if it was working at all. I don't suppose you want to hear it then," I teased.

"I certainly do. Come on then, play it!"

I clicked the play button and waited. There was a lot of hissing until my first question came up:

"Is there anyone here?"

"I am here," came the instant reply. Amazingly I had captured a voice. I looked up at Nathaniel and saw that he was looking almost as excited as I was.

"What is your name?"

"Evan Lindhurst - what is yours?"

"Mark. Mark Hopkins. Are you alone here?"

"No."

"Are you the spirit of an American serviceman?"

"What do you mean spirit? I AM an American serviceman."

"Oh my goodness," said Nathaniel, it's amazing! But I don't think he realises that he's dead. Do you think we should tell him?"

"Well he has a right to know." I said. "Maybe that's why he's stuck here. Perhaps it's because he doesn't realise he's dead that is stopping him from crossing into the spirit realm."

"I think we need a medium to help him," he added, "come on, let's go and get Clarice."

Inwardly I groaned but Nathaniel *did* have a valid point and it would be a fantastic achievement to know that we had helped a trapped spirit to cross over into the spirit realm where he could meet up with his friends and family again and find peace.

We could hear Madame Clarice before we could see her, that distinctive shrill little giggle carried along the empty corridors like a baby banshee coming to get us.

"And that was 'ow I managed to get my name een the peppers! Don't evere say that Madame Clarice ees not weethout the cunneeng of a monkee!"

You got that right, I thought.

"Clarice dear, I wonder if we might pull you away for a moment or two? We have made contact with a spirit and it would be marvellous if you could help him to cross over. Would you be able to do that?"

Nathaniel meant no offense in his words but Clarice clearly heard them differently from how he meant them to sound.

Nathaniel! Am I not a world-renowned medium? Am I not known eenternationally? As I was just telling 'ubert here, I was on the redio only a wek ago revealing my eener most seecreets about the world of speereet, so when you say, 'Am I eble to do that,' I am most tekken abeck. 'Owever, as a dear, dear friend I say yes, I weel do eet and you may come along too 'ubert, eef you weesh?"

The guide looked stunned for a moment.

"Oh no Mademoiselle, that sort of thing is not for me. Give me a pride of lions on the vast plains of the Serengeti or even an errant tiger skulking through the steamy jungles of darkest India, but a ghost? No. I prefer things I can see! That's why I tend to sit by the door. When it comes to spirits I prefer mine in a glass!"

"Ooh very well you naughty man. You weel mees the 'ilight of your lafe but eet ees your choice, non? Come along then you two, let's 'elp thees airman to go 'ome."

Suddenly I felt a bit warmer towards Clarice. Perhaps she wasn't so full of hot air after all.

Chapter Fourteen

We silently made our way upstairs. It felt as though we were on a legitimate mission now, genuine ghost hunters, not just ordinary people out on a fun event but part of an actual psychic experiment and I must be honest, it was very exciting!

The corridor was still just as cold as it had been and still misty with strands of mist free floating like ghostly fingers. Almost immediately, I noticed a blue light dart from one side of the corridor to the other but I kept my mouth shut as I felt that the moment was not for me, but for Clarice and the airman. I discretely switched the voice recorder on again and whispered into the microphone. "Are you still here Evan?"

"What was that," said Clarice. "Deed you hear a voice?"

"Oh that was me, sorry, I was doing a few more EVP's - it's too good an opportunity to miss!"

"Very well Mak, but please do not be too loud, normally I do these theengs een total silence!"

"OK," I'll hang back a bit then." Suddenly I realised what I had just said. I was going to be alone, more or less, whilst Nathaniel and Madame Clarice were further down the corridor.

"Don't go running off Mark," called Nathan.

"Fat chance of that," I replied. I decided to ask some more questions.

"Evan, are you aware that you are dead?" I waited a moment or two and then listened back to it.

"Dead? No, that's impossible. I'm waiting for my orders."

"You ARE dead Evan. Honestly, I wouldn't lie to you. What year do you think it is?"

"1943 of course."

"No it's not. It's 2008."

"Holy smoke, get outta here. 2008? You sure have a big imagination - I guess everyone is living on the moon now, huh?"

"No, I'm afraid to say that we ran out of money after the first few moon landings."

"Oh, ho-ho, you're a joker for sure. Moon landings in deed!"

"You ARE dead Evan, I swear to god. We are here to help you. There is a lady here named, Madame Clarice and she can help you to cross into the light where your friends and family are waiting to see you - wouldn't you like to see them again?"

"Sure I would, but I was just waiting for my leave. You say they are in a light? Why?"

"Because they, or at least some of them, will be waiting for you there, it's heaven for want of better words."

At that point I could hear Clarice calling to him.

"Evan, please listen to what Clarice says, she can help you to move on."

"I'm not sure about this, I don't know if I want to go anywhere... What's that?

"What's what? Does it look like a bright light?" Said Clarice, taking over.

"It's beautiful. It feels so pure, it's like a magnet, it's pulling me - I can't resist it - Mom? Is that you?"

"That's eet my friend, go towards the light. Do you see anyone you recognise?" Said Clarice.

"Mom, is it really you? Kathy Lee, wow, you're in the light too."

"You see them, my friend? Tek their 'ands and they weel 'elp you across. Do not be afred, eet weel only take a meenit and like a breath of air you weel be over een 'eaven."

Clarice's words seemed to be working because I could clearly see Evan's blue spectral shape moving towards a spinning white light.

"Tek 'old of their 'ands Evan and you'll be alright, you'll be in 'eaven een seconds," urged Clarice.

The spirit turned and looked at us all, firstly with a look of puzzlement on his face and then he smiled. "Goodbye friends," he said. "I had no idea that I had passed over and needed to move into the light. I had seen the light before but I was frightened by it. I thought it was one of Hitler's dirty tricks. Hi Mom, you're looking great!"

They were the last words we heard him say.

It felt amazing to think that I had been part of something so 'out there' - I had actually talked to a spirit and helped him on his way. How cool is that?

"Mak, well done. I could sense the enershee flowing from you. You are a geefted young medium - do you realise that? 'E is gone now, I saw two ladees 'elping 'im."

Suddenly I knew that Clarice was genuine, otherwise she would never have realised that Evan's mother and the other lady, Kathy Lee, had helped him over. I decided not to mention that I had seen them all, it would have just seemed too braggy and that was the last thing I wanted either Clarice or Nathaniel to think. That would be revealed another time, perhaps.

"You know, 'elping eem across made me realise sometheen vitally eemportante…"

"Yes Clarice, and what pray tell might that be?" Answered Nathaniel.

"Do you know Mak? Can you guess whut eet made me realise?"

"Uh, that it is wonderful to be able to help a troubled spirit? That life should not be taken for granted?"

"Yes to both but 'elping eem made me realise that crossing speerits over really made me 'ungry!" Clarice laughed and pulled us both into an embrace and I realised then that she actually had a sense of humour as well as a heart of gold and I felt a bit awful for pre-judging her. After that we made our way back to the guide's desk to tell him what had occurred.

"You got rid of one of our residents? Are you trying to make us bankrupt?"

I think he was half joking but Madame Clarice assured him that there were still plenty more speerits 'anging around ere'. That shut him up. Suddenly his eyes were darting all over the place.

Outside, the weather still looked decidedly grim so we all decided that the thought of a nice warm house had more appeal than any more ghost hunting. What we had experienced was more than enough for one day.

That night, as I lay in bed, just before dropping off to sleep, I thought about Evan and smiled. As Tina Turner might say, this weekend had been *simply the best*.

Chapter Fifteen

I knew that the next morning, Clarice was going to be heading back to France and despite me not liking her at first, over the past few weeks I had grown used to her eccentric ways and had actually got to like her. There was one thing however, that I wanted her to explain to me before she departed – the photograph. How could I be in it when it was taken so long ago?

"Eet look like you non? But ees eet you Mak?" At this point Nathaniel came ambling towards us from the back garden. He was laden with a basket of mixed berries for Clarice to take home with her.

"Nathaniel? Mak 'ere wants to know 'ow come 'e is een thee peecture I 'ave?"

Nathaniel gently placed the fruit basket on the deck and sat down beside us. He lifted the photograph from Clarice's hand and studied it. He then smiled and looked up over his half moon glasses, first at Clarice, then at me.

"Puzzled are you, Mark? Tell me, how do you think you will look when you are my age?"

"I don't know," I replied.

"I think you might look a lot like me! That little boy in the photo is me, Mark, not you. Genealogy is a mysterious thing, if all the ingredients to make a person are in the correct proportion, a repeated likeness can occur, and with you, clearly it has!"

"Blimey. Really? That's you?

"Eet certainly ees Mak, tekken a long, long time ago, before you were even a tweenkle een your mothers eye."

"It was! Why, even your Grandmother, Katherine wasn't born then," added Nathaniel.

"Well I'm puzzled," I said. "And it's something that has been on my mind a lot lately. If it's not too personal, Uncle, can I ask you how you came to be in France at such a young age? Why were you living so far away from the rest of your family and also, how is it that you turned out to be so different to Nanna Katherine?"

"Oh your Grandmother never told you? I'm shocked! Where do I start? Well, my Great, Great, Grandmother was French you see, and as children, my mother, your Great, Grandmother, Flora, would take me to Provence to spend each summer with my Great, Great, Grandparents who, amazingly, were still alive. We both loved taking the steam train to Dover and then on the boat across to France. People rarely travelled abroad in those days and looking back, I suppose we were lucky to be able to afford to do so. Of course this was many years before your Grandmother was born and later, because of the thirteen-year age gap, we never really got to be that close. As it happened, mother and I were in France on the day the World War 2 broke out. I was 10 then. When we heard the news on the wireless she immediately sent a telegram to your Great, Grandfather, Robert, suggesting we would possibly be safer staying where we were until it had all blown over, thinking it wouldn't last long. He agreed, after rather a lot of coaxing, so mother told me, and so, unexpectedly, for the next two and a half years, we were exiled in France. It was there that I first met cousin Clarice. She lived in the house next door to ours in Provence. We quickly became great friends, along with her best friend, Justavia. Clarice taught me French and I taught her English…"

I wanted to say something funny at that point but decided to let it go. Nathaniel carried on. "We have remained close ever since, haven't we dear."

Clarice nodded and indicated for Nathaniel to continue by making a rolling movement with her hand.

"Little did we know," he continued, "that stranger things were set to happen - for we were soon dashing off under the cover of night to Switzerland with the Nazi's hot on our tails!"

Talk about *The Sound of Music*, only without the music part! I couldn't believe it, MY family, practically living the lives of reckless adventurers! "Tell me more, tell me more!" I demanded, and probably sounding like a spoiled child or backing singers from the movie, Grease!

"Well, after more than two years away from Robert, your Great Grandmother decided to try to get us back to England on a fishing boat as it seemed as though the war was going to drag on forever. It was a bit of a hair raising adventure just getting back but we finally managed to set foot on good old British soil again in late February 1942 when I was almost 13."

"Your father must have been so happy to get you both back safely."

"Yes, he certainly was and it seems the result of his happiness was your Grandmother, Katherine coming along 9 months later!" Answered Nathaniel with a wink.

"But what about the Germans? What happened in Switzerland?" I asked.

Nathaniel suddenly looked world weary and said, "Not now Mark, all in good time eh?" And that was that, I had no choice but to wait, even though I was practically chomping at the bit to find out what happened next. Suddenly, for the first time in my life, my family seemed, well, cool!

So that was it, a bit of family history I had never heard before. Nanna hadn't been born when Nathaniel was abroad. I always knew that there was a rather large age gap between them but I also discovered that it was made even bigger when he later left home to go to university, in Oxford. Up until then I had assumed he was the only exceptionally bright one in the family. Now I know better - hopefully the smart gene skipped a generation and I'm more Nathaniel, than mum (or, heaven forbid, Dad!)

My train of thought was suddenly derailed by a stray notion that seemed to leap to the forefront of my mind, something suddenly recalled from a few months ago. It was the odd amount of windows in Nathaniel's house and that mysterious sliding door sound - I still had no answer as to what they might be. I felt I was missing something and as soon as Madame Clarice was safely on her way, I intended to come up with some answers to the many nagging questions sprouting like seeds of doubt in my head. Alas, fate, it seems, had other plans for me.

Chapter Sixteen

Exam time was finally upon me - one minute I was goofing around, blindly oblivious to the pressure building up at school and the next minute I suddenly became painfully aware of how little time I had spent actually revising for my GCSE's. I wanted to do well, I really did, so I decided that I had to be strict with myself and settle down to some serious cramming.

"Here's a tip," said Nathaniel, one Saturday as he saw me hunched over my text books. "Read your notes aloud, you know, all of the things that you think may come up in the exam and you'll be amazed at how they will magically stick in your memory after you put them out to the universe! Oh yes, and if you don't understand something, re-read it until it sticks - if you fail to understand something, it will never remain in your memory."

Well, you know what? Turns out ol' Natty D, was right! It absolutely does work. Despite the protestations of my friends, I made a conscious effort to get down to some serious studying. At one point it simply became too intense and as I was desperately needing a break, I wrote a short story which I called, Shimmer; inspired by the clouds one beautiful day as I stood daydreaming at my bedroom window after too much cramming. Here it is.

Shimmer

I stood at my bedroom window and watched in fascination as two clouds gracefully floated towards each other. I fully expected them to merge, to become one huge cloud but that wasn't what happened. Far from it. Instead, one cloud butted against the other reminding me of two rubber cauliflowers floating in an ocean of blue gravy (Thomas Hardy, I aint!) Then, like a tiny red dart, I noticed a splinter-slim glider sailing between them. The whole scene looked almost too good to be true, like a Rene Magritte painting, a perfect blue sky, two perfect clouds and a perfect red plane. Then something both remarkable and unexpected happened - the glider shimmered, lit up as it tilted its wings to face the sun and then it simply disappeared. Gone - just like that! I immediately wondered if I was seeing things, a trick of the light perhaps? I blinked several times in case it was something in my vision and then I waited for a few minutes to see if the glider re-appeared anywhere else. But there was nothing.

    I must have remained rooted to the same spot for an hour or more, but something compelled me to keep on looking for it. I don't know why but I felt concerned for the fate of the pilot - too much time spent reading about alien abductions and the Bermuda Triangle I guess! So there I stayed, scanning the sky until - was it my eyes or were the same two clouds, which should have long ago merged, moved on or even, simply dissipated, now getting closer to my window by the second? I started to feel afraid, this had to be something supernatural - things like this simply didn't happen unless, and I was almost too scared to think it, unless it was the second coming of Jesus Christ. But there was no angelic fanfare of trumpets as mentioned in the Bible and much as I would love to see the big, 'J. C.', one day, I didn't feel ready at 16 to face the end of the world!

The clouds were now close enough for me to literally reach out of my window and touch them, so I opened the window in preparation. I was surprised to see the movement of my action reflected in the cloud and amazingly, I could suddenly see myself, only the other me was dressed altogether differently. He looked like me facially; only he had longer hair whereas mine is short. Even the curtains behind him were different. It puzzled me to say the least! In spite of feeling trepidatious, I extended my arm to try to touch him, to check that he was real and not simply a figment of my imagination. Like a true reflection, the image did exactly the same. The minute our fingers touched, there was an explosive shower of bright white sparks causing us to both let go. I wondered what on earth had happened until I noticed the other me now had short hair and my curtains! Full of panic I felt my own hair - it was long! I quickly spun around to check my bedroom - everything looked different, totally groovy, like something from the 1960's. I raced back to the window and called out my name. To my horror, the clouds were starting to move away. The other me suddenly appeared at the other window with an equal look of panic written upon his face.

"Quick! Touch hands again before it's too late, or we'll be stuck in the wrong worlds" I cried. The clouds were now even further away and we had no choice other than to scrabble out of the windows and out onto the flat roofs that jutted out beneath our windows. Even so it was still an extremely dangerous situation. We both had to lean forward as much as we could in order to make contact with one another. I was aware of the garden far below me and at one stage I almost lost my balance, but then suddenly our fingertips brushed and once again there was a shower of sparks. The impact could have proved fatal for us both, had we been thrown forward but, as before, the force threw us backwards.

I landed on my behind, beneath my bedroom window. I immediately felt my hair to see if I was me again - I was! I then jumped up to see if the other me was fine - the cloud was obscuring my view and I could see nothing. Then I heard his (my) voice. "Are you okay?"

"Yes I am, you had me worried for a moment there."

Briefly, the clouds parted and I could just about see him waving to me on his flat roof. "Hey, we'll have to do this again some time," he called as he faded from view.

"I'll take a rain cheque, looks like it might be cloudy," I replied. He smiled and then faded from view.

After a while with no more contact, I scrambled back inside my bedroom window, glad that things were back to normal at last but at the same time feeling as though I had lost something valuable. I still had a nagging worry about the glider though and so I went and stood by the window once more. To my delight it suddenly reappeared sailing back through the gap between the clouds - it looked as though the pilot didn't have a care in the world and then a thought struck me, was I the pilot? When I needed a momentary escape from my worries, the shimmer had occurred exactly at the right moment - it was as though I left this reality! Like many moments of realisation in a dream, I suddenly awoke. I must have nodded off on my bed after resting my eyes because the next thing I was aware of was Mum calling me, saying that Nathaniel was on the 'phone and that he wanted a word with me. Groggily I but made my way downstairs and took hold of the receiver. "Hello?"

"Mark - are you alright? You sound tired," he said, sounding even more upbeat than usual.

"Oh, I'm okay. Just this minute woken up from a much needed nap - at least all of my cramming has produced another weird story."

"Sounds intriguing. Not studying too hard are you? Remember to leave a bit of time for fun."

I assured him that I would and that was when he delivered what I call his double whammy!

"July 19th - be sure to put that in your diary. Your mother has given me the nod to take you to France to stay with Clarice for a month..."

"Whoohoo - really?"

"Yes, really. And Minty too!"

"What? WHAT? Minty? No - why?" I whined.

"Because your parents are going on a cruise - a bingo and karaoke cruise that they have been saving newspaper coupons for months, for - apparently. They will be sailing around the Mediterranean and your brother Paul has already arranged to stay with friends in Scotland. Surely you don't begrudge your parents or your twin sister a holiday do you?"

"No, it's not that. It's just that Minty and me, well - you know, we're just so different and we don't exactly get along - plus she's going to be bored silly the minute we get there, I just know it!"

"Minty and I, Mark - grammar, remember?"

Fortunately he couldn't see me roll my eyes.

"Then it will be up to you, Clarice and myself to keep Minty occupied will it not? Now relax, chill out, as you young people like to say, and think about this - you have a whole month ahead of you - in France!"

Yeah, with Minty, I thought. *Oh joy!*

Well I'm clearly not always right. I fully expected my darling sibling to be grouchy as hell at the prospect of being away from Sky TV for a month but no, miracle of miracles she assured me that she was actually looking forward to getting out of England. I only hope she isn't expecting Provence to be as chic as Paris. Still, perhaps Nathaniel is right - it will be a good chance for Minty and me, oops, Minty and I, to bond a bit - we should be alike - we ARE twins after all! Apparently!!!

Chapter Seventeen

July the 19th was suddenly upon me - and thank goodness. All of my rotten exams were now over and done with and I actually felt pretty confident that I'd done as well as I possibly could, under such a stressful and unnatural situation! Minty has been suspiciously quiet all morning - busy, no doubt, cramming as much as humanly possible into her suitcase ready for our journey to Dover, to catch the 4.30 ferry to Calais! Woohoo!!!

I too have been racking my brains to make sure I didn't forget anything essential, as we are going to be away a whole month! How cool, no, how, *kewl* (now that's cool!) is that? Mum and Dad are to set off on their dodgy cruise early tomorrow and by then we should already be settled into Clarice's magnificent château (according to Nathaniel).

At 12.30 we said our goodbyes to Mum and Dad. I noticed Mum had tears in her eyes. She said that she wished she was coming with us but Dad just pulled her tightly to him and said,

"Don't be such a ninny, we are ALL going to have a marvellous time."

For once Dad was spot on, how could we not have a marvellous time, particularly as we had only ever seen the sea once before, well, kind of, for technically, what we saw, was where the sea had been - it was Weston Super Mare after all, where the sea is like a phantom, or should that be, a rumour?

The sea crossing was smooth (ish), I had some anti sickness wristbands to wear but as I could see that Minty was looking a tad green, I offered to let her have one so at least we would both feel half OK (or half sick). She smiled and then puked over my shoes! After I had cleaned myself up I headed for a room that was showing cartoons. I had only been in there for about ten minutes when I saw Minty heading towards me desperately holding onto the wall rail. As I felt pretty much OK, I dared to give her my other wristband and it seemed to do the trick. Within half an hour she was much better and I felt fine too, as long as I didn't move about too much. Nathaniel had remained where we left him, apparently looking out of the window but in reality, snoozing!

I don't know what I was expecting as we landed on foreign soil but Calais was not the prettiest place I have ever seen but I guess it's more of an industrial area to drive through rather than a tourist attraction in its own right.

As soon as we got away from the port we drove through some very pretty villages with houses that seemed to be dusty and ancient but none-the-less, full of charm. France reminded me of Britain in the old black and white movies I had seen. Many hours later, when we finally pulled up in front of Clarice's château, I thought, *OMG - I was not expecting a ruddy palace!* Yes! Madame Clarice lives in a dirty great château, all by herself! Well virtually! I couldn't believe that we would actually be staying there - the place really is like a fairytale palace, truly - well, in comparison to our house it is. What grandeur - four weeks for one and one's twin to live as royalty!

"Blimey this place is smassive!" Cried Minty, creating a new word! "We could spend the month here, not seeing one another YAY!"

No, I'm not going to state the obvious, tempting as it is. I actually WANT to get on with my sister for once - I just hope she's willing to meet me half way, after all, I *did* give her the wristbands! As Nathaniel unloaded the car and placed our luggage upon the gravelled driveway I noticed movement behind the stained glass panel in the impressive front door. Suddenly the door flew open and out rushed, not Clarice who I was expecting to see, but someone far younger and very pretty.

"Allo, please follow me. I am Maugret, Madame Clarice's maid." She said, stretching the 'au' in her name, breathlessly.

Maugret, which I assumed was a French version of Margaret, attempted to gather all of the luggage in her hands but clearly, short of a magic trick, it wasn't going to happen. In any case, Nathaniel would hear nothing of it so we each carried our own bags and together we trudged our way along the gravel path and up the grand curved steps that took us into a huge hallway that had the most amazing painted ceiling. It brought to mind a scene from, *The Sound of Music*. Clarice suddenly made a dramatic entrance, seeming to float down the magnificent marble staircase in an extremely sparkly dress and I wondered if she had been waiting for her cue to make her grand entrance. I know, I shouldn't have such negative thoughts about others but honestly, it's probably what most of us would do if we lived in such opulent surroundings. Not that I'm saying I would come down the grand stairs in a sparkly dress! Come on, you know what I mean!

"Nathaniel, Mak and, 'oo do we 'ave 'ere? You must be Meenty no?"

Minty gave me a, 'is she for real' look, so using only my eyes, I urged her to behave.

"Yes that's me, Meenty!"

I almost choked on a humbug that I had just popped into my mouth, at Minty being so rude to the person, providing free board and lodging to us all.

"Clarice dear, it's Minty, like toothpaste. Her real name is Minnie but for some unfathomable reason she doesn't like it!"

"Like the eendian, Meenee Haha," laughed Clarice.

"More like Minnie Winge bag," I joked.

"Don't push it, Mak," said Minty out of the side of her mouth, who then proceeded to plonk herself down on the bottom stair looking about as dejected as an overlooked orphan.

"Oh look at 'err, poor bebby, all worn out! Come on young leddy, there ees some lovely French cuisine ready for you to sample in the dining room - I am sure you are 'ungry, yes?"

"Flippin' famished, answered Minty, suddenly looking alert.

Clarice then led us all up stairs to show us to our rooms.

"Thees ees your room Mak, right next to the bathroom - I know what you dirty boys are like!"

I didn't quite know what to make of Clarice's comment and assumed that she thought that even at 16, I'd be climbing trees and rolling about in the mud. Clearly Madame Clarice is not used to having teenagers around her. My room was nice though. It had a huge mahogany sleigh bed that matched a colossal triple wardrobe and matching dressing table. My room even had a fireplace!

"And thees ees you room, Meenty." Clarice proudly gestured for Minty to enter the room next to mine. If ever a room could be classed as girly, this was it. Pink floral wallpaper adorned, not only the walls but the ceiling and doors too! It made me want to sneeze, just looking at it. Everything imaginable was chintzy, the bedding, curtains, carpet - blooming crazy if you ask me. Did you see what I did there? A joke - blooming, like flowers? Oh never mind! Minty gave me a quick glance as if to say - 'how many flowers?' Her face soon changed though when Clarice pointed out some issues of Vogue and Paris Match she had put next to Minty's bed to help her acclimatise.

Once we had put our bags away and refreshed ourselves (poash for using the lav) we made our way downstairs to the dining room. The room was dominated by probably the biggest chandelier I had ever seen, hanging directly over a huge oval Mahogany table. Madame Clarice must be doing something right because the furniture was similar to items I have seen in photos of Buckingham Palace. Instead of eight normal looking legs on the table, this one had eight carved ebony cherubs embellished with gold - dead fancy, but the fanciness didn't end there, oh no. It continued around the edge of the table and upon the matching, deeply upholstered chairs. I was thinking, *am I dreaming? Peench me!* Then I noticed the cutlery. It was in the Art Nouveau style featuring carved ivory goddesses with tiny stylised ivy leaves wrapped around each handle picked out in green enamel. Quite honestly, I was in seventh heaven! This place was fan, flipping, tastic!

To one side, beneath a rather unusual oil painting that featured flying apples wearing bowler hats, there was a sideboard that matched the table and chairs and it was laden with all manner of food. The smell alone made my tummy rumble in anticipation. Some food I could identify, but a lot was going to involve me taking a gamble to taste it. My eyes were naturally drawn to the cakes and desserts - no denying it, the French have the upper hand when it comes to nosh, that's for sure!

"I 'ent eating that," said Minty out of Nathaniel and Clarice's earshot, and pointing to what look like strips of chicken in a sort of brown gravy. "Could be anyfin!"

"Minty, don't be so awkward. How are you going to experience French cuisine if you aren't willing to try something new?"

"Ooh get you Mr La-di-da. I'll eat what I flipping well like awright, bruvva?"

"Oh suit yourself but stop showing yourself up - it's only chicken for goodness sake!"

"Yeah but is it? Could be human flesh for all I know and what's that brown poohey stuff?

I gave up and rolled my eyes at her saying, "Yeah, whatever!"

"Oh Clarice? Came Nathaniel's voice. "These chicken goujons are simply delicious - would that be a truffle sauce upon them?"

"Eet ees - you know your food non? The truffles are from my own wood. I 'ave three dogs trained to sneef them out!"

"Really," He said. "How marvellous. Do try the chicken and truffles you two."

"I have, already and they're delicious but moaning Minnie here didn't like the look of them."

"Oi! I can speak for myself Einstein - I'm trying to be a vegetarian - it's better for my Inner Temple!"

"Indeed? An Inner Temple is just an empty vessel unless you nourish it," Said Nathaniel.

"Yes Uncle, I know that," answered Minty. "It said so in *Hello!*"

"You have no idea what he meant, do you," I whispered quietly when we were back at the buffet. Minty looked at me as though I had a fly on the end of my nose.

"Come on then Einstein - what did you make of it?"

"Alright. What's the point in having an Inner Temple when there is no substance to it - you can only acquire an Inner Temple by sampling all the pleasures in life, not by being afraid to try something new."

Minty looked at me for a moment without saying a word then she squinted her eyes and shook her head saying," How can you and I be twins? You're such a prat."

Well, to say my flabber was well and truly gasted would be a major understatement and with a heavy heart I sadly realised that it was going to be an extremely long month!

Chapter Eighteen

Our second day started with an air of mystery about it. Minty and I had been so tired from all the travelling the previous day, that we'd both chosen to go to bed much earlier than we normally would. Nathaniel and Clarice had been chatting in the kitchen as we had made our way upstairs - goodness only knows what time they went to bed! As we were both so tired, the fact that we were sleeping in strange rooms had little time to sink in and the next thing I recalled was when a laser-like beam of sunlight zapped me square in the eyes the next morning. It was an odd situation that Minty and I found ourselves to be in, as we had no agenda as such, at least not yet.

I got up and had a fantastic breakfast, absolutely everything was available to me and afterwards I felt really stuffed and I hoped that nobody would notice how much I had consumed - it wasn't that I was greedy, just that there was simply too much choice! Afterwards, I sat in the decked area of the sunlit garden for a while and after a minute or two I noticed Minty looking out of her bedroom window so I waved to her. She completely ignored me! A split second later I felt a distinctly grabby hand on my shoulder, when I turned my head to see who it was, it was Minty!

"What the heck? I just this minute saw you in your bedroom window!"

"Hardly. I haven't been upstairs since breakfast - must have been daydreaming, you twit!"

"No! I was NOT daydreaming and I am not a twit! I saw you as plain as you are (inwardly I smiled at my clever insult!) looking out of your window. I waved to you and you completely ignored me, so does that sound like you or not?"

"Oh really? I probably WOULD ignore you but I'm telling you, it wasn't me. Maybe it was what's her face, whatsherface - Maugret - she's about the same height as me!"

"Yeah, but she's pretty!"

"Oi, cheeky monkey. If I'm not pretty, you're not handsome - we ARE twins after all." Minty stared at me for a moment before blurting out theatrically, "Oh my god, you ARE ugly, then I must be too," before she suddenly burst into laughter.

"Oh hardy-har. But that's what I find particularly odd about being twins - we are nothing alike, I mean - I'm super-intelligent and devastatingly handsome!"

"And just a teensy bit modest? Anyway there'd better not be a ghost in my room. I'm not sleeping in a haunted bedroom, no way. As for your pathetic attraction to the cleaner - get over it, she's beneath you!" With that, Minty decided to go upstairs to investigate (she's very brave in the daylight!) After 5 minutes or so I saw her in the window again, this time she opened the window and called down.

"Oi, poohface - nuffin''ere - you must be going off your trolley, brother dear."

Well, I know what I saw in spite of what Minty thinks, I definitely saw someone who looked very much like her at her window earlier, I just know it. Suddenly I heard a noise behind me, it was Uncle Nathaniel - he had stepped onto the patio to take a good lungful of air.

"Sparkling day, eh boy- ah, this is the life!"

I smiled, it WAS terrific being in the country and it felt like a million miles away from home.

"So what's planned for today, Uncle?" I asked as he stood peeling a very ripe pear with a pearl handled knife.

"Mmmm, here, try this." He handed me a slice. It was sweet and delicious.

"From Clarice's own orchard!"

"She's got a little patch of heaven here," I said. He nodded and smiled in agreement.

"Oh, you want to know what today's plan is? Well let me see - shortly we are going to take a nice leisurely drive down to Carcassone to take in the wonderful sights of the fortified city - that should be good, eh? Then, we shall be visiting Clarice's good friend, Madame DuVin, another psychic - I thought she might be able to help you both appreciate life beyond mortal life - sounds heavy going but it really isn't!"

"Groovy," I replied, with great enthusiasm. "Sounds good to me, dunno about Minty though."

"Mark please, the Queen's English! Hopefully Madame Minty will enjoy it too," he said, smiling.

"As long as there is food and fashion, maybe with a couple of bead shops thrown in for good measure, Minty will be happy, I can assure you of that."

We were soon on our way, coasting along on a bump free road (take note, councils of England) and passing through umpteen pretty villages. And what a car! Clarice had decided to take her Rolls Royce Silver Cloud so that we would have plenty of room. She had instructed Maugret to pack a picnic for us so that we could stop at a place called Montolieu, Village du Livre, just west of Carcasonne - also known as the book village of France, a lovely place with like, a billion bookshops, well, quite a few, anyway, that I was itching to delve into but unfortunately we weren't there for books - we were there to nosh!

Nathaniel pulled in to a lovely leafy park so that we could have our much-needed picnic. Good old Maugret, she certainly managed to pack a lot in to what I had thought looked like a fairly small wicker hamper but of course it wasn't. She managed to cram in just about every conceivable delicacy you could ask for, but typically, even that didn't exactly go to plan. Where Nathaniel had laid the tablecloth, just happened to be on top of a red ant's nest and as we were innocently relaxing in the dappled sunlight, the ants were busy staking their claim on our food and our limbs.

"Ugh, what the?" Cried Minty, "look out there's flippin' red ants everywhere!" She jumped up and started to franticly shake herself down. Suddenly we were all doing the crazy new dance while the locals happily watched our antics (feel free to ignore the pun!) and laughed and I could have sworn (but I'm not supposed to) that one of the kids said, "crazy British!" Luckily, the ants had only gone and figured out that there was food above their heads when we were almost finished our picnic and so packing up wasn't quite such a wrench as you might imagine.

The weather couldn't have been more perfect, with the bluest sky you could possibly imagine, in fact the sky was so blue that it made the vast sea of greenery appear to practically glow in richness. Briefly I found myself suddenly thinking about Mum and Dad on their Bingo and Fags cruise but then, just as briefly I forgot about them again. What I hadn't forgotten about though, was Nathaniel's extra windows - they still continued to bother me!

We stopped briefly for a few minutes in a rustic village pub to use the rest rooms and then we would have been ready to roll again, had it not been for Nathaniel. He was engaged in a conversation with Mrs Bloomington on the 'phone.

"And be sure to water the borders, there's a dear. Enjoy your break and feel free to invite the ladies from your writing circle over for tea if you like. I'll phone you again in a couple of days - oh and one more thing - don't go into the attic, it's not safe! Must dash now, take care dear, ta-ta." He flipped his phone shut saying, "bless her, she's a real brick!"

Don't go into the attic eh, I thought, *it's not safe? It is!*

....

Oh yes, it truly was a fabulous day, the warm wind was blowing into the car as we sped along, I kept my eyes shut because I didn't want to get dust or bugs in them but even with them shut I could still tell exactly what my dear sister was doing. She had spent the better part of an hour trying to look like Amy Winehouse by piling her hair up and applying a stack of mascara that swept upwards at the outside edge of each eye and guess what? Yep, she totally did NOT nail it and ended up looking like a right old fright. It's not the smartest thing to try to put eye makeup on when in a moving vehicle! Plus, unfortunately for her, the wind had clearly taken a dislike to her decidedly un-

French idea of fashion and had quickly managed to unravel her 'do' by making it look more like a 'don't', causing her to have to resort to sitting in the foot well to try to avoid it.

"Oh what's the use," she cursed. "You try your best to look chic and mysterious..."

"And end up looking like the bride of Frankenstein," I joked.

"Oh yeah," she cried. "As if YOU'D know anything about fashion, look at you in your knock-off hoodie, keep your arms down or your sleeves might fly off."

"Yeah right, Cruella de Vile - very chic I'm sure!"

Apart from our battles with the wind in the car, no, not that kind of wind, you KNOW full well what I mean, it was a relatively good journey and we made Carcassone for almost dead on 12.30.

First stop, once the car had been parked, was for Madame Clarice to 'veeseet' her 'gud friend' Justavia. Clarice led us along a bright, sunlit cobbled alleyway that nestled between a patisserie and a fruit shop and which lead to a sunny little cul de sac occupied on three sides by a building with painted windows depicting the Crystal Ball, the Tarot and the Palm. Clarice swept through the doorway in the centre part of the building set within a magnificently ornate gold painted portico. She let herself in, as the door was unlocked (*a bit risky*, I thought) into a room that hurt your eyes from all of the colours that immediately appeared to be doing battle with each other.

"Preeety non?" She asked.

"Non," I replied honestly.

"Ha, you are notheen but a boy and whut do leetle boys no of colaire?"

I deliberately kept quiet and tried my best to avoid Clarice's quizzical look.

"I reckon it's lush," said Minty. "One should nevah shy away from bold colours yeah? 'Ent that right Clar?"

Clarice looked taken aback at being thrown into sudden alliance with Minty. "Steek weeth me Meenty and a weel mek a beautiful woman of you," she replied.

"Best of luck with that then," I said, ducking, just in time as Minty tried to whack me across the head with a rolled up copy of Vogue. Just then a person who I assumed to be Clarice's friend, stepped out from behind some bright orange and purple floaty curtains. What is it with elderly people? They all look alike! Despite Clarice being a slightly heavier build, they looked almost identical.

"Justavia, how well you look," cried Clarice rushing to embrace her. "You look almost as young as me!"

"Yes without the 'elp of the surgeon's knife eh? Thees," she said flicking her hand from her head to her hips with a theatrical flourish, "ees all natural!"

"Naturel?" Clarice muttered. I quickly noticed that Madame DuVin was quite unsteady on her feet but there was something more, something strange about her face that made me want to keep staring at her. Unfortunately she caught me looking and made her way, lurching all over the place, towards me and then it dawned on me - she had no eyebrows, not a hint, not even badly painted on ones (like most old ladies).

"And 'oo might you be," she asked, offering her cheek for a traditional double kiss. I was thinking, *oh gross, another over powdered doughnut*, but I kissed her out of sheer politeness. It was then that I got a waft, over the top of whatever dreadfully fusty perfume she was wearing, of wine - the woman was practically pickled! She looked at me with one eye squinted and the other one decidedly bloodshot.

"Why you kip moveen? Please stand steel for me to feex my eye upon you," she said in another hard to understand slurred French accent.

"Uh, I AM standing still - it's you that's swaying," I replied trying to be honest without upsetting her. Madame Clarice came waddling over to intervene.

"'Ow ees beesneece Justavia? Seems, eef I may be so bold, to be a leetle beet dusty in 'ere - beesneece not so good?"

"Dusty? Een 'ere?" Justavia glanced around and quickly had to grab onto a table for support as if the sudden head movement had brought on vertigo. "Oh dear, must 'ave a beet of an 'ead cold - perhaps I need a leetle neep of wheesky?"

"No," said Clarice. I think you 'already ave 'ad a beet too much to dreenk. Come on, let's mek you a nice cup of tea, particularly feeting as we 'ave Engleesh guests weeth us today."

"Engleesh are they?" said Madame DuVin. "Ees that why they dress so strengley? That odd leetle woman weeth the theek eye mekup has hair the 'air of a birdsnest non?"

"Now now Justavia, that's just the wine talking, try to be polite to our European cousins!"

Justavia Anotherbottle! That's what I was imagining her surname should be. I could have listened to the two of them for hours, it was like watching and episode of, *Allo Allo*.

"Oi, nerdface, did that wobbly old biddy just insult me or wot?" Said Minty.

"Or what! She's a," and I whispered the next bit, "a bit of a drinker! Flippin' pickled, actually!"

Minty looked stunned. "Blimey, that's it then, I ent gonna be a drinker no way, people'll fink I'm fick, yeah?"

"Minty - the Queen's English! Thick not fick," I said, trying to help her and accidentally sounding more like Nathaniel.

"Ooh, 'ark at you, get yer 'ead out yer butt Mr La-di flippin' da, you're 16 not 60!"

What was the use? I sighed and made my way through the mysterious orange and purple curtain. Inside was a small kitchenette and as I glanced around, a depressing site met my eyes. I had to carefully step over the many bottles that littered the floor. Madame Clarice was busy looking in the fridge for some milk, and she picked a bottle up and carefully sniffed it.

"Ugh mak! Be a dear and get us som meelk from the grin grocerre next door, 'ere are two euros - thees meelk 'as seen better dess!"

"Okay Clarice, no problemo." I could see Minty watching as I made my way to the door.

"Oi, were you goin off to? Don't leave me 'ere, it stinks funny, yeah?" She said.

"Crikey, I'm only going next door to get some *meelk* but you can tag along if you must - just behave yourself!"

"Awright Dad, you flippin' moron!" She continued moaning as we made our way into the fruit shop. "Cor, it stinks funny in 'ere too, what is it with foreign countries, yeah?"

I deliberately ignored her, she was so embarrassing to be around that I just wanted to get the milk and get out of the shop as soon as I could. I turned around having paid for it but she had vanished. I immediately stepped outside into the sunshine, shielding my eyes with my hand as I scanned all around me, wondering where on earth she could possibly be.

Chapter Nineteen

Flipping girl, where are you, I thought - then I spotted her. She was looking in the window of a second hand store.

"Hey, pimple head! Come 'ere, look!" She called. As I made my way across the square, squinting from the sunlight. I immediately spotted what she was pointing at - a cruddy looking old necklace with glittering green crystal beads.

"Look at that, smashin ennit - it's only 15 euros, what do ya reckon - should I blow my allowance on it?"

"I dunno, it's your money- just don't come begging to me if you see anything else - bit old for you though isn't it?"

"Hello? This in an antique shop you duffer, of course it's old!"

"You know what I mean, stop being so obtuse."

"I will when you stop speaking the ruddy Queen's English, right?" She said, manoeuvring herself in front of the window so that her reflection was in line with the necklace. I watcher her as she stood pouting and posing and moving her body up and down like a demented chicken until she looked as though she was actually wearing it. "Mmm, gorge! Right, I've decided, it's too lush to miss - I'm 'aving it." With that, she barged inside.

It's odd, but as my crazy sister was making her way to the till, I started to feel as though something was trying to grab my attention, almost as though invisible hands were trying to pull me towards the back of the shop. Whatever it was, I found that I was unable to resist the strange lure, so while Minty was busy trying desperately to haggle over the price of the necklace to far lower than it was marked, which impressed me for once, I have to say, I gave in to the strange pull and let myself be guided towards a tatty bookcase full of equally tatty books. I knew I was under surveillance from the beady eyes of an ancient-looking woman, probably the younger assistant's mother, I guessed.

Now, I can't explain it any better than this, but suddenly I felt as though my hands had invisible strings attached to them, like a marionette's, and without any conscious thought from me, both hands were pulled forward, making me reach out for a thick volume directly in front of me that had two fab-looking metal clasps upon it. I was fascinated, not only by the ancient looking book, but also by what I figured must be some sort of spirit guiding me and I thought, ha, Minty will be so flippin' jealous at my superior psychic skills! I was still busy examining the book, trying my best to undo the rusted clasps when Minty grabbed my elbow to pull me outside.

"Wass that crap? Put it down, you don't know where it's been. Now go on then, praise me. I just got meself a great deal, knocked the silly French twit right down to 10 flippin' euros!"

I rolled my eyes in despair. "Okay, don't get cocky, dear sister. They probably put an extra five euros on the price anyway, to allow for bartering from potential tightwads from the UK!" I replied putting the book down.

"No way," replied Minty, as we left the shop. I would have liked to have spent more time there but Minty was intent on rushing back to show Madame Clarice her bargain buy.

"You're just jealous 'cause I'd make a better antiques buyer than you!"

I rolled my eyes again. Girls eh?

Back inside Madame DuVin's, Clarice was sitting down and chatting to Nathaniel who was standing in the now opened, back doorway looking disdainfully out at the garden, full of cigarette butts and wine bottles and about a million dandelions.

"We're back," I announced.

"Ah bon, I thought you 'ad gone to thee farm for eet!"

"Sorry, Clarice, I got side tracked by my beady eyed sister," I turned giving her a raised eyebrow.

"Oh hardy har, he's just jealous 'cause I beat him to this." Minty held up the necklace proudly before Clarice's eyes.

"Oh, like I'd want a stoopid necklace that probably came off a dead person - if you ask me you just wasted ten euros on a bit of tat."

Clarice looked surprised. "Is that all you ped for eet?" She reached for it and examined it carefully. It's exquisite - you 'ave a good eye, Meenty." She then went uncharacteristically quiet, running the necklace through her hands. Suddenly she jerked, almost falling off her chair and inadvertently letting one go.

"Ooh my," she said. "Thees, remands me of somsink that 'ave escaped me for a while..." She said cryptically.

"That's not the only thing that escaped," whispered Minty out of the side of her mouth to me. My shoulders immediately began to shake, I wanted to laugh but didn't want Minty to see that I was sinking to her level so I rolled my eyes instead as if I was disgusted with her. Madame Clarice then spoke again. "So odd, I feel I am being blocked by somsink but whut eet ees I do nut know. Eet'll come to me, you wet and see!" She looked at Minty. "You know, eef you laf beads, Meenty, I 'ave plenty you can 'ave back at the château."

Minty looked at me with the smuggest face I have ever seen, but I, being the elder one by three whole minutes, let it go because frankly, I wanted nothing better than a nice cup of tea. I looked around and spotted Madame DuVin lying slumped in a chair snoring, I could see that she had no teeth and for some strange reason I suddenly felt sorry for her.

"Will she be alright," I asked Clarice.

"Oh she'll be fine, leetle man, a nice cup of, 'ow you say - 'char', weel do 'er well."

"Okay, that's good then," I replied, wondering why she constantly chose to belittle me by referring to me as, 'leetle man'. Nathaniel suddenly spoke.

"He's hardly little, Clarice, I'll have you know that young Mark here is my protégé - he's very intelligent, you know!"

At last, I thought, *someone on my side for once.*

Clarice smiled. "I know thet, I am not bland, Nathaniel, nor do I believe in over-prezzing, as eet will go to their young 'eads. But enough of the cheet-chetting, as you Breets would say - it's time for a cuppa!"

Amazingly enough, the cup of tea *did* do the trick when it came to bringing Madame DuVin around, it was nothing short of a miracle, because no sooner had she finished her second cup than she was setting up her 'creestal ball,' to give us all a ridding. Once she was ready, she ushered everyone around her rickety old table with a request for us not to lean on it for fear of sending the crystal ball flying out of the window. Naturally I wanted to laugh as I was imagining the scene vividly, but decided to keep my lip well and truly buttoned, as Dad would say, for fear of distracting her. Minty stood peering over her shoulder.

"Not so close child, please, give an artiste some spess," she urged, pushing her many bangles up her spindly arms out of the way. "I nid to 'ave some elbow rum - ridding the creestal tekks gret dexterity, non?" Minty stepped back about a millimetre, yeah, she's just too helpful (not!)

"Ah oui," cried Madame DuVin whilst partly shading the ball with her sparkly, ring adorned hands. "Theese ees por vu, Nathaniel - I can see you steppeen through a secret doorway into nothingness!"

I wondered, was it me, or did Nathaniel go red in the face after she had mentioned the secret doorway, and did I not see a conspirational glance from Madame Clarice? It all sounded very odd indeed. She hadn't finished with him yet though.

"You are a mysterious man, non? You 'ave a 'idden secret do you not?" She looked at him intently as she said this but I was more aware of Clarice smiling, knowingly.

"Secrets are not good for the soul, Nathaniel, you mash reveal all or you will nevairre be successful! There, that ees what the ball 'as to say to you, leesen well and heed my words, now, oos next for a gleempse of the fyushaire?"

Minty pushed forward again saying, "Ooh pick me, pick me - it's mega urgent that I know my 'fyushaire'," she mimicked, "if that's okay with everyone?" We all rolled our eyes and then Minty's message began.

"You are a dominant child non? You lack the social graces but this will not always be so, you are very eentelligent lak your brother, non?"

I could see Minty shaking her head.

"I see you studying 'ard at university working with fabreec. You, young ledee are going to be thee fashionista - a designairre oo weel be verr successful."

Well that was my theory up the swanee. I was certain Minty would end up on working on a checkout somewhere or serving behind a greasy counter in a fish and chip shop, but then again, who knows how we are going to turn out, eh? Apart, that is, from Him upstairs and Madame DuVin!

"Young Mak, what does the fyushaire 'old por vu?"

I eagerly took the now vacated seat.

"I am seeing somesink ancient, a manuscript of great antiquity and you alone are the one to unravel the text. I see you all grown up - you are seeting in an underground shamber weeth a seengle shaft of light illuminateen where you are workeen - eet ees not your 'ome, eet ees not 'ere - eet ees in Eshypt!"

Blimey, Eshypt? I'm off to Egypt then, I thought, *how cool is that?*

"Are you sure?" I asked her, fully realising my mistake after the words had left my lips.

"Sure? SURE? Am I not, Madame DuVin, greatest creestal ball readaire in all France?"

I could see Nathaniel moving his eyes as if to suggest I say 'yes' so I did just that. "Yes, Madame DuVin, you are simply the best."

"You'd better belive eet boy, better than Tinna Turnairre," she replied whilst shooing me away with a sweep of her bony bejewelled hand, which I took to mean I had proven myself unworthy of any more!

"Come back 'ere leetle boy, there ees one more theeng!" I cautiously moved close to her. "When you discovairre the truth, don't just stumble eenside because eef you do, you will nevairre be the sem agen!"

Oh boy, just what I needed, another cryptic clue. As I walked away, scratching my head, Madame DuVin beckoned Clarice to join her. Clarice made a theatrical gesture as if to say, 'moi? before edging forward to take a seat next to Justavia.

"Ivven famoos middiams lek you, dear friend, laaave to 'ave a ridding! Come, seet quiet and let me see wut the ball 'as to say to you." Clarice looked around at us all and smiled, raising her eyebrows to show her puzzlement.

"I see luff, I see 'l'amour comeen eento your laf, een fect I see you 'ead over 'eals in luff weeth a very wealthy man, non? Thees man, ee meks you 'appier than you 'ave been in ages and you weel wunt to settle down weeth 'eem for the rest of your laf." Madame DuVin then looked up to see how Clarice was reacting to her reading. "Eet ees good news, non?"

"It EES gud news, bon surpreese - eet would be a meeracle at my time of laff - weel thees new man be coming down my cheemney at Chreestmas?" She replied, trying to supress her laughter. Madame DuVin peered over the top of her diamante framed spectacles and looked at Clarice, deadly serious. "You will need a very wide cheemney for eem to weegle down, 'e will be enormously fet!"

Clarice pulled a face.

Now it was Madame DuVin's turn to suppress a giggle. "Got you deedn't I, no, 'e wunt be fet - 'ad you belivin' me for a moment there, non?"

Clarice suddenly burst out laughing, with relief more than anything else (I think).

All through this I was itching to have a go with the crystal ball myself, it's been something I've always wanted to try so I decided to pluck up the courage and ask Madame DuVin if she wouldn't mind letting me have a go, even though I was still a bit nervous of her - well, you just never know how she'll react!

"Madame DuVin?"

"Yis!" She snapped.

"Oh never mind," I answered timidly (for me!)

"Mak, ere's one theeng een laf you nid to learn, eef you want sometink badly enough, you 'ave to be prepared to face your dimons. Grrrrr!" She then smiled. "Don't be a bebby, wut did you want to ask me?"

She had issued me with a challenge and so, like the brave Kings of jolly old England, I accepted. "Can I have a go with your crystal ball - please?"

"You, a leetle boy? Wants to 'ave a go weeth my precious creestle ball - sometheen so precious as to be irreplaceable? So 'ighly mysterious and powerful that it could shatter eento a million pieces if used incorrectacallilly - of course you can - 'ere, let me show you 'ow to do eet!"

I had no time to laugh at the way she had murdered the word, incorrectly because, wasting not a moment, she attempted to show me in five minutes, something that had taken her years to master and it left me feeling like a failure before I had even started.

"You 'ave to look deep een the meedle deestance, not exactly looking at theengs but seeing whut develops around them, non?"

"Ohhh," I replied, hoping I had got what she meant. "Like you do with Magic Eye pictures?"

"Yes, YES, exactamon, perhaps you are not such a bebby maybe - although, weeth me, those Mashik Eye peectures mek me go cross-eyed!" She then took the opportunity to show me her cross-eyed look, which, I could clearly hear, made Minty snigger.

"Plis, 'ere Mak, 'ave a go, 'ave a go..." She then gestured for me to quickly sit down, with a wide sweep of her arms as she got out of her chair, so that I could tap in to the energy she had raised, apparently, but to be honest, I couldn't feel anything other than a hot leather seat pad! Anyway, I did as instructed, sat down and in my best theatrical pose I put my hands together and stretched, making my knuckles crack as a magician might do. I could see Minty looking at me with a look of sheer disgust on her face.

"Boys weel be boys!" Said Clarice.

Now don't ask me how, but I just seemed to know exactly what to do to get in tune with the crystal. I took three deep breaths with my eyes shut tightly and asked for a message for Madame DuVin. I wanted to feel positive but quite honestly, I wasn't expecting anything much to happen and at first, nothing *did* happen. I tried as hard as I could to make my mind completely blank and for a time it was, that is, apart from an image of the old battered book in the antique shop that suddenly appeared. Then, I started to see words floating around it - one, two, three, four - from the window to the floor!

Briefly, I opened my eyes to look at Madame DuVin and was stunned to see that there were tears glistening in her eyes. She glanced across at Clarice and then at Nathaniel as if they all shared some kind of hidden secret. It left me puzzled so I closed my eyes to see what else would be revealed to me but all I could see was the book again and as I was watching it, it came closer and closer towards me and then, to my surprise, I could see my own hands reaching out to take it - but then I lost the image and that was that.

When I opened my eyes, Madame DuVin, Clarice and Nathaniel were in the kitchen in a sort of secretive huddle. Minty was flicking through the copy of Vogue she had used to whack me across the head with earlier.

"Oi, Minty," I called. "I'm just nipping back to that antique shop for something if anyone asks - it's urgent."

"You're not going after that crappy book are you?"

"So what if I am, it's MY money."

"Jus' make sure it ain't useless like this useless necklace, I tried to do it up and found that the flippin' clasp is broken!"

Minty rolled her eyes at me and then lifted the magazine up to shut me out. I then rushed outside and hared across the square like a boy possessed only to discover, horror of horrors that the two women were busy locking the shop up.

Chapter Twenty

"Oh no, please. I have to buy that book?" I pointed to it as best I could, but the younger woman of the two simply shook her head.

"Please!" I pleaded but they acted as though I wasn't there. In one last desperate attempt I grabbed hold of the older lady's hand and kissed it, saying, 'please, Madame,' looking directly into her eyes. She looked at me and smiled warmly, tapping, who I took to be her daughter - the other lady, on the elbow and whispering something in her ear.

Twas a miracle! The younger lady tutted but then quickly unlocked the door and then the older lady gestured for me to follow her and made her way towards the back of the shop and uncannily, picked up what she thought I wanted. Amazingly she had guessed correctly! I gave her a, thumbs up sign, excitedly. Her daughter was waiting at the door tapping her watch as if to hurry her mother along and then miracle number two happened

- I offered the old lady the 10 Euros marked in pencil on the price tag and the old woman pushed the money away and folded my fingers around the note and let me have the book for nothing! TOTALLY FREE!!! Can you believe it? It was amazing - and now I totally love the French! I gave the woman a hug and she gave me a huge smile in return. With a wave goodbye to them I then raced back to Madame Duvin's.

As soon as I was back in Madame DuVin's shop, I quickly found a quiet spot where I could study my fine treasure, as I thought of it, in total privacy. Yeah right!

"God, what a load of old crap!" Said Minty creeping up on me like a bloodhound. "You don't half like wasting your money don't you, you - dweeb! Could have bought some sweets instead and we both could have shared them!"

"Yeah right, French sweets - Parma Violets, mmm lush! This book isn't a load of old crap for your liking - can't you see, it's an old bible!"

"Oh great, going all religious now are you? Well, like I said, s'crap! Look at the catches, I bet you can't even open it!"

"Yes I can, or will - just needs a bit of oil on them, or a bit of gentle persuasion."

"How about this for a bit of gentle persuasion - chuck it away, probably get cooties just by touching it - supposing the last owner had leprosy or something and it's been impregnated into the filthy pages - your fingers will probably drop off."

My twin, how could this be so?

"Steady on, you just said a word with 4 syllables - best you sit down for a minute, you might get light-headed!"

"Oh har bloody har! So it's a bible - do you have any idea how many bibles there are in the world? What's so 'must have' about that crappy thing?" Cried Minty.

"Don't you worry, I am the twin with the brains, you are merely the twin with a MASSIVE CAKEHOLE! I'll soon know why I was pulled towards it, mark my words, my precious leetle pomme de terre." I said, mimicking the locals.

"You were pulled towards it?" She replied. "Oh my god, you ARE a nutter after all!"

"Hmmm, flattery will get you nowhere, At least, what I was pulled to, might still be of some use."

"Yeah, might be if you could open the crappy thing! At least my beads are wearable..."

"Yeah if you're a granny!"

"Style transcends the ages yeah?"

"Twaddle! Listen dear sister of mine, would it be too much to ask for a modicum of privacy around here? Why don't you just clear off and go play with your beads, or the traffic!" The last bit was not meant to be heard, just a grumble really but 'ol radar dishes heard it clear enough.

"Oh charming, you'd love that wouldn't you, to be a single rather than a twin- what's the matter, brother, am I too much competition for you?"

I chose to ignore her, hard though it was, and eventually she went away. Of course, I then felt guilty so rather than explore my new treasure, which was a major struggle for my conscience and me, I went off in search of rent-a-gob, sorry, Minty - for I suddenly had the dumb idea that maybe we could look at the book together. *Crikey, what's the matter with me? I must be getting soft!* I eventually found her out in the small back yard amongst the bottles and the fag-ends, holding the crystal necklace up to the sun. She pretended not to see me, but I knew that she knew I was there.

"What ya doing?" I tried my best to break the ice.

"I'm wishing. Wishing I hadn't bought this piece of crap and enjoying being in my own personal space, that's what I'm doing," she replied, a tad frostily, I might add.

"Listen, I'm sorry Minty, honest I am. I know I can be a right old crab at times, but I wouldn't want anything bad to happen to you - you're my only sister and I lo, lov - err, like you – and back there, I was just mouthing off. That's all. Look, I've brought my crappy old book with me so that we can look at it together."

Minty looked at me, one eyebrow cocked as if trying to grasp if she had just, almost heard me admit that I actually loved her.

"Hello?" She said. "Why would I want to look at that?"

"Because I'm being magnanimous. Because I think it might be more important than it looks - I dunno, I just felt drawn to it within seconds of entering the shop. That's why I had to buy it. Go on, I dare you - touch it, let me see if you get the same feelings that I did when I first picked it up."

"Ha, its nothing to do with you being 'drawn' to it - truth is you're too flippn' weak to get the stoopid old thing open - well I'm wise to your little plan!"

I fought the urge to reply with a snappy comeback and bided my time. At first she continued to look at me like I had just sprouted a second head but then seeing that I was not about to respond to her funny look at me, she reached out her arm and wiggled her fingers at me as a sign for me to pass the book over to her. Which I did.

I watched her intently as she made contact with the book. I sensed there was something important about it and I wanted to see if Minty got the same feelings that I did. The minute she touched it I knew, for the look on her face said it all! She looked positively stunned as she was holding it - for she was acting as though it was on fire. Suddenly she dropped the book.

"Argh, what the hell?" She cried.

"What? What did you feel?"

"What did I feel? You know full well what I would feel - you just wanted it to burn me, you prat!" she spat.

"No, no I didn't." I said. "I had no idea that it was going to affect you like that, I only wanted to see if you felt anything about the book. So, what did you feel?"

"Listen Einstein, that flamin' book gave me an electric shock! I got a horrible burning pain that shot up my arm! Admit it - it's a joke book, isn't it!"

"No, it isn't, Minty, honestly."

"Well what is it then? You used me as a guinea pig!"

"No! I tried to tell you, it's whatever pulled me to buy the book that affected you - do you get what I mean?"

"I don't know if I WANT to get what you mean, this thing just hurt me - it's weird and it's freaky!" She said, picking the book up again, only this time using two fingers, to study it in greater detail. "And I saw things!"

"What? Like what? What did it show you?"

"I'll tell you what it showed me - three people, three ghostly looking people, that's what I saw! There was a man and a woman, then what looked like a young girl, oh, and there was a baby too, the woman had a baby in her arms! Then, as if that wasn't freaky enough, I saw a kind of sparkly ribbon of light winding its way around them like a lasso and pulling them all together tightly. Flippin' freaky book!"

"You saw all that - in less than a minute? Are you aware you have a psychic ability?"

"I am NOT flippin' psychic!"

"Yeah, whatever! So, Minty - what do you think it all means then?"

"It means you've bought yourself a haunted book, that's what it means. Make sure you keep it in YOUR room tonight. I don't want that thing anywhere near me. And let me tell you again - I am not flippin' psychic!"

At that she got up and tossed the book back to me but, as I hadn't expected her to do so, all I could do was to watch it as it sailed through the air towards me but naturally, me being rubbish at anything resembling sports, I failed to catch it and I could only cringe as it landed face down on the concrete path where one of the clasps immediately shot off and the other left hanging open at an odd angle.

"You prat! Look what you've done now!" I yelled. I was fuming, not only because of what had happened to 'my treasure' but because of the way Minty didn't seem to give a damn and just chose to flounce off, and after me being so unusually nice to her. I vowed never to make that mistake again, that's for sure!

I bent down and picked the battered book up. The clasp that had shot off had rolled into a straggly weed and fag-filled former flower border. I got down on my hands and knees to retrieve it. Luckily for me it was still in one piece. As I was checking it for damage I noticed that on the reverse it had an elaborate letter 'J' etched into it. I suspected, hoped actually, that it just might be something to do with whoever had owned the bible last). Without a moments rest I carefully opened the bible up and I couldn't believe what I saw and thought to myself, *surely not?*

Chapter Twenty-One

"What ya doin' now, Stig?" It was Minty, she had come back and had the nerve to show her face again so soon! In case you're wondering why she was calling me, Stig, it's because of one of my favourite books, *Stig of The Dump* - she always compared me to Stig but I actually think she meant the boy in the story, Barney.

"None of your business, Manky!" I couldn't resist snapping at her again, maybe it would have been different if she still hadn't had such a nauseatingly smug look on her face. I turned away from her so that she couldn't see what I was doing. I knew full well it would drive her mad.

"Hey! Look, I didn't mean to break your stoopid, sorry, I mean your *precious* bible. Lord knows - get it? I only wanted to get it out of my hands as fast as I could! I'm not interested in being psychic and I really didn't appreciate whatever it was trying to do to me."

"And you couldn't have simply handed it back to me? I said. Anyway, I think you *are* psychic and that's that, if you *are*, you can't simply stop being that way. I reckon you have more potential than you realise, so stop being such a negative nancy. Anyway, I've read that negativity attracts negativity so if you only want good things to happen, start being nice to people!"

"I will if you will, Einstein! So, what ARE you doing?"

I explained that due to her 'accident', I had discovered the letter 'J' on the clasp that shot off, and now I had discovered a different letter on the other clasp - it was an 'G'. That was not what had shocked me the most though, oh no. As I turned past several torn out pages and then past the first few, relatively normal looking bible pages - there it was - a star shaped hole!

"A hole - in the bible? That's a bit, you know, naughty isn't it?" Said Minty.

"Positively sacrilegious."

"But," said Minty. "Just suppose that it was never meant to be a normal, for reading, kind of bible? Maybe it was always meant to hide something and yet just look like a regular bible?"

I was stunned. My twin had acted like my twin should act, like a fellow smarty pants - and it worked too. Now, at last, I had seen a glimpse of the sister I always hoped for.

"Minty, you're a gen-e-ass!"

"Yeah, thanks for that, bro," she replied, but I could tell that she felt pretty good about it! Then, just when I thought I'd sit quietly to see if anything came to me, Nathaniel announced that we were heading back home and that Madame DuVin had decided to join us for a few days break. *Well*, I thought, *I hope Clarice makes sure her drinks cabinet is kept well and truly locked!* Yes, I was thrilled at the prospect of solving the riddle of the book but more thrilled by the thought of some food, as my stomach had been rumbling ever since I'd picked the book up. When it comes to my stomach, the book could jolly well wait!

"Minty, I've been meaning to say, I'm sure I can fix that necklace clasp for you when we get home if you want." She looked at me quizzically.

"O-K?" She replied, seemingly waiting for a punch line that never came.

....

We got back to the château at almost 5, dinner was scheduled for 7 (Clarice had phoned Maugret ahead of time with instructions). Perfect! Two hours for me to look at the book - then, right as out of the blue, Nathaniel got everyone together, saying, "So, whose ready for a pre-dinner story then, after all the travelling we have done I thought it might be a good way to relax and to ready ourselves for another of Clarice's gastronomic feasts - I've undone my top button already!"

I knew the night would be particularly torturous, nothing watchable on the television because, surprise, surprise, it was all in French and therefore unintelligible to me! Minty would be on a mission to moan about anything and everything, then, just after Nathaniel had suggested telling us a story, get this - Minty only suddenly piped up that she had just written one herself and announced that she'd like to read it out to us all. Has my annoying sibling no shame? Talk about stealing my thunder! I'm sure she suggested it purely out of jealousy because I get on so well with Nathaniel. I'm not unduly worried though, it'll be crap - trust me, she doesn't know one end of a pen from another!

"Another secret writer in the family eh." Said Nathaniel. "I must say, young lady, you are turning out to be quite the dark horse."

"Whut ees your little tale all about then? Ponies, dresses or ees eet abut boys, non?"

Minty raised one eyebrow and spoke directly to Clarice, "As if! You won't guess what it's about in a million years so I suggest, as Nathaniel said, everyone relax and be sure there's someone close by to hold your hand - that's all the warning I'm giving you."

"Whut deed she say?" Said Madam DuVin cupping her hand to an ear.

"It's OK, dear. Minty is about to tell us all a story," said Nathaniel loudly. "It would appear that we are a family of writers!"

"Be back in a flash," said Minty, "just have to go and get it from my room."

With that she rushed upstairs to get her journal. Minutes later she was back, unusually fast I might add, so we all settled down in the lounge and waited for Miss Cleverpants to begin.

"OK?" Said Minty. "Everyone ready?" She looked around to make sure. "I'll take your silence as a yes, then so I want to see butts on seats, pronto - come on! Right. I have called this story -

Touching the Past

"Don't you be touching anything in there, Eloise, there's too many precious items for little fingers to get hold of!"

Blimey! It was the same speech every time I visited Nan - she never seemed to notice that I was now a teenager, and no longer a child. Nan's china cabinet had always held a certain fascination for me. Design-wise it was hideous, festooned with cream painted swirls and embellished with little touches of gold lacquer and with poorly painted butterflies that looked more like moths, in oval panels at each corner. Totally gross but nonetheless fascinating. It reminded me of something you would find in Rapunzel's bedroom or the Queen's privy!

Most of the items inside weren't really my thing, porcelain children in garish colours climbing apple trees and some odd looking sheep with a shepherdess sporting hideous rouged cheeks in deep red circles - to me she looked more like a clown than a shepherdess. There was one, ugly looking item that I could just about see, tucked way at the back of the bottom shelf and it looked far more interesting. From what I could make out, it looked as though it had sprouted hairs! Probably a mouldy bit of wedding cake knowing Nan!

Nan was busy talking to her neighbour in the back garden leaving me with time to kill. The ornate brass key, with a hanging loop that featured a faded pink tassel dangling from it, was simply asking to be turned. I knew I would have to be fairly quick if I wanted to explore the wonders beyond the swirly glass door but in order to reach the mysterious hairy object, my shaky hand would need to navigate between many delicate ornaments without knocking any over as I did so. I quickly peeped into the kitchen and beyond to make sure the coast was clear. Nan was showing the neighbour a pair of thermal pants she had just bought! Good, she was still occupied.

I immediately took my chance and quickly turned the key. It opened the lock easily and was far smoother than I imagined it would be. I wasted no time at all and pretty quickly had my hand on the door pulling the slightly stuck door open. As I pulled it towards me it screeched horribly and for a second I froze where I was, fully expecting Nan to come in at any moment wagging an admonishing finger at me. I remained where I was, stock still, listening intently. Oh no! There was a definite pause in the conversation I was half listening to. Whether that was a natural pause or one for Nan to tune into what I was up to, I couldn't be sure. Suddenly she called out, "You alright in there, Eloise?"

"I'm fine - just reading!" I called back. The nattering resumed and so did I. I now had full access to the cabinet for the first time ever and I felt a distinct thrill run through me - it was like being a cat burglar (although technically I wasn't out to steal anything!)

As my hand carefully skimmed across the top of some of the tackiest ornaments I had ever laid eyes on, trying hard not to knock any over, it reminded me of the game, *Operation*, where you have to move items in an image of a body along an electrified route without touching anything else along the way and triggering a buzzer.

Just as I was feeling totally confident, the heel of my palm brushed the top of a plastic Spanish dancer doll, making it rock - I held my breath and a thought occurred to me - *why am I doing this?* Luckily it was OK, the stupid Spanish doll stopped rocking and I was able to carry on. At last, my fingers closed around the mysterious hairy object. It felt pretty disgusting but my curiosity had got the better of me and so I carried on lifting the thing over the busy figurines, barely managing to keep hold of it between two fingertips and when I had it at the front of the shelf I finally allowed myself a sigh of relief.

Whatever it was felt odd in my hand, it's hard to explain but it definitely felt kind of gross. As I turned it around and saw what it was, I gasped and immediately dropped it.

The thing landed face upwards, and to my disgust I could see that it was a shrivelled, blackened head, only in miniature. It had grey, wiry hair, tiny sharp-looking yellow teeth - everything a head should have and tied around its neck was a tag stating, 'head of archaeologist, Harold Porter recovered June 12th 1932 from a tribe in Papua, New Guinea. Then it hit me (no, not the head!) Oh my god! This was my Great, Grandfather's head!

I now understand what Dad meant when he joked that my Great, Grandfather had always had a head for danger.

Suddenly I heard the shuffle of Nan's slippers on the kitchen lino so acting with lightning dexterity I popped the gross little head amongst the coal in the coal scuttle.

"Ooh is it me or has it gone a bit parky all of a sudden?" She said spookily. "Let's have a bit more coal on the fire eh..."

....

For a moment there was total silence in the room. Nathaniel and Clarice were both smiling as though they had discovered a precious diamond - Madam DuVin just looked puzzled - and me? I was fuming! It was bloody good - what a little turncoat! Minty *was* good at English all along and probably only pretended she was crap just to annoy the hell out of Mum and Dad - and me!

"Whut was eet? The leetle 'orrible 'airy theeng, what wus eet?" Said Madam DuVin.

"It was a shrunken head! Eloise's Great, Grandfather's head, to be precise and it was that, which Eloise's Nan threw onto the fire thinking it was just a bit of coal!" Explained Nathaniel.

Madam DuVin pulled a sour face and said, "Ugh, 'ow 'orrible - but clever non?"

Minty! I could have hit her!

Chapter Twenty-Two

In spite of my annoyance, I couldn't help but admire Minty, the way she kept up the charade of being, well, a thicko, just to blend in with her friends. At least, now I knew what she was really like although knowing her, she will still want to keep Mum and Dad in the dark - I can't imagine why - particularly as my motto is, 'if you've got it flaunt it'!

By the time we had ploughed our way through several courses for dinner and still managed to tackle the rich chocolate pudding afterwards, there was little chance of me doing much at all with the book. I had a quick scan through it, but really I wanted to wait until I had more time to study it in great detail.

Later, after we'd had some cocoa and biscuits (occasionally it pays to give in and be treated like a kid!) I made my way up to my room. Minty, like a bad smell, was close behind me. Naturally she insisted on having the adjoining door open once again. I didn't mind though - she was more like a perfect twin should be tonight than she had been prior to reading out her story. Once she had settled down and stopped asking me pointless questions just to avoid the silence, I took the chance to have a good study of the book under the covers with my torch.

"Hey, what's that light," She asked, nosily.

"Never you mind, I'm just reading - go get your beauty sleep!"

"Alright Dad!"

Then, for the first time it actually went quiet so I carried on flicking through the book and tracing my fingers over the star shaped cavity. I suddenly realised that it was not a conventional five pointed star, but one with six points, like the Jewish, Star of David, and it looked to have been cut far too cleanly for a person to have done it by hand. No, this had been deliberately cut by machine. Then, just like what had happened to Minty when she had been holding it, I felt an odd vibration burning into my fingers and locking them firmly to the pages so that I was unable to let go. Suddenly I was able to hear voices, an argument by the sound of it. I heard quite plainly, a female voice crying out, "Tell him Joseph, tell him! Our lives are more important than a book full of diamonds!" Then I heard a reply, a male voice, presumably Joseph, whoever he was. "Please! Let my family go, kill me if you must but please spare the lives of my family."

After that there was a deathly silence and I suddenly discovered I could now let go of the book, thankfully. I felt as though I had briefly opened a window and remnants of the past had come flooding in with the breeze.

I looked across to Minty's room - she was right about one thing - the book *was* certainly spooky and clearly contained more than just paper and a huge star-shaped hole. The creepy feeling stayed with me and so I decided to tackle the job of concentrating on it, only in daylight. The whole thing spooked me so much that I didn't even fancy having it next to my bed while I was sleeping, so quietly I crept outside my room and left the book on the landing window ledge before closing the bedroom door to make myself feel safer.

Incredibly, after all that had happened, I managed to have a good, dreamless night's sleep.

The next morning I was awoken by several shafts of sunlight breaking through every conceivable gap in the shutters - I got out of bed and pulled them open - it was another fantastic, sparkling day and I couldn't wait to get outside in the garden and breathe in the scents of summer.

Bleary eyed, I made my way out to the bathroom. I glanced to where I had left the book the previous night, but it was gone! Minty couldn't have taken it because I knew full well she was still in bed like a great big slug and would probably remain so for the next couple of hours. Maybe Maugret picked it up? Well, I had no doubt it would turn up one way or another so I carried on and had a wash, brushed my teeth and then made my way downstairs for breakfast.

Breakfast had been arranged out on the patio once again and I wish I could have captured the absolute perfectness of the day to be able to recall it whenever our summer day's, back in England, are so dismal. Nathaniel was already sitting at the table, he had his back to me. I walked around to say hello and there he was, looking at MY book!

"Ah, good morning to you, Mark - sorry, I hope you don't mind but I was just having a gander at your latest purchase! Maugret discovered it on the landing window ledge and thought it might be mine. It's a rather strange book, is it not? I could hardly put it down, it feels almost magnetic, as though my fingers are pulled by an invisible force to the paper – reminds me of something, but something that I can't quite put my finger on - not a lot in it though, apart from a big hole!"

"Yeah, I know what you mean - the big hole was a surprise to me too. When I bought it, I couldn't get the clasps undone and I secretly hoped that the pages might be illuminated like the Book of Kells. Boy, was I ever wrong. But Uncle, there's IS something compelling and odd about it - more than that though, I sort of get the feeling that it's come home, somehow."

Nathaniel eyed at me curiously. "Come home? What on earth makes you think that?"

"I don't know. It's just a feeling that I have!"

At that, Nathaniel silently stood up and walked back into the house without so much as a glance back, muttering to himself.

I was puzzled by Nathaniel's reaction but the lure of the food quickly got the better of me and once again I sat back and enjoyed the delights of France. I then took the opportunity to take a longer look at the 'holy' book. The cover was made, as far as I could tell, from thick leather. It was black and very cracked with age. Inside, around the edges of the 'non holy' pages there were bad stains and a lot of spotting (foxing, as Uncle later corrected me) to the paper, making some pages look like the skin of an over ripe pear. The title page was particularly fascinating - it was beautifully painted and had an illustration of a bee hive with many tiny bees that had been picked out in gold leaf.

The complete pages preceding the hole inside had been embellished with what looked like hand drawn illustrations. This seemed to me, rather elaborate for something that was essentially nothing more than a safe! That led me to wonder what exactly had been hidden inside it? It must have been pretty valuable if such a lot of trouble and expense had gone into creating the fake bible. That night as I sat in my room, I thought back to my first spirit encounter at Woodchester Mansion and it suddenly dawned on me that, as apparently, I have a rather keen psychic ability that has been waiting to express itself all along, then what about Minty? As far as I can tell, we as twins, seem to share a unique psychic ability - something that appears to be manifesting itself at quite an alarming rate!

Chapter Twenty-Three

Later that day, Minty and I joined Nathaniel outside in the back garden. He was sitting on a bench that encircled a huge oak tree, reading a book. I had the bible in my hands which he saw and asked me to pass it to him. As Minty and I both explained what had just happened after we had touched the bible, he carefully laid his book down and motioned for us to sit next to him, saying, he had been mulling something over and had come to a conclusion - it was now the right time for him to reveal some things from his past, things that he felt might be significant at this time. *At this time*, I thought, *whatever that might mean.*

Nathaniel sat with his hands resting on the bible and seeing that both of us were now ready for him to commence, he began, at last, to tell us his amazing story...

"It was back in 1940, whilst your Grandmother and I were still in France, that we got friendly with a family who lived nearby and who's father worked for Cousin Clarice's father, Philipe. I thought they were all just servants until Clarice inadvertently let slip one morning that they were actually Jewish and very wealthy at that. Soon, they were hiding in our house, away from the prying eyes of the Nazi soldiers who had descended upon our village faster than flying ants in high humidity. Clarice's father swore me to secrecy, warning me that if the Germans ever found them, the entire family and anyone who had helped them, would be sent to an internment camp or worse, shot on sight.

The family, Joseph Green, who was the father, Esther, the mother, nine year old Hannah and tiny Ruth, who was just a baby, were, in fact, a family of diamond merchants and had been great friends of Clarice's family for many years, for both fathers worked together and were local philanthropists who did a great deal of fundraising for charitable causes. Their house had lain empty ever since the family went into hiding, but it was soon commandeered by the German army who then issued a warrant for the arrest of the family. The warrant also stated that, 'anyone discovered sheltering enemies of the Führer would be shot on sight'. Philipe DuVin knew that something needed to be done and done quickly. Fortunately he, like the Greens had good business contacts in Switzerland and consequently, they were all guaranteed a place of safety if and when they reached the politically neutral country.

For a number of weeks the Greens remained hidden away in the DuVin's attic. They had made it as comfortable as it could possibly be, but for a wealthy family with a young child and a baby, it was not ideal. Unfortunately, one night when a blackout was in force, the Greens, thinking they were relatively safe in the attic, kept a lamp on for both light and heat. Little did they know that there was a roof tile missing allowing a beam of light to be visible in the street below and unfortunately for them, a German foot soldier just happened to be walking by and he had spotted it.

The soldier immediately hammered on the DuVin's front door demanding to speak to the head of the household. Philipe opened it on the chain and asked what was wrong. The soldier shouted at Philipe to let him inside so that he could find out where the light was coming from. Philipe tried to reassure him that he would find it and turn it off but the soldier would not hear of it, leaving Philipe with little choice, other than to reluctantly, open the door up, fully. The soldier instantly struck him savagely across the face and barged past him. Philipe's wife, Madeline, who had rushed to see what the commotion was, screamed as she saw her husband's lip bleeding, but the soldier simply pushed her back into her bedroom and slammed the door shut before striding up the stairs towards the attic.

"Stop?" Cried Mr DuVin. "You have no rights entering my house! Where is your search warrant?"

Mr DuVin's words proved useless, as the soldier didn't so much as glance back. Then, pulling his gun from its holster he turned and shouted, "This is my search warrant! If you have nothing to hide, you have nothing to fear," he bellowed as he continued striding purposely upstairs.

When the soldier reached the top landing, closely observed now by the whole DuVin family along with mother and I, he suddenly stopped and listened. As fate would have it, at that precise moment the baby, no doubt picking up on the fear in the atmosphere, chose to cry out. With that, the soldier quickly realised that behind a demi-lune console table lay a hidden door beneath a heavy velvet curtain.

He thrashed about feeling through the material until he located what he was looking for - a doorknob. At that he tore the velvet curtain down and viciously turned the doorknob to gain entry - but to his anger, the door was locked. Full of rage, he kicked the console table out of his way upturning it and smashing a vase full of flowers in the process and was just about to swiftly kick the door open when he noticed something. Fallen out of the console table was a drawer. He then rummaged around inside it, keeping one hand pointing the gun at his onlookers and as he suspected, there inside was - a key.

Suddenly he became aware of a woman's voice sobbing from behind him but choosing to ignore her, he forcefully unlocked the door to the attic and burst into the room, slamming the door back in the process. There, to his glee, he discovered the entire Green family, bravely shielded by the arms of Joseph. The family were all huddled together in a dim corner of the attic. The soldier quickly stormed across the attic towards them, waving his gun. He then aimed it squarely at Joseph Green's forehead whilst, with his other hand, he shook open an arrest poster he had taken from his pocket. He looked at the face on the poster and then at Joseph.

"So, Green, you are hiding in the darkness like the vermin scum that you are, eh? Did you honestly think you'd get away from us? You're the last family of Jews on our list and handing you over will earn me a handsome bonus."

"Please," pleaded Joseph. "Let my family go, kill me if you must but please spare the lives of my family."

"Brave words Jew! But what makes you think I'd want to kill any of you? You should be happy to go to one of our camps where you will be safe until we win the war. Now tell me, where are they?"

"Joseph looked shocked. "Where are what?"

The soldier looked at him coldly, "You know damn well what I'm talking about - the diamonds - where are they!" He spat.

"No, I don't know what you mean - I'm just a salesman!"

Suddenly the soldier's patience ran out. He pistol-whipped Joseph across the head. Joseph sank to his knees, blood pouring down his forehead and into his eyes. Esther rushed across to comfort him and both children began crying uncontrollably. The soldier savagely pushed her away with his foot and pressed the barrel of the gun into Joseph's forehead, shouting to Esther, "Shut them up before I shut you all up, forever!" He then turned back to Joseph. "Now tell me, Jew, if you know what's good for you and your family - where are the diamonds? If you still refuse to tell me I will shoot you one by one starting with..." His hawk-like eyes scanned their petrified faces. "The baby!"

"No!" Cried Mrs DuVin who was standing in the now open doorway behind Philipe.

"You! You stay out of this. You are collaborators and harbourers of war criminals - you will be dealt with later."

He then looked back at Joseph, who was trembling before him. "Well? Where are they?"

"Tell him Joseph, tell him. Our lives are more important than a book full of diamonds!"

Joseph's eyes inadvertently flicked towards the direction of a bed beneath the small dormer window. The soldier didn't miss it and shoved the injured man to the floor with his foot.

"You, all of you - move to the back of the attic - come on, do it - I said, MOVE!"

Everyone, the Green's, the DuVin's, mother and I, all meekly huddled together and headed towards the far end of the attic. All we could do was to watch as the soldier rummaged through the

Green's belongings breaking things with careless abandon. He threw a sheet at Esther Green ordering her to rip it into strips. Joseph was now more than aware how precious his family were to him and how he had now, also thrown his friends into danger, along with us too - and yet, still he hoped that the soldier would not find the diamonds - for they were his family's hard earned legacy. Just then the soldier raised his right arm triumphantly, in his hand was a bible. He immediately glanced across and could see from Joseph's expression, that he had struck gold, or rather, diamonds.

The soldier wasted no time in frantically opening the two metal clasps on the bible and quickly discovered that hidden inside, past a section of perfect Christian biblical pages, was a star-shaped cavity - a 6 pointed star at that - a Star of David. He knew that the bible had been made purely to deceive and secreted within the space, was a small parcel wrapped in tissue paper. The soldier, now with a look of avarice upon his face, carefully opened the parcel and there, before his greedy eyes sparkled a king's ransom in diamonds.

He looked across, purely to sneer at Joseph.

"So, you know nothing of this eh? So much for your precious star eh? You'll pay for your deceit, Jew."

Then, one by one he ordered each of us to walk towards him, backwards. We were all crying, expecting to be shot in the back but the soldier had other plans, he simply wanted to tie our hands behind each of us using the torn material and then gag us so that he could leave us, bound and unable to shout out, locked in the attic whilst he went to fetch reinforcements.

"I'd like to set this house alight to burn the sorry lot of you to ashes, but I won't, I'm not risking a promotion by lying to my Reichsmarschall, not even for scum like you."

Then, with one last glance at us, terrified and bound, he slammed the door shut and locked us all in. I was sure he was expecting high praise for capturing such a high profile family."

....

Nathaniel could not have known that once the soldier was outside the attic he had another, purely selfish thought, of something he needed to quickly take care of. As he stood alone on the landing, his ear still to the attic door, he quickly shook out all the bullets from the gun's cartridge and then, equally quickly, proceeded to fill it with several small packs of diamonds that he had hastily re-wrapped using torn out pages he had pulled from the now emptied bible. Then, with all the stealth of a cat, he began to search around in nearby rooms adjacent to him for a place to temporarily hide his ill-gotten gains. After a quick search, he discovered a loose floorboard in what appeared to be a child's bedroom, of which he promptly lifted. Then, scanning the room for something suitable to hide the gun in, he spotted a wooden cigar box crammed full of crayons lying on a desk. He grabbed hold of the box and tipped the crayons out, upon the floor. The soldier then carefully placed the gun, wrapped up in a comic he had found nearby, and reverently placed the box in the floor space beneath the window. He then replaced the floorboard as though burying something beloved. Cunningly, his sole intention was to retrieve the diamonds later, once the family had been dragged away for interrogation, knowing full well the chances of them returning were less than zero. Ironically, like his captives in the attic, he also planned to escape to Switzerland but, unfortunately for him, fate had other plans, for no sooner had he left the house, than he walked straight into a hellish gunfight between Allied soldiers and his own comrades where he, along with several of his kind were quickly cut down during the ensuing battle.

....

"We could hear the sound of machine gun fire from where we were in the attic, but although we were all terrified, we knew that we had very little time if we were to have any chance of escaping. Fortunately, Philipe had been prepared, as luckily for us, he'd had the foresight to keep his wrists slightly apart while he was being tied up so that the extra amount of room, allowed him to loosen the strip of rag that was used to bind his hands together. Very quickly he managed to free himself and then immediately, he set about releasing the rest of us.

Once everyone had been set free, Philipe peered discretely down from the small attic window to see what the commotion was that they could all hear, happening down in the street below. We didn't know then but Philipe had immediately realised the severity of what met his eyes, the carnage - bleeding, twisted bodies, upturned vehicles and a tank with black smoke billowing out of its hatch. He had clearly seen that the battle had been a desperate one and he instinctively indicated for us children to stay back - for the last thing he wanted was for our young minds to be polluted by seeing such horror. After a moment of quick mental debate, Philipe then reached down and tore off a section of one of the white sheets to make a flag, and then he went back to the window and waited a moment until he had found enough courage to shout down to the Allied soldiers he could now see, milling about in the street, whilst waving the flag out of the window. Minutes later we all heard the sound of thunderous footsteps climbing the stairs, making us all tremble at what might happen next. Suddenly the footsteps stopped and were replaced by the sound of the doorknob rattling.

"It's locked," shouted Philipe, "we've been locked in!"

We could all hear mumbled voices and then we heard the sound of the key being turned in the lock. As quiet as mice, we all stayed well back, still suffering mentally by what had happened to us earlier but as the door gently opened and the first Allied soldier quickly realised that we were simply innocent victims and not the enemy, he smiled warmly and walked over to us. At one point we all panicked when the soldier reached into one of his tunic pockets for something, until he pulled out a couple of bars of chocolate and handed them to me and the other children. This certainly helped to make us feel more secure. Philipe and Joseph tentatively smiled back at him and both reached out to shake the soldier's hand vigorously.

Having seen so many days of fighting, the soldiers appeared to be only too glad to have brought the look of relief to our faces, rather than the usual hate-filled stare or just plain terrified looks they were normally faced with. Philipe quickly took the opportunity to officially welcome them into his house and offered them food and drink and somewhere warm to rest awhile. He soon discovered that the German army had now been completely repelled from the city and naturally, this came as joyous news to us all, and for a short while he, and the rest of us, felt almost safe again, safe enough to enjoy an all too brief celebration. But then, after Philipe's thoughts had turned once more to the potential fate of Joseph and his family and to mother and I, and how our fates could so easily be turned again if the Allies were ever overtaken, he shared with us there and then, that until the war was over, we would all continue as we had planned - heading to neutral Switzerland.

Chapter Twenty-Four

Nathaniel continued with his story.

"Our journey would have been perilous had we not been fortunate enough to purchase tickets for a train that was packed full of Allied troops. It was on the 22nd of July, 1940, that we arrived in Basel for a far longer holiday than any of us expected. Joseph said he felt both truly blessed and cursed, blessed for his family's safe delivery and cursed for the loss of his diamond legacy that he vowed one day to find. Fortunately both he and Philipe had the foresight to deposit their earnings into Swiss bank accounts as did most European businessmen of the time - this, at least, ensured they would be financially independent.

As promised, their Swiss friends did not let them down. Each family was provided with a place to stay, which, as luck would have it, were only a short walk away from each other. It was during this time that something happened that revealed to me, the extra special gifts that both, the DuVin and the Green family, shared.

....

It had become a Friday ritual for mother and I to join the Green Family at the DuVin's house for dinner, and it was on one such occasion that I was to discover that there was more to Philipe DuVin than first met my eye. Philipe and Joseph had often been absent for dinner; they would have their food ferried out to them to an adjoining barn, usually brought by Madeline DuVin who told us that the men wanted to be undisturbed as they were 'working on a project of national importance to the war effort'. Naturally to the ears of a young boy, such as I, I translated it to, 'Please do all you can to find out what the two men are up to!'

It didn't help that there was nothing much other than propaganda on the wireless or, if you were lucky, or unlucky - you choose, there would be a waltz or two wafting along the airwaves. To someone of my age, this was tantamount to torture and could only lead to one thing - a spot of investigation!

I wasted not a moment and looked around to see what Cousin Clarice was up to but she seemed to be engrossed in knitting what appeared to be a giant tapeworm that I later learned was in fact, a pair of long socks for the soldiers on the front line - I pitied them shivering in the trenches, hoping to have something warm and dry on their feet, for, from what I had seen, the chance of them receiving two socks the same were dreadfully slim - however, her heart was in the right place and that fact alone, warmed my heart towards her. In a way I was glad that Clarice was preoccupied, this meant that I could do all that a boy needs to do, alone, with no female intrusion - for in my simple opinion at that time, espionage was a dirty game FOR MEN!

As if tuning into my thought patterns, Clarice immediately glanced across at me and raised her half knitted sock triumphantly. "You should 'ave a go," she mouthed.

"I'd rather be skinned alive," I replied, before scuttling out of view. It was my aim to slip unnoticed outside without anyone being none the wiser - not an easy thing to accomplish in such a packed household, though. With great stealth, I crept across the cobbled approach to the barn, keeping within the shadows wherever possible. The sky was indigo blue with an impressive scattering of twinkling stars and there was a full moon that threw pale blue moonlight across the yard. I noticed a beam of yellow light spilling out from beneath the double doors so I crept close towards them. I knew what I needed was a knothole to peer through and it didn't take me long to find one, it still had the knot in place but that didn't deter me for, with the aid of my trusty pocket knife, I was soon able to poke the knot out. I put my eye to the hole and peered inside and I must tell you - what I saw was a very strange sight indeed! I could see Joseph Green sitting down at a tatty old table, writing something - so far, not unusual, but upon his head was what looked like an upturned colander, only minus the holes. The contraption had wires attached to it, which then went beneath, what appeared to be a bandage, wrapped around his temples, seemingly to keep the wires in place. Philipe DuVin was standing just behind him holding some sort of device that he was occupied, controlling. "Operation Fracture? Are you sure?" I heard Philipe say. "So, they 'ave managed to infiltrate Guernsey, that ees not good, not good at all. Joseph - try to kip your thoughts trenned on eet, I nid to send a coded message to our people rat away."

I felt a sinking feeling in the pit of my stomach - they were spies! *No wonder, they have been so secretive since we came here*, I remember thinking. Suddenly I felt as though I too was a spy, only in my case, to anyone discovering me, it would look as if I was working for the Nazis. I continued monitoring the two men for a moment more until I felt something soft brushing up against my ankle. I looked down and there at my feet was the biggest rat I had ever seen.

Suddenly all of my thoughts were focussed on the giant rodent about to sink its yellow teeth into my foot, or so I imagined. I couldn't help myself but to let out a cross between a yell and a yodel, which naturally alerted the two men inside the barn. Philipe rushed out to see what was happening and caught me on the hop.

"Whut are you doeen 'ere? You were under streect eenstruction to stay een the 'ouse, were you not?" said Philipe, looking left and right to see if anyone else was lurking in the shadows. Then, satisfied that I was alone, he gestured for me to enter the barn. Immediately Joseph turned around, his concentration on what he had been doing, all but broken. "Now look what you 'ave done you stupid boy!" He said.

I *did* feel stupid, actually, I felt like crying, it was bad enough being so far from home and now I had made enemies of two people I had become highly respectful of. I couldn't forget how brave both men had been back in Provence and now, I thought, *they have been spies all along?* That suddenly elevated their bravery even more!

"What were you doeen 'anging around the barn?"

I was lost for words - struck dumb.

"Nathaniel," said Philipe, "I nid to know. Why were you loitering around outside the barn een the dark?"

The stern look on Philipe's face suddenly made me cry. I felt foolish, deceitful and thoroughly wretched for being so sneaky and in particular, for being caught.

I looked up at Philipe sheepishly and said, "I was watching you through a knot hole. When you tell a bored child not to do something it only makes us want to do it even more - I'm sorry I let you both down. I wish I could turn back the clock and stay indoors knitting socks with Clarice."

It was the mention of knitting socks with Clarice that seemed to soften Philipe's approach towards me. I think he realised just how suffocated I must have been feeling, being stuck indoors with the all the women. "Oh, now I understand. Tell me, Nathaniel, I 'ave to know. Whut exactly do you theenk we are doing 'ere een thees barn?"

I felt awkward again, thinking, *should I tell Philipe the truth or fudge it, in order to not get into more trouble than I am already in. The truth,* I thought, *at some point I have to start being honest and this, when dealing with two heroic men, is more than the perfect opportunity to do so.* "I was spying on you, I wanted to know what kind of project you were working on that was, a project of national importance to the war effort."

"Pardonez Moi? Oo told you thet?" Said Philipe, raising his eyebrows in surprise. "What we do 'ere is nothing othere than... sorting seeds, getting theengs ready for the summer months–."

I spoke again. "Mrs DuVin said that you were not to be disturbed because you were both working on a project of national importance to the war effort, so naturally I thought you were probably working for the Resistance. Was I wrong to think that?"

Now it was Philipe DuVin's turn to be truthful. "Nathaniel, we are not playing a game you know. Pipple's lives are at stek by the very things we see and act upon. I cannot tell you exactly what we are doeen, but you are correct in that whut we are engaged in is, as you say, of not only, national eemportance but world importance too, and someteen that must nevairre be revealed to anyone. Eemagine 'ow easy eet would be to get the truth out of you, a mere child, if you were to be captured by the Nazis. No, eet ees bettere I theenk, to keep you out of thees altogethere."

At that point, Joseph Green came across and spoke. "Tell us, Nathaniel, what exactly deed you see?"

I then told them everything I had seen and what I imagined they had been up to - listening in to wireless transmissions sent by the German army. I added that I thought the helmet, Joseph had been wearing, was a device to strengthen the signal.

"Very good," said Philipe, "I see that you are a smart boy."

Even though my head was still hanging low in shame, I saw Philipe looking across at Joseph to catch his eye and then, tellingly, Joseph shook his head, frowning, but Philipe simply smiled at me.

"Perhaps you'd like to work alongside us? We could use someone lak you to seet outside the barn and kip a look out when we are beesy workeen. Would you do thet?"

I pretended to consider it for a moment, trying to hide my pride at the thought of being classed as one of the men, then I thought about the rats.

"Uh, socks are part of the war effort too though aren't they?" I said. "Maybe I SHOULD help Clarice to knit socks for the allies rather than hanging around here and getting in your way?"

Philipe frowned.

"Oh," I innocently added. "One more thing before I head back indoors - who, or what exactly is Operation Fracture?"

I suddenly caught a look on Philipe's face that told me I had just said too much. At that, Philipe gently slid the door shut whilst Joseph led me over to the chair that he had been sitting just minutes before.

"There are crucial, mystical theengs 'appening 'ere thet nobody othere than Joseph and I should know about, Nathaniel, said Philipe, cryptically. "But now, I theenk you'd bettere tek a seat."

Chapter Twenty-Five

Whilst Nathaniel was taking a much needed sip of his iced tea, after so much talking, I found I couldn't resist the urge to ask him a question - something that had been troubling me ever since he started talking. But instead, turning to Madame DuVin, who had now come to join us, I asked her, "Madame DuVin, do you mind me asking where you were, when all this was happening?"

Madame DuVin looked at me queerly, screwing up her eyes as though she considered me to be nothing more than a meddling child. She then cupped one hand to her ear, looked at Nathaniel and said, "Whut deed 'e jus' say?"

I rolled my eyes in frustration and instead, also turned to Nathaniel who was now sitting with a half smile on his face.

"Justavia's a bit Mutt and Jeff, Mark," he replied. Then, instantly realising that he had made the already muddy waters even muddier by using a term he realised I was, most likely, not familiar with, he added. "Mutt and Jeff - that's cockney rhyming slang for deaf, dear boy. Mutt and Jeff were characters in the comic papers a long time ago - very long, actually! In answer to your question - well, let me just say that you must hang on a wee while, you'll get your answer soon and, by the way, well done for being so observant - Minty, please take note!"

Minty, who seemed preoccupied making her right shoe dangle on her big toe, scowled, and then she leaned across and flicked me hard on my ear. I immediately shot her a warning look and then waited patiently for Nathaniel to continue, which he did.

....

"No doubt you are wondereen whut the strenge lookeen 'elmet on the table, ees? Am I correct?" Said Philipe to me.

"You are," I replied.

"Well, I shall tell you, but only when I 'ave your solemn blood oath thet you will nevere pass the eenformation I am about to geev you, onto anothere, for thees work is of vitalle importance to the war effort."

I desperately wanted to know what was going on so I readily agreed, not because I wanted to help the war effort, at least, not then, but simply because I was incredibly intrigued and knew that I would never be able to sleep soundly again until I knew what was going on around me.

"You are familiar with a blood oath, yes?"

No, I am not familiar with a blood oath," I said, and then I suddenly found the prospect of pain entering my head. "Why, what are you intending to do," I asked, attempting to raise myself from the chair.

"Don't fret, my boy. Do you see that boiling kettle of water just there?"

I looked at where Philipe was pointing and I shuddered. There was indeed a copper kettle boiling away on a small wood-fired stove, red flames licking up the sides of it. "Uh, yes, I see it," I said, somewhat hesitantly.

"Eet's OK, trust me - I am seemply going to sterilize a niddle een the steam so thet when I preeck the skeen on your 'and, the puncture sat weell not become infected - are you weeth me so far?"

I nodded. I didn't like needles but I was well aware that there was a war going on all around us and I knew that it was time I started acting like a man. "OK," I said. "Can we just get this over with as quickly as possible?"

At that, Joseph stepped over to the kettle and taking a needle out of a black velvet wrap, he held it in the steam for a moment - then he walked across to where I was sitting.

"Pliss, 'old your 'and out, Nathaniel," he said.

I did as asked, my eyes quickly seeking reassurance from Philipe who nodded slightly as if to say, 'it's OK, and then I stretched out my hand and awaited the pain. I couldn't watch, to me it's unnatural having your skin pierced. I flinched as I felt the skin on the heel of my thumb being pinched together and rubbed by Philipe even before the needle went in.

"All done," he said. Only then did I open my eyes. In front of me was a piece of paper with a drawing of a triangle upon it with what looked like a crude image of our planet in the centre. Two points of the triangle each had a dot of fresh blood upon them, then my drop of blood, which Joseph had on a the end of a quill, was then placed upon the triangle's topmost point.

"Now," said Philipe, "two must pledge their loyalty by signing their name beneath their lafe blood at the two lower points and you, Nathaniel, above your lafe blood, on the topmost point."

At that, Joseph signed the lower left hand point. He then slid the paper to me and signalled for me to sign the uppermost point, which I did, and then I instinctively passed it along to Philipe, for him to sign the final point, but for some reason he did not. Then he stepped aside and I was amazed to see Cousin Clarice standing there. I had no idea that she had even entered the room. She looked at me and smiled and then she signed the lower right hand point.

"Good," said Philipe with his arms around all three of us. "We now 'ave a full Trine of Earth to use in the battle against oppression. I imagine you are eetching to know what you have signed up for 'aven't you, Nathaniel?"

I nodded in agreement.

"The Trine of Earth represents, power, protection, good 'ealth and universal love, sometheen all of us 'ere who are striveen to breeng about to our planet. Thet ees why I chose eet as a form of protection, and the pyramid shape itself because of its power," said Joseph. "Clarice, Joseph and you, my boy, all have one theeng in common - do you know whut that is?"

"No," I replied. "I am no good at knitting socks if that's what it is."

Philipe laughed. "No, it eesn't kneetting!" He said. "You all 'ave the psychic abeelity about you! 'ow do I know thees, you might ask yourself..."

"I knew," said Joseph. "Because I saw it een a veesion," You see, Nathaniel, you and Clarice, 'ere, like I, come from a reech bloodline of seers and pipple enreeched with the psychic geeft! Now we are all uniteed and tomorrow, you shall learn all about the art of seeing, sometheen that 'as been practeesed for meellenia but known to but a few. Now, 'ows that leetle wound of yours doeen?"

I looked at my thumb, feeling like a fraud - there was hardly a mark to be seen. "It's fine," I replied.

"You're a brev boy," said Philipe, laughing. "Now, 'oos for some suppere, I theenk we all deserve somtheen rather delacious, non?"

With that, we all headed indoors and I must admit, I felt rather excited, but it was more than just that, because, for the first time I could recall in my life so far, I actually felt useful."

Resonates

Somathing to offer!!!

Chapter Twenty-Six

Nathaniel continued.

"I would have liked to have put all thoughts of the war far behind me for the night as I knew that mulling over all that had happened today and trying to contemplate where my strange initiation might lead, would most likely, lead to insomnia and I do so like my sleep. I decided to try to have a quiet word with Clarice on the quiet. I found her busy chatting away with Hannah as both of them were fully engaged in knitting socks and scarves for the fighters. It was after eight o'clock by the time I finally managed to get her all to myself, after Hannah had gone upstairs to help her mother bathe the baby before she went to sleep. As I headed towards her, she was still knitting her dreadful socks as if her life depended on it.

"Do you actually enjoy doing that," I asked her.

"Oui - I lak to do my beet. Maman theenks I am geefted in the kneeting. Would you lak me to kneet you sometheeng too?"

I shook my head. "No, that's kind of you but I think the soldiers deserve your socks more than me," while at the same time thinking, *if they are brave enough to fight, they are certainly brave enough to wear such fearful socks.* I immediately felt wretched for having such a bad thought towards Clarice's selfless act and so I said. "Actually, Clarice, I would love you to knit me a pair of socks when you have the time, a long pair, nice and warm."

She looked up at me and smiled. "Of course. I would be delatted to. Whut colairre would you lak?"

"Yellow please, if you have yellow wool that is, otherwise black will be fine."

"How about yellow and black stripes then, like the bumble-bee, then you weel be all prepared to go and steeng the enemy right in the derriere, non, with your new skill!"

That made me smile. Then, recognising that I suddenly had the perfect opportunity to bring up the, Trine of Earth, I said, "Clarice? Can you tell me anymore about the clairvoyance that your father mentioned earlier."

She then gently rested the knitting on her lap, looked up at me and said, "I could, I could tell much, but eet wouldn't be rat. There's a certain order of command in what we are doeen, so you will 'ave to wait until Papa and Monsieur Green are ready to tell you. Be patient, Nathaniel, I feel sure you will know everytheeng you want to know, tomorrow."

And with that, Clarice returned to her knitting again, affectedly dismissing me. As I had nothing else to do, I chose to join her, to simply sit and watch the flickering flames dancing in the fireplace as if they were celebrating something, as yet, unforseen.

Chapter Twenty-Seven

"At 8.30 the next morning," said Nathaniel, "I was escorted outside and into the barn again. Accompanying me were Clarice, Monsieur Green and Philipe DuVin. I noticed Hannah in the yard, she was occupied pegging sheets on the washing line and didn't seem the slightest bit interested in what we were all up to and it made me wonder if she was in on it all or whether she genuinely wasn't interested. I quickly got my answer.

"Papa," she called. "What are you all up to?"

Joseph Green turned and walked over to her. "Hannah, whut we are up to ees no concern of yours, my sweet. Whut you are doeen by 'elping your mothairre with all the washing, cleaning and cooking ees equally as important as anytheeng we may be doeen behind closed doors. As long as you always kip your mouth closed, eef and when anyone should ask you any questions, we shall all remain sef. Do you understand, my brave daughtairre?"

Hannah smiled. "I do, Papa. I will breeng you food and dreenk in an hour, yes?"

Joseph smiled back at her. "Thet weell not be necessary my daughtairre, we 'ave all thut we need eenside the barn, but bless you for askeen, anyway. Now you go along and 'elp your dear mothairre, there's a good girl."

"Yes Papa," she replied. "See you letaire then." And with that, Hannah picked up the now empty washing basket and headed back indoors. I couldn't help but notice, though, how she patted something, I could see was rectangular shaped, in her pinafore pocket, as she went inside.

Once we were all inside the barn, Joseph pulled the double doors shut and slid the two bolts across, securing them. Philipe pulled out the chair from the table that Joseph had been sitting at yesterday and indicated for me to take a seat. I must admit it, I was feeling somewhat apprehensive, half expecting to have my brain fried or something equally as dreadful.

"Thees ees whut I want you to do, Nathaniel. Please put thees 'elmet on your 'ead. Don't worry, it won't 'urt you at all!"

He handed me the strange helmet that really *did* look like a colander minus the holes. It had two wires attached to it that went into two soft pads where my ears were, they were what worried me the most. I noticed that inside it, the helmet had been lined with a soft cotton wadding, presumably to make it sit more comfortably on the head.

"Thees ees merely a whaaat noise sheneratore! Eet's notheen to be alarmed about. All eet does is to fill your 'ead weeth a noise to cancel out all othere noises and een doeen so, will 'elp your mand to feelter out any random thoughts you maght be 'aving. I weell be spikking through a macrophone that you weell 'ear thru the two speakeres, there ees one by each of your ears and I shall be giveen you eenstructions all the whalle to guide you to where we want you to view. Do you underestand?

I said, yes, I think so. To which Philipe said that there was no time like the present, to give the helmet a test run. He explained further, stating that the helmet was a white noise generator which would essentially allow me to block out everything other than his direct questions and that, using my new-found psychic ability, he would be able to note down what I could see, remotely. Suddenly the penny dropped, Somehow I was going to be able to view things happening miles away without having to leave my seat - apparently. I was not convinced in the slightest, though.

"I 'ad a good talk to your mothairre, Flora, last night, Nathaniel. She told me thut I was raght regardeen your psychic abeelity, almost all the males een our family 'ave eet..."

....

At that point I stopped and put my hand up. Nathaniel raised his eyebrows and said, "Yes Mark, you have a question?"

"Yes I do. I know now, after Woodchester Mansion, that I have a psychic ability to a degree, but then again, so does Minty - and, unless she is hiding a certain part of her anatomy, as far as I can tell - she is a female!"

Nathaniel looked over the top of his glasses at me quizzically. "Yes, indeed she is, but she is also your twin and I suspect that when it comes to twins, anything is possible, for it is only at the very last stage in the development of twins that the sexual gender is set. I believe that in your case, meaning both of you - you each have a psychic ability. Let's not forget Clarice though, for although the majority of males in our family have the gift, so do several females who are not twins."

"Oh terrific," moaned Minty. Not only have I got a weird name but now I also have a weird head!"

"You don't need to state the obvious," I enjoyed telling her.

"Butt-hole," she replied.

"Now, now, children. Let me finish my story..." Said Nathaniel, after taking another sip of his iced tea.

....

"That morning was interesting to say the least. Not only did I have to wear the strange looking helmet, but I also had to wear a strange looking pair of goggles that reminded me of a couple of half egg shells. These, so I was to quickly learn, ensured that I would have positively no visual interference on top of my auditory isolation.

Once I had relaxed in the chair as much as I could - for I was still half expecting something painful to happen, don't ask me why, Philipe's instructions started making their way through the strange isolating white noise silence, if you could call white noise silent, that is. The effect of hearing Philipe's voice coming out of nothing else made me feel rather out of it, as if I was inside an isolation chamber or, strangely enough, in heaven.

After a while I started to see images in my mind's-eye, odd red-tinted images, at first anyway, but soon they were coming thick and fast to me in full colour and to my amazement, I was soon viewing scenes as if watching a movie.

The test location I had been assigned to view, was on whatever was occurring at that moment in the Berghof - Adolf Hitler's private residence in Obersalzberg, Austria. Unfortunately, at that particular time, all I could see were masses of cleaning staff - all of them running around like clockwork soldiers occupied in preparing the place for what appeared to me to be some sort of celebratory dinner. I saw huge rows of tables being dressed in red and black tablecloths to match the enormous Nazi flags hanging down all around the perimeter of the room. The maids and the servants were all wearing black uniforms with red armbands, in fact red and black were the only colours that seemed to be allowed in the room.

    I ended up being so engrossed in what I was viewing that I failed to realise the effect the experiment was having on my mind, for suddenly I began to feel decidedly strange, almost as though I had lost my sense of gravity and was suddenly starting to float upwards, out of the chair. This made me feel nauseous and I had to signal to Philipe that I needed a break. The last thing I noticed was a vase of red tulips on the table and I reached out to them. Amazingly, as I came back to reality, there in the barn, I held a single red tulip in my hand!

    Philipe and Joseph were stunned. Not only had I been able to see as much as I had done on a first attempt, but that I had been able to apport something from the remote site, back to the viewing space. This, I was to learn, had not been done before and it left me feeling a bit like a celebrity. Then, once I was freed from the helmet contraption and the goggles, I was left with two oval indentations around my eyes that made Clarice laugh out loud, bringing me instantly back to earth, and blinking in the light again, even as pitiful as the barn light was.

    Fortunately, I began to recover very quickly and when questioned by the two men about whether I felt any side effects, I told them that all I felt was as though my soul, somehow, had briefly left my body and then, how it had softly floated back down to re-join with me when I came back. I didn't have long to consider this in any great depth though, for suddenly, I was confronted by a large sugary pastry filled with fruit and cream and a beer stein filled with apple juice as my reward.

It is strange, but far from being apprehensive about the experiment, I was in reality, already thirsting for more.

I won't bore you with the many exploits we all undertook during that time, particularly as many of them are still classified as top secret. There was so much that we were all viewing clairvoyantly several times a day each, suffice it to say that I mentally travelled far and wide and that, hopefully, my time spent viewing the activities of the Führer - Herr Hitler, himself, might have helped somewhat in the war effort to bring peace back to our troubled little planet.

Chapter Twenty-Eight

"Wow, Nathaniel - you dark horse! When we were at Woodchester Mansion, you never even mentioned that you had any psychic ability. Why was that?" I asked him.

"Mark, my boy, I think you'll find that most people who have lived through any war will, for the most part, be reluctant to relive it. I told you what happened in France purely because your natural ability has been leading you, and Minty too, towards events that I knew I was a part of and, I must be honest, keeping everything bottled up inside of me for so long was starting to weigh down more and more heavily upon me with each passing year and so I thought, now is the time - better out than in. And now, so long after the events, I felt it was safe at last to reveal secrets that I was warned never to talk about by my late friends, Philipe DuVin and Joseph Green."

Minty suddenly got up and walked over to Nathaniel. She bent down and kissed him on the cheek. "You're a hero, Uncle, a true, unsung hero!" She then walked over to Clarice, who had also now chosen to join us, and kissed her on both cheeks in the French way, "you deserve the highest of praise, not only are you a role model for womanhood but you are a true heroine."

Clarice cast her eyes down to hide her emotion and gently patted Minty on her arm in a show of emotional gratitude.

"I am jus' 'appy that mama and papa were able to 'ave peace een the remaindere of their laves," she said, dabbing at her eyes.

I could see Nathaniel's eyes glistening as he tried to hold back tears that I suspect had needed to be shed for almost 66 years and suddenly he seemed his actual age of 79, instead of how I usually thought of him, as ageless.

"There is a bit more to my story that you should know," he said, "and you asked me a question earlier regarding Justavia, remember?"

I said yes, I remember. I asked you where Madame DuVin had been during this time and then something about her surname suddenly hit me.

Nathaniel smiled at me. "You are a smart boy, Mark. Allow me to explain what happened next.

After months of taking turns remote viewing with Joseph and Clarice, Joseph was sent instructions that he was needed elsewhere. He was assigned to a unit in Belgium and in all my years, I have never discovered what he had been sent there for, to do. With him went Esther and baby, Ruth, but not Hannah. She wanted to go, but her parent's thought that whatever they were doing in Belgium posed far more of a risk to the family and so, Hannah, at an age when she could easily, accidentally let sip information, should she ever be interrogated, was reluctantly put into the care of the DuVin's. She was given a new name as her birth name sounded too Jewish, so instead she became known as Justavia DuVin and given false papers to prove it, if ever needed."

So I was right, I thought. *Justavia was Hannah all along, sneeky monkeys!*

Nathaniel continued. "Yes, Hannah, here, had a new name and a new life. Of course she never lost touch with her family, in fact we often viewed them remotely, but for some unknown reason, we eventually lost track of them completely, almost as though our collective viewing ability had been blocked.

Sadly, many years after the war had ended, I soon discovered just why we had been unable to view them. I learned that the family had eventually been captured and incarcerated in the dreadful, Dachau concentration camp. Immediately, Joseph and Esther were wrenched apart, being sent to the male and female sections of the camp. Esther was allowed to keep little Ruth with her but the baby quickly became sick and was the first of them to die, as she soon came down with dysentery and rapidly wasted away to nothing.

The loss of Ruth, naturally had a dreadful effect on Esther who quickly lost the will to live, having to contend, not only with her all consuming grief, but also from the relentless questioning from her interrogators who deprived her of sleep every night. In a matter of weeks she had physically wasted away from lack of nourishment, to little more than a skeleton, and it was just under two months since she had been captured, that she too was dead.

Joseph held out as long as he could. He was tortured repeatedly and taunted about the death of his wife and child, he even made several attempts to escape but, during one attempt in which he was forced to run as fast as he could to avoid the searchlights that constantly swept the perimeter, his heart simply gave out and he suffered a massive, fatal heart attack. All of the Green family are the true heroes," said Nathaniel, dabbing at his eyes.

Madame DuVin was now standing right next to him, with one hand resting on his shoulder in support and I noticed her giving it a squeeze of affection. I couldn't help it, the high emotion of the moment had hit me like a bullet - now it was my turn to show my appreciation.

I walked over to Madame DuVin and kissed her on both cheeks saying, welcome back, Hannah. Madame DuVin heard me well enough. Immediately, her eyes filled up with tears and she reached her arms out and took my hands in her, then she lifted my hands and kissed them. It was then that I realised why she drank so much, it served to help deaden the pain she had carried for all of those years. I smiled at her warmly and then I turned to Nathaniel and, as I indicated with my eyes, he handed me the bible which I then passed to Justavia, or should I say, Hannah. She looked at it, then back at me as if for confirmation, as if she could hardly believe her eyes, and then she looked at Nathaniel and Clarice and she began to cry, hugging the bible tightly. Nathaniel handed her a tissue to wipe her eyes. Justavia sat down and then carefully opened the bible. She immediately let out a gasp upon seeing what was inside.

"Thees is our family crest," she said with her eyes brimming with tears. "See the bees? They are making the honey of gold? The 'umble bee 'as been our mark de la famille for centuries - now I know thees ees truly Papa's bible!"

Then, tentatively she ran her hands over the stubs from the pages that had been torn out and then she turned the section of pages that remained, until she came to the aperture and gasped. I suddenly realised, uncomfortably, that she must have been expecting the diamonds to still be there, inside, and then she began to cry again, closing the bible and hugging it in a rocking motion as though it were a baby, seemingly lost in the past for a moment. I reached out and gave her shoulder a squeeze and she looked up at me and smiled, wistfully, patting my hand with her own. It was heartbreaking to witness. I couldn't help myself, I knew I needed to give Nathaniel a big hug too. He seemed to have shrunk in size all of a sudden and I could see that he felt embarrassed by us seeing him getting so choked up with emotion. To give him a chance to recover, I went across to where Clarice was sitting. I was now well aware that I had made a huge mistake in my pre-judgement of her.

"Madame Clarice," I said. "I must say how proud I feel to be considered a fellow psychic along with you, Nathaniel, and, of course, Joseph. Oh, heaven forbid - and not forgetting my twin sister, Minty, ooh, and of course, Justavia!" I turned to smile at her and she smiled warmly back at me.

"All of us are fortunate," said Clarice, "to have been blessed with such special abilities..."

"Yeah. So listen up, universe," I said looking upwards, "thanks very much!"

"Oh Mark," said Minty, "you can be such a knob sometimes!"

"Ah thanks, Sis, I love you too," I replied, but I meant it, and not in a sarcastic way either, not in the slightest.

"So," I said, turning to Madame DuVin? How come nobody knew that you had a psychic ability then, or did it develop later?"

She looked at me and then her face broke into a huge smile. "Mak, I always thought I was not psychic at all, so I seemply learned the craft of the Tarot because I was feeling left out. I knew everytheeng that was goeen on, everytheeng - thees peeperes are as sharp as they were way back then. I wanted to 'elp the war effort to but I 'ad no natural abeelity, so I wracked by brains to find sometheeng I could do! When pipple thought ah was fast aslip, I was learning the craft of the Tarot and by the time the war 'ad ended, I was preety damn hot at dooeen the Tarot riddings!"

At that, Madame DuVin gave me a theatrical wink. "And thet, dear one, breengs us beng up to det! Seems I 'ad a beet of my Papa's geeft all along, oui? Even eef eet deedn't manifest itself unteel I was een my teens. God bless hees soul."

So that was it, Hannah, or rather, Justavia, as she was now known, *had* inherited her father's psychic ability despite it being mostly a male trait in our family. That must have been what Nathaniel had noticed in her pinafore pocket - the rectangular shape, a deck of Tarot cards!

Suddenly something else Nathaniel said earlier, rang a bell with me. "Nathaniel?" I asked him.

"Yes, my boy."

"Was that why certain things appeared in your house each time you told me a story, like the vase of daffodils for instance?"

Nathaniel looked at me with his face slightly down-turned but I could see a smile forming. "You rumbled me! Honestly my boy, you are becoming positively dangerous!"

Dangerous? I thought, *what on earth do you mean by that!*

That night, Nathaniel's words plagued me, and I lay awake for hours praying for sleep to come but no sooner had my eyelids grown heavy, than something completely unexpected happened in the room next to mine...

Chapter Twenty-Nine

"Oh my god, O, M flippin' G!" Cried Minty, looking white as a ghost as she suddenly came rushing towards me from the adjoining bedroom.

"Oh my god, what?" I replied tiredly, but still feeling a bit freaked out by seeing her, well, freaked out!

"Oh my god I've just seen a weird blue light in my bedroom! A weird, floating blue light! I was watching it, yeah, for like, five minutes and it was, like, oh my god, as though it knew I was watching it, yeah, and, oh my god, it came floating towards me, like, real close until it was like, inches from my nose!"

"Yeah right, you don't honestly think I'd fall for that do you - stop taking the micky."

"No, nooo, honestly! When the weird blue light thingy was closest to me, yeah, I could see that it was actually made up from hundreds of faces and they all seemed to be trying to talk at once, only I couldn't hear anything! Man, I tell you, it's waaay too creepy for me, there's no way on earth I am going to sleep back in there tonight, I can tell you that, now come on, shift over!"

"No! No way, you're not sharing my bed you big jessy..."

"I flippin' well am, c'mon shift yer butt!"

"Oh flippin 'eck, Minty, you're a right pain in the derrierre (well, we WERE in France you know!) Look, how about we swap rooms for tonight, yeah?"

"Uh, well I guess so, but I'll still be alone though, won't I - supposing it's only after me?"

"Look I'll just be next door, like what, a mere 15 feet away? Tell you what, as you're such a big scaredy-pants, what about if I leave the connecting door open - how about that?"

At that she lunged at me like a girl possessed and then gave me a big hug of gratitude. This truly *was* alarming and more shocking than seeing an apparition!

Before I climbed out of my warm bed, I made sure that Minty was okay by pulling the light cord to turn the main light on to eliminate the possibility of any shadows and then I made my way through to her room. To be perfectly honest, by this time I was feeling a bit creeped out, myself, but I had no intention of showing it to little miss eagle-eyes, who was now holding a sheet up to under her nose and inadvertently doing a very good Mr Chad impression.

I immediately looked around her room and thought, *what is it with women? She hasn't been here five minutes and already her bedroom is like a boudoir, full of trinkets and girly things.* I was going to say crap but that would have been tres vulgar! The room was so girly that I found it hard to believe Minty had seen a blue thingy, surely it should have been pink thingy and a sparkly one at that! Talk about speaking too soon. I hadn't been in bed for more that ten minutes with Minty constantly saying, "seen anything yet?" when I spotted something that looked exactly as she had described - a fizzy, blue orb of light floating softly about by the window. I frantically rubbed my eyes to make sure it wasn't simply a floater in my vision, but it was still there when I opened them - and bigger, much, much bigger.

Determined not to freak out, I gently got out of bed, because I didn't want to scare it away, and then cautiously started to make my way towards it. I glance across at Minty and all I could see of her was her eyes peeking over the trembling sheet. I looked back at the blue orb. Whatever it was, it appeared to be oblivious to me creeping up to it and the closer I got to it, the more I could see what Minty had described - faces within it. It was like looking into a faceted gemstone or that weird thing in the Superman movies where people are trapped in the phantom zone. It was both amazing and puzzling at the same time and a thought instantly crossed my mind - *what on earth did it want?*

Suddenly it began to glow much brighter and then it proceeded to float slowly down until it literally sank into the floorboards beneath the window. For a moment or two I was puzzled until it occurred to me - *it might be trying to show me something.* Just then I felt a distinct presence - it was Minty with eyes as big as saucers (okay, a slight exaggeration, they looked bigger than usual - satisfied?)

"I saw you moving around, so I'm guessing you've just seen it too?" She said.

I explained to her what I had just seen and the look upon her face was one of pure relief.

"See, I told you! Maybe it's trying to tell us something!"

Well that's spooky for a start, I thought, *for I was just thinking the same thing myself.*

Suddenly Minty's expression began to change, her eyes started flickering all weird like and then she started speaking, only the voice coming from her lips was not her own. At first I thought she was mucking about but then, call it instinct if you like, I realised that she was totally unaware of what was happening to her.

"Don't shoot!" She cried. "They are only cheeldren! 'ow deed you know? Who told you we were 'ere? We thought we'd be sefe, 'idden away up 'ere. We thought we were going to be alrat, 'idden een the attique - 'ow were we to know that a sleeped slet 'ad allowed lat to escap?"

"What about you and your family? Who are you and what happened?" I asked. Minty stared at me - at least she looked like Minty but the voice clearly belonged to another so I decided to ask her who she was.

"Esther. My name ees Esther Grin. Please 'elp me, I 'ave been wetting to spik to my daughtairre 'annah for a long, long tam," she replied.

I couldn't believe my luck, Minty was being used as a psychic channel by the spirit of Esther Green and I could hardly wait to hear the rest of her story when suddenly, she stopped, mid sentence. I sat looking at Minty, disappointed. Her eyes then flickered open and for a moment she seemed puzzled about where she was before suddenly saying, "Uh, what just happened? And why are you looking at me like that?"

After explaining what had just happened to her, Minty got all stroppy and shouty, saying that it wasn't right for her to be taken over without her say-so. I told her that now was hardly the time for complaining and that I needed to go and get Madame DuVin. Minty naturally complained but I knew what I needed to do. Turning to the blue orb that had reappeared, I said, "Your daughter, Hannah is here, Esther, please wait a moment while I run off to get her."

The orb flared brightly. "Keep her occupied, Minty, I'll be back in a tic." I cried. I was gone before she had a chance to start whinging.

Chapter Thirty

I rushed across to Nathaniel's door and knocked lightly. No answer. I knocked harder, I felt terrible at having to disturb him at such an ungodly hour but I knew that it was necessary. I suddenly heard movement and he came to the door in his dressing gown, hair sticking up in all directions that made him look like a mad scientist, in fact, he reminded me of Merlin in Walt Disney's, *The Sword in the Stone*. I quickly spewed out everything that had just happened, prompting him to exclaim, "Oh my," before we both quickly headed off in the direction of Justavia's room at the far end of the wing.

Waking a partially deaf person without giving them a heart attack is no mean feat. Nathaniel had to resort to using a peacock feather from a floral display next to her bed, to tickle the tip of her nose with. That quickly did the trick eliciting a huge sneeze from the shocked woman. I turned the bedroom light on to allow Justavia to see that we were not intruders. Nathaniel then leaned across and spoke into her ear at close range. "Justavia dear - it's your mother - she's asking for you."

At that, Justavia's eyes opened wide and she was suddenly out of bed with all the vigour of someone a third of her age. She quickly pulled a frilly housecoat on, tying it tightly and then proceeded to follow Nathaniel and I back towards Minty's room. Suddenly we heard a door creak open and there was Clarice peering through the gap, eating a biscuit. "Whut ees eet, are we being burgled?"

"No, it's fine, Clarice," said Nathaniel, "but you might want to come with us." She didn't need asking twice and within seconds she had joined us on the landing, still doing her dressing gown up as she caught up with us, with the biscuit between her teeth.

"It's in here," I said, turning to everyone.

"Oh, about flippin' time too," said Minty. "That thing gives me the serious willies!"

The blue orb was now as tall as a human adult. It was still virtually fizzing all around the edges as though it was generating static electricity. As Justavia stepped into the room, the orb flared again and became so bright that when it stopped flaring, we were all amazed to see a full apparition. Esther Green had materialised.

"Maman, oh Maman," cried Justavia. The spirit of Justavia's mother glided towards her.

"Hannah, my beautiful daughtairre - I 'ave wetted so long to look upon your fess once more. I wanted to spik to you through the cards but the choice I med deed not allow eet. I 'ave come to tell you where your legacy lies."

Justavia's eyes filled with tears. "But Maman, a legacy means leetle to me - you, Papa and dear Ruth - you are my legacy, you are the only precious theengs I desire."

"Hannah, you weell always 'ave us - we shall all be togethairre when God sees fit to allow eet, but for now my child, you deserve a taste of laff's pleasures, all the theengs that you 'ave denied yourself because of your griff. Our family's legacy weel now be returned to you weeth our blessing…"

At that, the room became even brighter with triple the light intensity seen before. With a distinct sharp blast of cold, fizzing air, the light suddenly dimmed and there next to Esther stood Philipe and another beautiful young woman.

"Daughtairre," said Philipe, holding out his arms to embrace her. Justavia stepped forward, saying, "Oh Papa," she cried, "'ow I have meesed you."

Then, as his spectral arms enfolded her, Justavia felt as if she was a child again, for to her, his embrace felt solid and eminently mortal.

"Hello my sister," said the young woman, stepping forward.

"Ruth?" Said Justavia, clearly stunned. "Ruth? Look at you, all grown up!"

"Yes, I am all grown up. You are seeing me at 25, for thees ees the ege I choose to appear as. We can appear at any ege we choose to."

"Oh my," said Justavia. "You're all alright - Oh my goodness, I can't tell you 'ow 'appy that meks me fill."

"We cannot stay lak thees for long, 'annah, to do so requires too mush of our energy. Leesten to me, I must now return to the light form - I shall be beck ret away so please watch carefully for me and then watch where I go."

At that, all three spirits became bright orbs again. One immediately dipping beneath the floorboards under the window.

"Yes," I said to the others. "That's where the light went before, down under the floorboards."

Minty and I both knelt down for a closer look. I tried to lift the floorboards but they all felt pretty well fixed but then Minty pressed down on the edge of the one that met the wall and the other end of it promptly popped up. We looked at one another excitedly. There, tucked into the space between the joists, we could see a rectangular object covered in dust. I had to fight to stop Minty getting to it first because I wanted to be the one to claim the discovery of whatever it was - I know, selfish of me especially after Minty had found the right floorboard to go to - but I AM only human, although Minty would probably disagree! Then I felt petty and decided to let Minty do the honours (nice of me wasn't it!) I think she must have been stunned by my second thoughtful act of the day towards her.

"Thanks Mark, you're not such a prat after all," she said lovingly - I think!

"What's in it, what's in the box," cried Nathaniel excitedly. Justavia, however, remained calm. She merely stood silently watching the proceedings hand in hand with Clarice.

"With a quick look at all of them watching her, Minty carefully wiped her hand across the box to clear the dust away until everyone could clearly see that the box was nothing more than an old pictorial cigar box, one that had been decorated (well I think desecrated is closer to the truth) with flowers done in pen and ink.

"Huh," gasped Clarice, for she seemed to recognise the box. *I wonder*, I thought, *was this hers?*

Briefly I wondered if it was a box full of crayons (did you think I was going to say cigars?)

As Minty carefully lifted the lid, there was something wrapped in comic papers, inside it, which she began to unfold very carefully and suddenly we all saw what was inside - a gun!

"Bloody hell," said Nathaniel, totally out of character. "Don't touch it, Minty, it could be loaded!"

Minty immediately backed away. "You look then," she said. "You're the most senior - aren't you?"

At that, Nathaniel knelt down, inadvertently making his knee joints crack in the process. Then, very carefully, he lifted the gun out of the box and placed it gently upon the floor as if it were an unexploded bomb in danger of going off at the slightest touch.

As he was doing this, the remaining two orbs suddenly flared brightly and then vanished with a snap, leaving a strong smell of ozone as if their work had now been done. Nathaniel kept one hand on the gun.

"Who do you think this belonged to?" I asked him.

"I am not sure, I don't seem to be able to tune into its energy so you're guess is as good as mine."

"Hey, maybe we should try some psychometry!" Said Minty.

"Some psycho what?" I said, amazed.

"Psychometry - you idiot. You know, when someone is able to tell the history of an object purely by holding it for a while," said Minty, which shocked me even more than the spirits had done.

"Oh yeah?" I said. "So you reckon you can do that huh? Since when, pea brain!"

"Now, now children - tis no time for pettiness." Said Nathaniel, carefully picking the gun up.

Minty had her arms folded defensively and one eyebrow cocked quizzically. Naturally I simply had to bite back.

"Listen Aerohead," I said. "Only with a stack more bubbles - *I* can do things you've never even dreamt of - I'm actually a natural psychic!"

"Pah! Unnatural psycho more like - you're no more psychic than me..." She replied.

"How can you say that? It was you who saw the spirits of my book and that blue thingy here, first, so I guess, even though you are having trouble accepting it, we ARE very much alike after all, right down to our, 'spooky' abilities."

"No way José. You're not trying to tell me that I'm going to be as weird as you from now on, are you?"

"You already are, stoopid! Now ferme ta bushe for a moment while I hold the gun for a moment."

"Have you both quite finished," said Nathaniel, not angrily but clearly beginning to get irritated, particularly at such an ungodly hour of the morning. "I don't think it would be a very responsible thing for me to do, letting you hold the gun, Mark."

"Please, Nathaniel, you know I am responsible. I have a strong feeling that I need to hold the gun! It's the only way we are going to get any answers," I said. "Please Nathaniel, I repeated. "Let me do this."

He didn't have a chance to continue for suddenly, by some weird miracle, Minty actually nodded as if to say, *yes, give him a go*, which in itself is supernatural, while I held out my hand for the gun.

Nathaniel shook his head slowly, as if he wasn't totally convinced that he was doing the right thing and then he carefully handed the gun to me. As he pulled his hand away, he was still shaking his head. "Just promise me you'll not go anywhere near the trigger!"

I nodded. Of that I had no intention. The first thing that surprised me about the gun, was that it was a heck of a lot heavier than it looked and I too was concerned that it might be loaded so I made sure that my hand was well away from the trigger at all times and made sure that I kept the gun pointing downwards, away from my feet, just in case, after all, I didn't want to ruin any chance of me becoming a professional tap-dancer! I then closed my eyes and tried hard to tune into its energy, concentrating on who had last held it. It didn't take as long as I expected, for something to start coming through to me, in fact it happened pretty much instantaneously.

In my mind's eye, I could see a filmy sort of figure stepping forward from what looked like swirling black mist, whatever it was, it looked like it was trying to form itself. It appeared to be wearing what looked like a greyish blue uniform and I could also, just about make out what looked like shiny, knee length black boots. Things then seemed to suddenly speed up and very quickly, what I was now looking at became sharper and sharper before my disbelieving eyes and my attention was drawn to a fairly distinct gold swastika over a red background. It was then, as if a psychic camera had been pulled back to reveal more of the image, that the collarless neck to a jacket decorated with gold stars and an eagle, came into view, followed by a name, Otto Kruger, that also sprang into my mind along with the word, 'Führerhauptquartiers'.

I started to then sense that Otto Kruger considered himself a 'herdsman,' for it had been his job to round up groups of innocent Jewish people.

By now, the gun seemed to be getting heavier and heavier by the minute and the compulsion to look and see if it was loaded proved too great to resist, so I opened my eyes to seek reassurance from my onlookers.

"What? What is it? Cried Nathaniel.

"Wait," I replied. I couldn't help glancing across at Justavia, for I half hoped I might receive her blessing to check the gun for bullets but she was leaning on Clarice with her eyes closed. I returned my attention to the task at hand. I tried to block it but something in my mind was telling me to shoot the Jew but I was stronger and fought it, for I knew I had to end something that had started oh so long ago.

It seemed strange, but I simply knew how to open the gun's cartridge chamber, it felt as if the gun had been my own weapon. I flicked it open and I heard Nathaniel gasp. "It's Okay," I reassured him. "I am not going anywhere near the trigger - trust me."

I could see a wad of paper had been forced into the cartridge so I set about trying to remove whatever it was. I noticed that in the box were a couple of sticks, one of which I knew would be just what I needed. And so, armed with the stick, I proceeded to pry the wad of paper out and having done so, I passed it across to Nathaniel.

"Well would you look at that! It's bible paper," he cried.

I looked up in amazement and suddenly noticed that Justavia now seemed to be on full alert.

Everyone was leaning over Nathaniel as he carefully opened the paper up. "Stand well back," he said, "Just in case." His warning was duly ignored, as nobody appeared to want to miss seeing what was inside it. Very carefully, Nathaniel opened the wad of paper up. Inside were several smaller wads of paper. He opened one of them up and suddenly gasped. Incredibly, inside the dirty looking bible paper, was not a bullet or even fragments of a bullet - inside were gemstones, clear, sparkling crystal gemstones...

"Huh," came a quick intake of breath. "Are they diamonds?" Cried Minty.

"I can't be sure," said Nathaniel.

"What did your psychobabble tell you? Dear brother," said Minty looking at me, one eyebrow raised as if to say, *well?*

I was just about to explain to her what I had picked up earlier regarding Otto Kruger, when suddenly, I was thrown backwards, hitting the wall and knocking the gun out of my hand in the process as I slumped to the floor. For a moment I just sat there, stunned, not knowing what had just happened to me. Minty and Nathaniel came rushing to my aid and were helping me back to my feet when an odd feeling came over me and I started to feel light headed.

"Are you feeling alright, dear boy," I heard Nathaniel ask me, as he stood rubbing the hand I had banged, but I didn't feel right, not at all. Then, inexplicably, I saw a flash of black and red and something blurred coming towards me at great speed and it made me jolt. Suddenly, someone else's voice started coming out of my mouth. "Leave ze diamonds where zey are!"

Whoever it was now hijacking my voice box, I knew instantly, was someone used to barking commands at people. "Put ze diamonds back in ze gun NOW!" I couldn't help it, I had lost control of my movement as well as my voice and my head was now looking directly at Nathaniel. Nathaniel understood immediately what was happening and he addressed the voice directly.

"Who are you?" He asked.

"Who am I?" Came the voice from my mouth. "I am your superior, little man. I serve the Nazi party - who are you? A Jew? Or just a snivelling sympathetic traitor to the Motherland?"

"Who I am is of no interest to you," relied Nathaniel. You, whoever you are, are dead and the dead have no rights in the physical world. Now I order you to tell me, who are you and who do these gemstones belong to?"

"You order me? Hah! Zey *are* my diamonds, MINE! And I have every right to them, for zey now belong to me, as ze rightful plunder of war."

"Rubbish! Where did you get them, come on, it is Karmic Law and you must answer me honestly…"

For a moment the voice ceased.

"I took them from a Jewish family I dutifully captured in the attic of this very house, they 'ave no rights, so the diamonds belong to me!"

"Oh, you like bright, sparkly things do you? How about this then?" Cried Clarice, suddenly stepping forward. At that, she conjured a huge bright white light, right in the centre of the room and I could feel a distinct pull from my chest. I couldn't help myself, from crying out. "Nooooo, get away from me, I must stand guard over my diamonds," when suddenly, the black and red glow that had been engulfing me, seemed to be smeared sideways and sucked into the intense white light that now resembled a vast tunnel into infinity.

"Noooooo," the voice continued but it quickly got quieter and quieter until it could be heard no longer, for the vengeful spirit of Otto Kruger had entered the light completely.

Everyone stood in awed silence, bathed by the first few rays of the early morning sun, that was beginning to rise. Somewhere in the distance I could hear a cockerel crowing and it sounded utterly wonderful, but more to the point, normal.

The possession had taken a lot more out of me than I realised and I suddenly found that I could hardly stop myself yawning. Being taken over by spirits certainly takes the energy out of you, trust me! I couldn't help but notice that Minty too, was also struggling to keep her eyes open. Nathaniel still found enough energy to carefully spread the diamonds out before him and we were all stunned, not only by just how many there, but also by the sheer size and clarity of most of them.

"Must be worth a small fortune," I said, peering over his shoulder.

"Indeed, my boy, indeed, but that can wait until tomorrow, I think we should all try to get a bit of shut-eye for now, otherwise we'll be a household of zombies come the morning."

"Yeah, rich zombies," said Minty, smiling.

Chapter Thirty-One

Though it was hard to quieten my overexcited mind, I did eventually manage to get a couple of hours of downtime, not that I got the chance to wake up naturally, oh no. I woke up because Minty, who had been trying to sneak past me en-route to the bathroom, accidentally tripped over the still-raised floorboard we had all forgotten to put back in place.

"Owww, my flippin' toe," she cried, hopping backwards and then landing heavily on my bed. That was what woke me!

"Minty! Flippin' 'eck, I was fast asleep," I moaned.

"Well clearly, not anymore, so you might as well get up you big slug - looks like it's going to be another sparkling day - did you see what I did just there eh, sparkling - like diamonds?"

I sighed. "Yeah, I got it. Didn't particularly want it mind you, but I got it!"

Later, after I had washed and got dressed, I headed down to breakfast, eager to ask Nathaniel more about the diamonds and to have a really good look at them, and at the gun. Naturally, being my annoying sister, Minty wafted along behind me like a clinging, pungent odour.

When I got to the patio, all three WW2 heroes, Nathaniel, Clarice and Justavia, were busy sitting at the table, sorting through the diamonds. Even though Justavia was the only remaining member of the once renowned Green & Green Diamond Importers, she had no understanding of gemstones at all, bearing in mind that she was only ten when she had last seen her father. Now, she was content simply holding each diamond up to the sun as though cleansing them of their dirty association, and marvelling at the pure clarity of each stone and the range of colours of which, shone, from each of them like a prism.

"Undoubtedly, these are very fine diamonds indeed," said Nathaniel looking at one through a jewellers loupe - they are all very clear and with precious little in the way of inclusions. I think you are going to be surprised at the value you have here before you, in this little pile, Justavia. Any thoughts what you are going to do with them?"

At that point I stepped forward. "Good morning," I said. "How's the treasure appraisal going?'

Nathaniel half turned his head. "Ah, Mark. Well, perhaps you should be asking Justavia that. Personally, I think she should sell the diamonds and come here to live, with Clarice."

"And why wud I want to do thet," Justavia replied. "I am quat capable of lookeen after myself!"

Nathaniel studied her and put down the loupe to address her directly. "Yes, but from the looks of things in your kitchen, you are also more than capable of drinking yourself to death. Surely a bit of company might be better for you?"

"You can come here to live eef you want, Justavia, lord knows, I 'ave plenty of room and it would be nace to 'ave someone of my own age around me," said Clarice.

"Excusez moi? I am one year younger than you, I'll 'ave you know!" She replied with a naughty look on her face. "But could you put up weeth me?"

"Oh I am sure I could - and if you misbeyave, why, there ees always the attique - ooh, I'm sorry Justavia, that was très insensitive."

"It's OK, Clarice, I know you deedn't min anytheeng by eet. Anyway, it's all water under the breedge now. I feel almost as though I 'ave come full circle and that now I'm ready to finally let go of the past. I 'ave no need to 'ide in the bottle any longer - Nathaniel!"

Nathaniel smiled at her.

"Good Morning!" Said Minty, brightly, who had been hanging back silently. "Shall I go make us all a fresh pot of tea?"

"Hey!" I said. "Who are you and what have you done with my sister?"

"Oh hardy-har," she replied. "I am not half as bad as you make out, the problem with you is that you just don't know me!"

"No," I replied, "you're right about that, but it's partly your own fault, you've always been prickly around me, mind you, I guess I can be a tad judgemental. If you like Jordan, well, I guess that's up to you!"

Minty rolled her eyes, "I rest my case. You see Mark, I never really liked Jordan, I only pretended too just to make you annoyed. I was rebelling because you always seemed so, well, independent, unique, you know, just different to everyone else and I wanted to be like that. God, I can't believe I'm spilling my guts out over an empty teapot!"

"Minty," said Nathaniel, breaking the sudden silence. "You are twins - both of you are unique - never forget that and the offer to come and visit me in Cheltenham is open to you as much as it is to Mark, OK?"

Minty smiled. "OK. Thanks, Uncle Nathaniel - tea?"

"Don't worry about the tea dear, Maugret will see to that, thees leetle bell eesn't jus' for decoration you know. Come on, take a seat and 'ave some breakfast," said Clarice, patting the chair next to her.

The rest of that memorable, lazy summer day was spent by all of us doing absolutely nothing other than enjoying the sunshine and Minty and I attempting playing badminton, badly!

In the evening Justavia gave us each, another Tarot Card reading. She told me that despite my tendency to be a loner, I would do something amazing that would draw people to me like 'the Pied Piper of 'amlyn' and that through my fingers would come words of immense significance to many. I was happy with that, I wanted nothing more than to be a writer and if that meant writing something truly worthwhile to the people who chose to read my work, I would be more than happy.

Minty's reading was similar, in a way. But whereas mine seemed to focus on the written word, Minty's reading appeared to refer to design, clothing design at that. Not surprising really, particularly as she seemed to carry a copy of *Vogue* wherever she was. What *was* surprising was when Justavia said this, and I quote, *'you shall marry into a jewel of a family and you shall excel in the creation of beautiful adornments'*. To which Minty replied, "me, married - I don't think so!" Leaving Justavia winking at her with a smile.

Nathaniel waived his chance of a reading, feeling that some things are better left unknown. I wondered if perhaps, he was still guarding a secret or two. Clarice, however, couldn't wait to have another reading, or, 'ridding' as she pronounced it. Justavia told Clarice that she would be lonely no longer and that very soon, she would have someone marvellous coming into her life, someone who would bring extra brightness to every dark recess, someone who sparkled like diamonds - at which Clarice suddenly twigged what Justavia was saying and then burst out laughing.

"Ooh, Justavia - you really 'ad me going for a minute! So you're coming to live 'ere are you?"

"Yes, Clarice, I think I just might," she replied with a smile, "eef you'll 'ave me!"

Chapter Thirty-Two

Justavia spent a lot of time thinking about what to do with the diamonds once they had been valued. As it happened, and I don't think anyone, other than Justavia, was surprised, the diamonds turned out to be worth a small fortune because of their clarity and the rarity of some of the colours of them. There was I thinking that some looked a bit too yellow and that some strangely pink or green but, as I soon discovered, those colours are pretty rare occurrences in diamonds and worth far more than the clear ones, referred to as white, particularly when free of inclusions (little dark marks inside) as hers were.

She decided that half of the proceeds from the sale of them would be going to the Holocaust Memorial Museum at Drancy, a town just outside of Paris. She wanted the world to remember what her people went through, but not only Jews, this would also be in remembrance of Gypsies, Communists, Poles, Homosexuals and the millions of innocents born with disabilities. She knew that her parents would have approved, because in spite of the wealth her family had amassed, she was well aware that she came from a long line of philanthropists.

The biggest surprise of all came when Justavia told Minty and I that we would be getting £10,000 each in the form of a college fund to set us both up for the life, something she said, young people of her generation hardly ever had. She said that it would be her chance to live vicariously through both of us.

Another amazing thing was when Justavia, after a brief word with Clarice, insisted on paying for our parents, along with Paul, to join us here in August so that our whole family could be reunited for the first time ever. For once, both I and, I'm pretty sure, Minty, felt happy knowing that our parents would be having a quality holiday for once, lord knows, they both need a bit of culture in their lives especially mum, she definitely deserves it considering all the cooking, cleaning and ironing she does for us all. The thought of them both here made me smile. I could picture Dad on the beach, cultivating a diamond-pattern tan from, as per normal, wearing a string vest in the sun thinking that it made him look like Bruce Willis in *Die Hard*! Yeah right! Die of embarrassment more like.

Seeing Nathaniel alone, I walked up to him and tapped him on the shoulder. "Nathaniel, mind if I ask you one more thing that has been bothering me?"

"Certainly young Mark, what itch do you need scratching?" He said with a wry smile.

"Well," I said. "You have more windows outside your house than there are inside your house - what's that all about? I have been trying to figure it out for months and it's been driving me crazy, well that and the strange clicking noise coming from your bedroom every now and again - I've been imagining all sorts of things, like maybe you had a secret suite of rooms or something..."

Nathaniel rolled his eyes. "Mark! I see with you I truly have my work cut out. Now, I am going to tell you something, but only after you promise me you'll never reveal it to anyone else - I mean it, not to Minty, not to your parents and certainly not to any of your friends... Pinky swear?"

"Ooh, sounds a bit worrying, but yeah, I promise, pinky swear." At that I hooked my pinky through his to complete the transaction. "There, now it's totally between the two of us. So - what is it," I said, eagerly.

Nathaniel took in a deep breath as if to ready himself. "Oh very well. I have worked for an intelligence gathering agency ever since leaving university, always have and always will I guess, or as long as I am able to, after all, I am no spring chicken."

"Do you mean GCHQ?"

"I didn't say that, Mark. Some things I cannot divulge for reasons of national security but what I *can* tell you, is that my work as a remote viewer never stopped and contradictory to what I have read about remote viewing in the press lately, rather than hurting my intellect, it has actively enhanced it, I mean, look at me, I'm 79 for goodness sake! Over the years my skills have increased to such a degree, that now I am able to influence people by planting things in their mind's - only for the good of mankind mind you, and never for anything bad! Now you know why my stories are so vivid to the listener. I can't help myself, it's as though I am on a mission when I am reading a story, a mission to entertain and to influence, but in a positive way."

He caught me frowning. "Um, I'm not too sure I like the sound of that. Sounds very much to me like just another form of brainwashing."

"Mark, let me reassure you - I only ever influence people of ill-intent and most certainly, never, ever family. As I said, my abilities are only ever used for the good of mankind, as were all the gifted people I have had the honour to work with. Now, in answer to your questions, yes, I *do* have a couple of rooms dedicated to my work because, surprise, surprise, I work remotely! That was why I had to be rather secretive about the latest model of Transmitting Helmet I had been sent, do you remember, when you and Clarice were out in the sun room?"

"Ah, yes, I wondered about that too! And the clicking sound? Let me guess, one of the doors to your secret rooms?"

"Correct, they connect my bedroom to my attic space, beyond what you thought was the back wall - actually, a false wall. It's there in the attic that I have several discrete transmitters hidden away - like, for instance, the one you saw as a box with a certain risqué picture of Pandora upon it. In reality it is just a plain grey metal box with a keyhole, but I was letting you see it as something else. Kind of hoping that you might of figured that out, what it *really* was, that is, but hey, plenty of time for Minty and your good self to develop further and I feel sure that you both will. Can't say that I am surprised you never figured the box out though - too blinded by a certain little bear from Nutwood!" He laughed.

"Hey, don't knock Rupert, he's from your generation and equally as cool as you!"

"Me cool? As if!" He replied with a grin.

1. James Bond Asserts

1. Alana's 50s HW
2. OWorshipers
3D Reckless Love of 4
God chords
Reckless Love of God
Youtube
Consentyoutube
Youtube.com.

Notes from the Author

I saw my first ghost back in the 1970's. I was out walking my dog, Toby, along Matson Lane with my sister Carole. For some strange reason, on that cold October evening, I felt compelled to look into the grounds of Matson House, a grand old building that stands directly opposite the Moat Junior School - *my old school.* Ever since childhood I had heard stories of a resident spirit said to haunt the grounds of Matson House, a female spirit, known simply as, The Blue Lady. Like most people, until I saw the spirit for myself, I thought the Blue Lady was just something made up, a scary story purely to frighten children. Boy, was I ever wrong. When I saw her, I cried out to my sister, "Look at that!" Next thing I know, is I'm standing a mere 18 inches away from a full ghostly apparition – all alone! Carole had hared off down the lane, causing Toby's little legs to practically leave the earth, all because my tone of alarm had seriously spooked her! *I* wasn't spooked though, truthfully. I was actually fascinated. I mean, how often does anyone get to see something so utterly amazing?

True to the legend, the lady before me was dressed all in blue and she was crouching down, searching amongst the autumn leaves looking for something. It took me a while to register what I was actually looking at, because suddenly I realised that I could see the trees clearly through her body.

The legend told of how the mystery woman had been caught up in a skirmish during events in the Siege of Gloucester, back in 1643 when King Charles the First was in hiding at Matson House. It is said that as she had been running for cover, one of her blue silk shoes had come adrift. When she went back to retrieve it, she was caught in the crossfire and killed. Excavations in the grounds 40 plus years ago, unearthed a whole blue silk shoe from the time of the siege, covered in delicate embroidery, along with the sole of another. Clearly all had once belonged to a very wealthy woman. These artefacts are now on public display at the Gloucester Folk Museum in lower Westgate Street and are well worth a look.

Also, there were also rumours, in my childhood, of tunnels, said to run beneath Matson House and St Katharine's, church just across the road from it, and it was also rumoured that the tunnels reached as far as to Gloucester Cathedral. True or not, I don't know, but what I DO know with great certainty is what I saw, and let me assure you - the Blue Lady is real.

....

I must give thanks to my sister, Carole Anne Pittaway, for being my test reader and for her diligence in pointing out the elusive boo-boos I missed when I read it, like, a billion times, or so it seems! I must also thank my Aussie pal, Enid Young for also test reading an early version of this novel and Lorna Hedges for her diligent, final read through. Finally, as I have said before, any mistakes in this novel are entirely of my own making - some may be genuine oversights and some, deliberately allowed, to fit the story. Just let me say -11 times out of 10 I don't make mistakes!

My dog, Cisco and me

Seek me out on *Amazon*, *Facebook* and *Twitter* and say hello!

Interview with the author, Ed Newbery-King

Hi there, Ed! So - a ghost story, why is that?

Not just a ghost story! As a person with a great interest in all manner of paranormal subjects, the sighting of ghosts is one element in particular that strikes a resonant chord with me. My first full apparition sighting happened back in the late 1970's and left me, not afraid as you might imagine, but full of wonder and wanting to see more. Since then I have been on something of a personal quest to seek out the truth concerning the afterlife. I am a member of two psychic circles in which, not only do I learn new things myself but I also help others to understand spiritual matters. I reckon it will be a long while before I have exorcised the lure of the spirit realm from my system! Look out for more of my paranormal-themed books.

Do you only write ghost stories?

No. There may often be spiritual or ethereal elements within my stories but ghosts are not the main ingredient in any of them so far. My first published book, Do You Believe in Magic?, is a contemporary fairy tale. I am currently working on several more stories that I guarantee will take the reader to many strange places and times.

Incidentally, I have written several pre-school stories too, all about a magical land called, Wellinever! - a place where anything can happen and usually does.

Can you tell us what are you working on at the moment?

Certainly! I am writing another YA (young adult) story, which, (no pun intended) blends witchcraft and Norse mythology, entitled, *The Cauling*. The story centres around a teenage girl, Willow Hawker, who, on the cusp of witching ceremony, begins to question why she is so different from everyone else in her village. Not only does she have blonde hair and blue eyes but she seems to lack the powers of witchcraft that her friends and family members all have. One night her mother confides in her of something that occurred on her wedding day. From that moment forth, Willow sets out to discover unanswered things concerning herself and what happened to her brother, Lark, who vanished whilst both were very young. Willow discovers that his disappearance is connected, somehow, to an old willow tree she has always been strangely drawn to, which stands forlornly next to an ominous looking black lake.

Yet another YA book I am currently writing is called, *Darkly Mysterious*. If you like Sherlock Holmes, you would most likely enjoy this story. Darkly Mysterious is the name given to the main protagonist, a wealthy young man named Duncan Meek, by the local schoolchildren who spy on him through the school railings as he comes and goes from his nearby house, whilst investigating each new case he is working on. Yes, you guessed correctly - Duncan is a Private Investigator. He enjoys giving out little snippets of information from each case to the children to foster their over active imaginations and sometimes, he discovers that some of the children's comments help him to view a case from a different viewpoint. This story is set in the late 1890's in Edinburgh and centres around Burke and Hare, the infamous body snatchers and the story begins with a poor woman approaching him with a request to find her missing brother who was last seen heading off for a meeting with Mr Burke and Mr Hare.

The third book I am working on is entitled, The Library of Dust. This is a biblical mystery concerning a fallen angel named, Arcturus and his request to a mortal youth, an Italian teenager, named, Paolo, to help him prove his innocence, and then allowing, hopefully, for him to get his wings back, for they had been torn from him, shattered into several fragments and then scattered over the Earth.

This is another YA novel and features ghosts, golems, time travellers and inter-dimensional travel, amid a variety of strange and esoteric events.

Sounds like you have a lot of work ahead of you then.

Yes, I do, but I don't see it as work. To me, writing is a much needed, outlet - if I couldn't write, I think my head might explode! On top of all of the books I am working on, I am also trying to get a TV musical comedy sitcom, named, Along Came Dad, that I have written (an homage to one of my favourite TV shows of the 70's - The Partridge Family), to be picked up by a network. I have written ten songs, each one themed to fit into each episode. Like my books, the sitcom story has elements of subtle learning, how to behave, how to be considerate, how to live a great life by being the best you can. Hopefully such things are discrete enough to not come across as preachy (or, heaven forbid, cheesy), but however they are perceived, they are part of who I am and I cannot write from any perspective other than my own.

So there you have a glimpse of my life at the present (27/7/2016)

Thank you, Ed - sounds like there is much for us all to look forward to!

Indeed there is, and you are most welcome :-)

The Leader

Dawn of the Light
Paul
Alah
Christlike
Integrity
Be Noble
Thing
Christ
Christlike
The Law
Beatitudes
Love Thy Neighbour

Christlike Community
K... Joy (Alan Paul)
Tony, Ian, Nicola, Kate
Sharon, Janes Hayden, Paul Pentrell
Kim Pentrell, Lukas, Michael
April, Ian Bayley, Andrew
Vicki, Peter K..., Janes White
Paul, Dey, Mary Ian?

Printed in Great Britain
by Amazon